MW00639617

The Lost Children of Gloam's End

by

CLEMENTINE DARLING

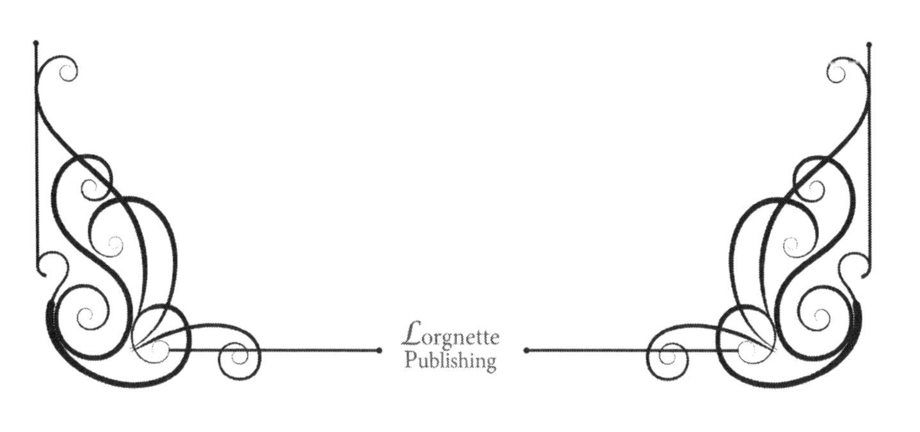

THE LOST CHILDREN OF GLOAM'S END

Copyright © 2022 Janice Yong

All rights reserved. No part of this book may be reproduced or used in any manner without the prior written permission of the author, except for the use of brief quotations in reviews.

Interior doll photography © 2022 Janice Yong

First edition • April 2022
ISBN: 978-981-18-3434-9

Also available in a full-colour edition
ISBN: 978-981-18-3671-8

Lorgnette
Publishing

For
the two Rs,
K,
and of course,
my number-one boy,
Mr Beetle

The Lost Children of Gloam's End

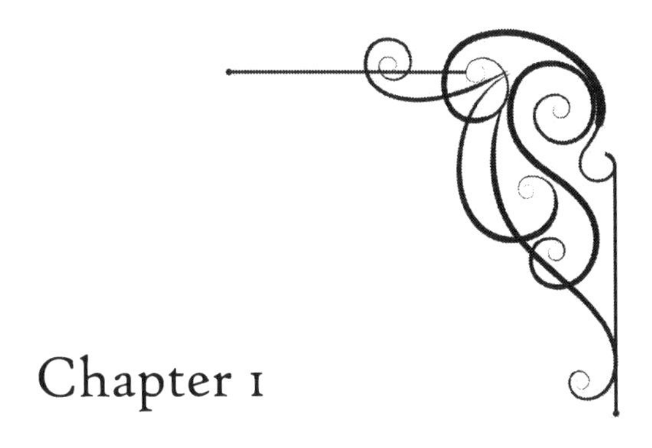

Chapter 1

There was once a girl named Josie. She was small and very pale, with dark, round eyes, and black hair cut in a curling bob about her ears. Josie lived in a very old house at the edge of a wood. It wasn't a very nice house, nor was it a very nice wood, but Josie didn't have much choice because it was the best her father could do.

Mr Harwood – that's Josie's father – was a widower, ever since Mrs Harwood died three some years ago. Money was a little short, and Mr Harwood had to work hard to make ends meet. He was what they call a bespoke tailor, and fortunately a very good one, and people would come to him for things to be sewn or mended. His speciality was 1940s-style suits – being a great vintage menswear enthusiast – and he took much pride in delivering his orders with matching boutonnieres.

Sometimes, he did voice recordings as well, for Mr Harwood had lovely intonation. On those days Josie would follow her father to the big recording studio in the town, where Mr Harwood would do voice-overs for documentaries, or read things like, "If you require assistance in French, press one".

The Harwoods had moved to Gloam's End after Mrs Harwood fell ill and lost her job. People in the town had been amazed when they learned the family had bought the old house at the end of the road, for it was a lonely place and had been empty a long time.

They told the Harwoods that it had not always been so, that the wood had not always been so dark and gloomy, and that a hundred years ago there had been a bustling village where you could get fresh eggs and homemade bread and locally-brewed ale. But then one day the villagers started leaving, and the people who were living in the Harwoods' house at the time said it was no place for children, and left too. One and a half miles away, Mrs Bramstone, their nearest neighbour, sent her little daughter safely away and closed her school for young girls.

Children had gone missing from there, the story went – disappeared completely without a trace – but though Mrs Bramstone suffered a dubious sort of fame in print and gossip for a time, neither the villagers nor the law ever found anything incriminating on either her person or her property, and the story gradually grew cold as one season melded into another.

No one knew how all this was so, for a hundred years is a long time, and facts get muddled and lost in the telling, but Gloam's End fell into an uneasy slumber and the townspeople stayed away. They wondered that Mr Harwood did not think it unfit for his little girl too, but these things appealed to Mr Harwood's antiquated heart, and the mortgage was cheap besides, so he merely smiled, and said that it was all right and it would do.

It was some time in autumn that it all happened. Josie usually spent most of her school holidays at home playing alone, but, being an only child, she was used to it and didn't mind really. Josie loved looking for things under leaves, and poking about in dark, disgusting crannies, make-believing sensational, spooky exploits, and putting to much use a bright pink pocket torch given her by her mother. Though little, she was venturesome, and had a bold spirit well-fed by a voracious appetite for reading and carbohydrates.

One Tuesday afternoon that October, her father came in looking grave and sad. He told Josie she had to start packing her things and preparing for a little trip. He had received a telephone call from a city quite some distance away, he explained. It was a nurse at the hospital calling about Mr Harwood's brother, Eddie, the famous photojournalist; it seemed he was dying, and had a few last things he wanted to say. Mr Harwood had never been very close to his brother, but then you couldn't very well say no to a person who was dying, could you?

And so Mr Harwood had to get ready for his trip to the city, and Josie had to get ready for *her* trip down the road. Mr Harwood explained to Josie that what his brother had was "quite bad" and might be "contagious if his spit got on you" and that he "wasn't taking any chances" – Josie could stay with Miss Gordy, their nearest neighbour, while he was away. This was an old lady who lived at Bramstone Hall; she was, in fact, the ex-headmistress' granddaughter and had been a friend of Mr Harwood's mother. Josie had not known her grandmother and so felt nothing for Miss Gordy, but Mr Harwood was fond of her for sentimental reasons.

"You'll be in very good hands with Miss Gordy, my pet, and it will only be for a few days or so," Mr Harwood told Josie.

"Oh, must I, Daddy?" Josie said miserably. "She's *awful*! She looks at me funny!"

"Why, what a thing to say, Josie!" Mr Harwood said in surprise. "Miss Gordy does nothing of the sort. She's always saying she wishes she had children, poor thing".

"So she can eat them I suppose," Josie said sulkily.

"Now you are just being a silly," Mr Harwood said, turning away to look for his suitcase. "Just think of the fun you will have exploring that big old house".

But Josie could not think of the fun she would have, for after all, not everyone is comfortable with strange old people. Josie had hardly ever seen Miss Gordy really, but what she had seen of her, she hadn't particularly liked. The old lady seemed quite mad to her, and sometimes said unsettling things like "The wind comes in like spirits of the murdered dead".

It was unfortunate that Miss Gordy tended to say such things to Josie and not to her father, who occasionally invited Miss Gordy over for tea. Mr Harwood felt sorry for the old lady, whom he felt sure must be lonely. He said, "Don't be silly, my pet" and "Go pack your things if you don't want me to do it" and went on folding his clothes. There wasn't much Josie could do but sigh.

The day of Josie's departure dawned bleak and dreary. The sky was heavy with clouds and looked very sad. As Josie went down to her breakfast, it started to rain, and the little drops ran down the windowpanes like tears. Josie sighed some more. It seemed the world was very much in sympathy with her.

Mr Harwood was just laying out some toast when Josie went in to the kitchen. "Come and have your breakfast," he said.

"Couldn't I just stay here at home, Daddy?" Josie asked. "I know how to open cans and use the washing machine. I'm sure I'll be perfectly fine alone".

"Don't be silly, my pet," Mr Harwood said. "You can't stay here all by yourself; it isn't safe. Miss Gordy will be company for you and take care of your meals too. Do be sensible, and eat your breakfast. Daddy has a train to catch".

He went off to check their bags and call for a taxi and see that all the windows were locked and the switches turned off. An hour later, the driver had gotten all their things into the car and they were on their way.

"Now Josie, be sure you say 'please' and 'thank you' and all that," Mr Harwood said as they rode along. Josie looked out the window and didn't say anything. She couldn't decide if she should start crying, and by the time she thought she would, they had turned off the road and into a long gravel driveway, passing under a rusty wrought iron arch that read *Harrowhead*, Bramstone Hall's original name – they had arrived at Miss Gordy's house.

This was large, brown-bricked and hip-roofed, with several chimneys poking up and partially covered with ivy. It was only two storeys high, but it was long, and extended a good distance in towards the wood. There weren't any flowers in the front like there were at Josie's house, nor pretty curtains at the great rectangular windows – many of which were in fact boarded up – the house simply stood there amid a very ill-kept, mostly dying lawn, cold and very plain, and stared out at the world in a grim, unblinking way.

Mr Harwood got out of the car and rang the doorbell. Josie had no choice but to get out too; there wasn't much point crying to the driver. She scurried up close to her father in the stately front portico. She didn't like Miss Gordy's house, which seemed to her overwhelmingly dismal. She had never been inside before, but she knew it had been a boarding school for girls a hundred years ago, when Mrs Bramstone, the headmistress, had been alive.

As Josie looked about with a mixture of curiosity and foreboding, the front door suddenly swung open.

"Ah, Miss Gordy!" Josie's father greeted her warmly. He bent down over her to give her something like a hug. The old lady was barely larger than Josie herself, which Josie always found very disconcerting. It made her look like some sort of wizened little elf.

"Say 'hello' Josie," Mr Harwood said, nudging Josie with his elbow. But Josie could only mumble; she never knew what to say to Miss Gordy.

"She's just feeling shy, Miss Gordy," Mr Harwood said apologetically.

"You just hurry along now, Christopher, or you'll be late," Miss Gordy said. "I'm absolutely delighted to have Josie here; there haven't been children in this house for years. Don't you worry about her now; she'll come around – they always do".

Mr Harwood turned to Josie and gave her a big hug. "I shall see you soon, my pet," Mr Harwood said. "Have a wonderful time".

Josie thought this was an exceptionally ill-considered thing for her father to say, but she waved to him glumly as he got into the taxi. It soon disappeared down the road. Taking a deep breath, Josie turned reluctantly to Miss Gordy.

The old lady was watching her contemplatively. Dressed in a faded lilac duster beneath a bright blue cardigan – evidently handknit – she looked thin and very fragile, but her eyes were bright and glittered like polished jet beads. She wore her short silvery-white hair in a wispy pixie-cut, while her face was pale and delicately creased – like paper, or boiled rabbit skin, Josie thought, suddenly thinking of some idiotic woman on television who'd boasted that the walls of her house were covered with it.

The papery face crumpled up now into a smile. "Let's go in, shall we?"

Miss Gordy took hold of Josie by the shoulders and pushed her firmly through the front door. The hall was unexpectedly dark and imposing. Josie stopped short and took another deep breath.

"Wouldn't you like to see your room, Josie?" Miss Gordy asked, walking towards the wide staircase.

Josie did not reply. She simply stood still, staring about her in amazement. The house was far, far larger than she'd ever imagined, and it looked, and smelt, very old indeed.

"It's a nice, big room," Miss Gordy continued hopefully.

But still Josie did not reply. She was awed by the sheer age and size of everything. Miss Gordy tried once more.

"Are you hungry? I've got some sandwiches which would go very well with a cup of tea".

"No," Josie answered curtly, still looking at the high ceiling and pillared gallery in wonder, and quite forgetting her manners.

"Very well then," Miss Gordy said, taking Josie's suitcase from her. "You can just stand there if you like, but I'll warrant you'll be tired of it before long".

She turned to go upstairs and left Josie standing alone in the hall. She could hear Miss Gordy going into a room near the top of the stairway. Then she heard the old lady open her case and begin putting her clothes away in a chest of drawers. Josie looked around her.

A great air of mystery hung about the place, which seemed to stem from the numerous closed doors, lofty ceilings, and cold, murky light, through which a million dust motes danced and twinkled like so many sprites. Josie now saw that while many of the windows were boarded up, others had really quite lovely stained glass, but then they too added to the gloom, for they were covered in dust and grime so thick that the panes had quite lost their colour and sheen.

Looking through the doorway to her right, Josie could just see a great sideboard and the edge of a large velvet sofa with flamboyantly carved legs. In the room next to it, she could see a library, with rows upon rows of books lining the walls. To her left was the kitchen, massive in size, with plates ranged along shelves that rose almost to the ceiling, and pots of all sizes hanging from hooks. Above her, the gallery with its heavy balustrade ran along the entire perimeter of the house, and seemed to echo with muffled footsteps and whispers. Everything was in shadow and looked solemn and depressed.

Suddenly, Josie felt the hairs on the back of her neck rise – she had the oddest feeling that she wasn't alone.

Her eyes darted back and forth, trying to penetrate the dimness of the dusky rooms. Whoever it was wasn't very far and this made Josie very uncomfortable indeed. Perhaps it was the murdered dead Miss Gordy always complained about, but Josie hurriedly brushed that thought aside. She still hadn't moved a step and now she felt like she really couldn't even if she'd wanted to.

Then, all at once, Josie's eyes flashed upward. They immediately lighted on a dim form halfway up the stairs. But it wasn't Miss Gordy. It was someone, or something else, and what Josie could see of it was *most* unsettling.

To begin with, it was apparently quite large, almost as large as a grown-up. But the horrid thing about it was that it didn't look like a grown-up at all. It was simply a shapeless, faceless, tall *thing*, dressed in what appeared to be a very dirty nightgown. And yet even that wasn't what bothered Josie most of all. What really unnerved her was the fact that the thing's feet, sticking out clearly at the bottom of its nightgown, were two very large *claws*.

Josie felt her mouth fall open. She simply could not take her eyes away from them. They were like the talons of a bird of prey, thick and curved, and looked very fearsome indeed. The sight of them made Josie glad that the thing's head was hidden. It seemed to her then that the thing was keeping very still – as still, in fact, as she herself was. It struck her that it was waiting, and worse, that it was waiting for *her.* There was something about its posture that suggested it wanted to see what *she* would do before deciding what *it* would.

Josie clapped her hand to her mouth to stop herself from squealing. But the very movement of her hand seemed to attract the thing's attention, and it immediately began to descend the staircase. Josie felt she *really* had to do something now, but before she could decide what exactly, she heard Miss Gordy's voice.

"Josie! Are you still standing there?"

The thing paused, then pressed itself against the blue papered wall, vanishing completely. Josie saw Miss Gordy's little slippered feet appear at the top of the stairs, and the rest of Miss Gordy soon followed. She went right past where the thing had been and didn't seem to notice anything at all. Her eyes fell on Josie's white, upturned face.

"Why, Josie! What a silly you are!" she exclaimed with a little laugh.

She went up to her, then paused and looked at the girl closely. A peculiar eagerness shone in the old lady's eyes. "Are you all right, child?" she asked.

Josie shook herself. She must have been imagining things. "Yes," she answered shortly. "Quite all right, thank you".

Miss Gordy frowned. "Very well, if you say so," she said, after a moment. "There are sandwiches in the kitchen if you want a bite. Usually we would eat in the drawing-room, but I thought you'd want to settle in a bit. Your room is the first one you see at the top of the stairs. I've left a towel on your bed if you want to wash up. If you need me, I shall be working in the drawing-room. Dinner is at six, bedtime at eight".

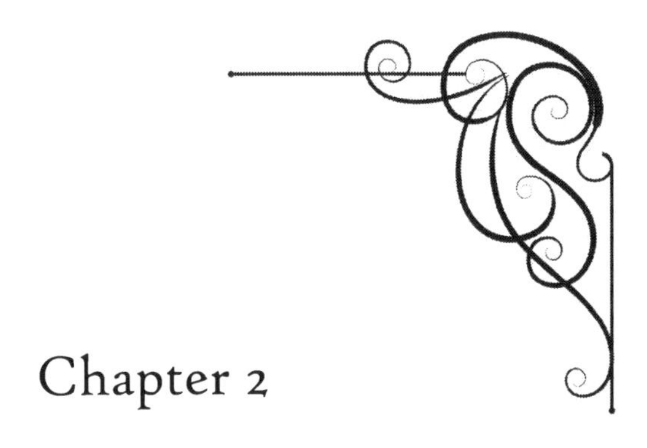

Chapter 2

Josie was left alone again. She considered what she should do next. Now that her fright had passed, she couldn't help feeling that this was turning out to be rather an adventure. Curiously, she made her way to the kitchen.

This room was large, and lined all around with shelves and cabinets. High above, paned windows stretched down from the ceiling; these, unfortunately, had been boarded up, save two, through which the daylight streamed in feebly. Besides the countless copper pots and chinaware, several wooden blocks and weighing scales were stacked against the wall, and above them, hanging from a dark beam, a variety of fearsome-looking knives, cleavers and saws. Josie wondered what Miss Gordy did with these and hastily turned away.

On a long oak table in the middle were a jug of cold tea and a plate of creamy-looking sandwiches, filled with what appeared to be coleslaw. Wrinkling up her nose, Josie poked her finger into one and tentatively licked it – it turned out to *be* coleslaw, but quite different from the sort her father picked up with the fish and chips, and she was surprised to find that it actually tasted rather good. She decided she would have a fine time eating these in bed, and, finding a little dish, she took two sandwiches and a mug of tea. Then, cautiously, she made her way up the stairs.

But the weird creature she had seen earlier did not reappear. Halfway up, Josie forced herself to stop and examine the wallpaper. It was very dingy, and even a bit mouldy, but Josie could find no trace of the ghastly thing.

Reaching the second floor landing, she found herself at the head of the gallery, along which she saw several white doors. The door to her bedroom, however, was the only one which was open. Looking in, she was amazed to see that it was not the cosy little room she had been expecting, but a long dormitory instead, with ten iron-framed beds arranged in a row down its length.

Closing the door behind her, Josie looked with interest about the room. Everything was very old, but tidy and clean enough. The narrow beds had all been covered with striped blankets and next to each stood a little chest of drawers; small placards had been tied to the iron frames at the foot of each bed. A folded towel and patchwork quilt had been placed on the bed nearest the door, and on the pillow were Josie's monkey and books. At the other end of the room, another door opened into a small bathroom.

Josie put her plate down and began munching on a sandwich. Thoughtfully, she went closer to look at the little placards tied to the beds, and saw that they were pieces of thick board, now yellowed and grubby with age, on which were written a name and a date in a curling, old-fashioned script. The one on hers read, *Margaret Helfrey, June 11th 1894*. At the next bed, she read *Harriet Wright*, with the same date written underneath.

Intrigued, Josie moved down the row of beds till she had read all the names. For a moment, she stood still, puzzled. She felt certain the names were those of the girls who had occupied the beds when Miss Gordy's house had been a school, but what was the date?

In some perplexity, Josie finished her sandwiches and tea. Next, she did some drawing, and then some reading, and finally she lay flat out on her bed with Monkey. Who was Margaret Helfrey, in whose bed she was now lying? What had happened on June the 11th all those years before?

Josie looked at her chest of drawers. She felt sure that nothing of Margaret's would still be left in it after all these years, but, nonetheless, she got up and opened each drawer carefully. The first two were full of her own clothes, while the last was empty. Josie was about to close it when something caught her eye. Peering in, she noticed a small patch of ripples in the upper right corner of the paper lining.

Excitedly, Josie felt about with her fingers. She'd always read about hidden compartments in old furniture; you just had to know where to press. But as Josie pressed at the rippled paper, she realised there was no hidden compartment. Instead, she felt something stiff and rectangular – something had been hidden under the paper.

With careful fingers, Josie picked at the edge of the lining. Someone had apparently tried to paste the paper back, but clearly they had not done a very good job because the paper lifted easily with a little crackling noise. Josie slipped her fingers underneath and pulled out the rectangular object.

It was a plain ivory card, about three by four and a half inches, stained with light brown ripples of old gum. Josie turned it over and sharply inhaled. It was a photograph of a young girl.

Josie had never seen a picture like it before. The image was printed on coarse paper that had been mounted on the ivory card. She sat back on her heels and looked at it.

The girl in the picture stared back at her. She was very pretty, and seemed to glow against the background of dark foliage. She wore her hair in a tightly braided coronet and her eyes were very large indeed. Josie couldn't tell what colour they were because the picture was only in shades of grey, but she could see that they were very light. She had been photographed full-length, so that Josie could see her white pinafore, and the long sleeves and hem of the dress underneath. In one hand she held a book; in the other, a basket. Perhaps she had been picnicking, for she was standing in the grass at the edge of a wood, with the trees rising up tall and dark behind her.

The girl's mouth, small and pouting, was slightly open as if she wanted to say something. She had an odd expression on her face, as though she had been surprised. Perhaps she had not been ready, Josie thought, perhaps she had not even wanted to have her picture taken.

Carefully, Josie loosened the photograph from the brackets which held it. On the ivory card beneath had been written one word and the year – *Margaret, 1894.*

Breathlessly, Josie looked at the picture again. The girl's large eyes were like those of a deer that had been startled. Josie suddenly felt she knew what the girl's expression meant. It said, "I don't like it here," and worse, "I'm frightened".

At first, Josie thought Margaret might be afraid of the dark wood, but then it struck her that the girl seemed to somehow be shrinking back, as if what she was afraid of wasn't *behind* her, but rather *in front.*

Josie shivered. The rain had gotten heavier, and the dorm had become shadowy. Instinctively, she was sure now that there was something not quite right about the Bramstone house, something strange and awful, something as ghastly as the thing she had seen on the stairs. Josie wondered how much Miss Gordy knew. It was all very puzzling, and a little scary, but she couldn't help feeling rather excited. Josie had never had a real-life adventure before.

Thoughtfully, Josie lay the photograph down and went to look out the single uncovered window. If Margaret Helfrey had been standing in front of those same trees, she would have been facing the house. Whatever had frightened her might have been *in* or *at* the house.

Several hard fingers suddenly touched her arm. Josie let out a little gasp and turned with a start. It was Miss Gordy.

"Everything all right Josie?"

The old lady had come into the room without a sound. Now she stood close by Josie's shoulder, her bright black eyes following the direction of Josie's gaze.

"Oh yes, quite," Josie replied. Her thoughts had flown to the photograph she had left by her bed; somehow, she didn't want Miss Gordy to see it. There was a mystery here all right, and Josie didn't know what Miss Gordy would do if she knew Josie had been poking about. But Miss Gordy kept her eyes fixed on Josie's face as if she were trying to read Josie's thoughts.

"Dinner will be ready in half an hour," she said at last. "I'll see you downstairs in the drawing-room". Without waiting for an answer, she turned and left as quietly as she had come in.

Quick as a flash, Josie slotted the photograph back into its frame and tucked it away where she had found it. She wasn't a moment too soon. Miss Gordy reappeared at the doorway. "I think you should come help me lay the table," she said. "I suppose your father doesn't ask you to at home".

Josie glared at her indignantly. "He does so!" she retorted.

"Then you'll have no objections to doing it here," Miss Gordy said, turning away. "Tidy up your bed before you come down".

Josie stared after her crossly. Her father had never minded her untidiness, being of rather a messy turn himself. She began corralling her pencils and crayons when suddenly, she became aware of a strange squelching sound at the other end of the room. Straightening herself up, she was just in time to see a figure slowly pressing itself through the wall by the last bed. Josie's breath caught in her throat. It was the thing she had seen on the stairs.

Scarcely daring to move, or even to blink, Josie watched the thing fully materialise. She could see it much more clearly now. It was indeed as tall as a grown-up, at least five and a half feet, and had, in some sense, the shape of a grown-up as well. But it was a very vague shape, for it was covered from the head down by the same dirty, loose-fitting cloth she had seen earlier.

She now saw that it was not a nightgown after all, but rather something more like a plain bedsheet, that hung down in voluminous folds. The sheet was draped over the thing's head much like one would do if one were pretending to be a ghost, but it had neither eyes nor nose nor mouth; indeed, it had no face at all.

After coming completely through the wall, the thing swiftly turned toward the nearest bed. Petrified, Josie watched it bend over the bed and start patting it with its sheet-covered arms. It seemed to be feeling for something, and it did so with a gracefulness and determination that was dreadful to see. In a moment, apparently satisfied that what it was seeking was not there, the thing rose. Like a hunting dog sniffing at the air, it hovered for an instant, swaying, before silently gliding to the next bed.

Josie sat frozen like a statue. She realised now that although the thing could not see, its other senses were acute, and more than that, it was obviously familiar with the room. Evidently, it had been here before, and probably more than once.

With increasing dread, Josie watched the thing continue its purposeful search. It was now just five beds away from where she was. It's looking for someone, Josie thought to herself, it knows the girls used to sleep here in these beds and now it knows that I am here. It will find me if I don't move; it will know which bed I'm sleeping in. Terrified, Josie scrambled to her feet and made a mad dash for the door.

Glancing over her shoulder, she saw the thing glide swiftly after her as if it were on roller-skates. With a half-suppressed scream, Josie dashed out into the gallery and flew pell-mell down the stairs. In the main hall, she ran full-tilt into Miss Gordy, who had come out of her drawing-room.

"What is it, what is it?" Miss Gordy asked, gripping Josie tightly by the shoulders. Her eagerness frightened Josie even more, and Josie drew back from her with a great shudder.

"It was nothing, nothing at all," Josie said, trying to free herself from Miss Gordy's grasp. "I– I thought I saw an earwig" (which, in truth, she really *did* detest).

She realised how improbable this sounded even as she said it, but she could not bear to be near Miss Gordy like this. Excitement had made the old lady's pale cheeks flush red, and her black eyes glistened even more strangely than usual. Did Miss Gordy know of the weird creature, Josie wondered, and did she have anything to do with it? Josie tried to step back, but Miss Gordy continued to hold her fast.

"What was it? What did you see?" she asked, her voice barely a whisper now. She peered searchingly into Josie's face.

"Nothing," Josie repeated, stilling her voice with an effort. "It was nothing".

Miss Gordy sighed heavily and let Josie go. The colour slowly faded from her cheeks and she suddenly looked very tired. When she finally spoke again, her voice was very sad.

"I am old, and I know children are afraid of me," she said. "I have suffered a great deal in my life, and been very lonely. I'm soon for the grave now and there are things – "

She paused and seemed to shake herself. "Well, aren't you being naughty, child, screaming about nothing and trying to frighten me like that. Naughty girls should be whipped and stood in a corner, my mother used to say".

Josie stared at Miss Gordy. She had never heard anyone sound so miserable before, and she felt a little sorry for her.

"I wasn't trying to scare you," she said. "I just thought I saw something, so I screamed. I wasn't trying to be naughty, honest".

Miss Gordy looked at Josie in surprise, then patted her arm with her gnarled hand. "Come then, won't you have some dinner?" she said with a little smile.

Josie realised she *was* very hungry. Besides, she thought, this could be a good chance for her to learn more about the house. So she nodded, and followed Miss Gordy into her drawing-room.

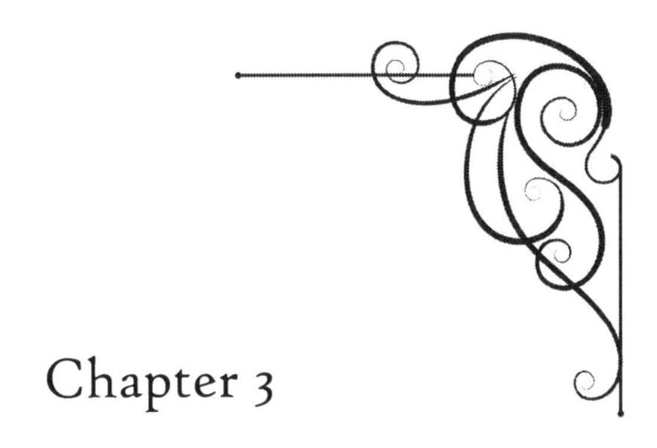

Chapter 3

This room was large and very cluttered indeed. Almost every space and corner was taken up by furniture and ornaments, most of which appeared to be very old. Besides the sofa and sideboard Josie had noticed when she first arrived, there were several small tables, chairs and ottomans, a bookcase cabinet, and an upright piano.

Photographs, shells and an elaborate clock under a glass dome stood on the mantel, and there were books and china everywhere; anything that could be draped in lace or muslin, was. Josie's eyes darted randomly from one object to the next, and then they suddenly lighted on something that made her gasp with surprise. It was a stoat's head floating in a pickle jar.

As soon as she saw it, she became aware of other similar jars about the room – a toad, a bat, a mouse, a parrot, a horned lizard. Those that had once had fur or feathers had been skinned, and all were a nasty ashen colour. There were other jars as well, but the things in them were no longer easily recognisable, and Josie could not tell what they were.

"That is a bear's snout," Miss Gordy said, following the direction of Josie's astonished gaze. "And that," she said, pointing to a jar nearby, "is a complete owl's flank".

"Oh!" Josie exclaimed. She could think of nothing else to say. The dead things made a strange contrast to the frills and embroidery that adorned them, and gave the whole space an uncanny air.

"Yes," Miss Gordy said with her odd, mirthless laugh, "my grandmother was a most remarkable woman".

Josie wandered about the room in speechless amazement. Dozens of insects, mounted in frames and shadow boxes, were meticulously labelled and displayed alongside mounted animals of all shapes and sizes, some of which had been dressed in fantastical costumes, and fitted with intricate clockworks and springs.

Still others had been transformed into strange, chimerical beasts, butchered and reattached in such a way as to be appalling versions of the originals – here was a two-headed squirrel; and there, a cat's head on a pine marten's body. On the large bow front sideboard, a group of dolls, almost eighteen inches tall and dressed in graceful Victorian evening wear, had all been decapitated, their heads replaced by those of a variety of birds, including a crow, a barn owl, a hawfinch, and a sparrowhawk.

"Oh!" Josie exclaimed again.

"Taxidermy was a common hobby for Victorian ladies," Miss Gordy said with a shrug. "My grandmother just brought it to, shall we say, another level. I have lived with them for so many years, they no longer affect me. I am accustomed to doing almost everything in this room; I find it less lonely to eat in here than in the kitchen or dining hall".

"The poor things!" Josie couldn't help saying. "Why do you keep them?"

"I must," Miss Gordy said simply. "It was a promise I made to my mother before she died. She didn't want them thrown out like trash; she felt that it was a way to honour them somehow…"

"Did Mrs Bramstone make all these?" Josie asked, staring at a snake, pale yellow and swollen, rolled up tight in a jar many sizes too small.

"Many of them, yes," Miss Gordy said. "My grandmother was very… unusual… Her father's family had made their fortune in the meat trade, you know; you have to be a certain kind of person to live in a butchery and work in an abattoir…" She began bustling about with the dinner she had laid on the sideboard.

"Put out the placemats and silverware there," she said, nodding toward a small table in front of the sofa. She brought the dishes over one by one as Josie laid the utensils and woven mats out.

"That's why I'm a vegetarian you see," Miss Gordy continued. "I know far too much about the cruelties of farming and the slaughterhouse..."

Josie glanced at Miss Gordy in surprise. The old lady had not seemed a compassionate, animal-loving type. Goes to show you really can't judge a book by its cover, Josie thought, remembering one of her father's favourite, somewhat trite, aphorisms.

As they sat down, Josie saw with relief that the dinner seemed normal enough, despite the outlandish room. There were mashed potatoes and rice, a bowl of fat snow peas, and massive mushrooms covered in a very tasty-looking sauce. It was almost like having dinner at home in front of the telly, Josie thought, except that instead of a TV, she had to look at a monstrous monkey automaton with dull, staring eyes, perched upon a covered platform.

She wondered what sort of person Miss Gordy's grandmother had been. She used to imagine that Mrs Bramstone was something like old Miss Willmott, the head at her school – neat and proper and fussy about everything, but harmless really. Now, as Josie looked at the squirrel with its four glassy eyes, she knew that Mrs Bramstone was nothing like Miss Willmott, who shrieked at the sight of a ladybug and wrapped her handkerchief around doorknobs before touching them. The person who had collected and made these creatures was someone much harder and much colder, someone with iron nerves who probably rarely smiled.

Josie's eye scanned the photographs on the walls and mantel. Many of them were very old, and similar to Margaret Helfrey's picture. Miss Gordy saw her looking at them.

"Those are photographs taken in the 19th century," she explained. "Some of them are daguerreotypes, and some are tintypes or albumen prints".

"May I look at them?" Josie asked eagerly. She felt sure there would be at least one picture of Mrs Bramstone, and perhaps some of her pupils as well.

"You may," Miss Gordy replied, "but not till you finish your dinner. My mother used to say that children who didn't eat properly should have their teeth knocked out".

Josie thought that was a stupid thing for Miss Gordy's mother to say, especially when she remembered her own irregular eating habits, but she held her tongue and chewed her mushrooms with a will. She would not miss this opportunity to find out as much as she could.

It struck Josie then that Miss Gordy was always referring to her mother, as though Mrs Gordy had not been dead at least thirty or forty years already. She must have had a very forceful personality, Josie thought, to have left such a lasting impression on her daughter, and she didn't seem very nice either. Josie felt sure Mrs Bramstone had left a similar impression on *her* daughter.

Gobbling down her last mouthful, Josie asked, "May I look at them now?"

"Don't talk with your mouth full, Josie," Miss Gordy admonished. "It looks most unattractive".

Josie got up and went to the mantel. Almost at once her eyes fell on the picture of a beautiful young woman, slim and tall, with dark hair tied back and dressed almost entirely in black. The face was a delicate oval, with features very fine and regular, but the mouth was unsmiling and the expression stern, so that she looked both haughty and forbidding.

"This lady looks very proud," Josie couldn't help observing.

"Yes," Miss Gordy said, coming to stand beside her. "That is Mrs Bramstone".

Josie stared at the picture in fascination. She had not imagined Mrs Bramstone so young – the woman in the picture could not be past thirty – or so lovely. She recognised Miss Gordy's jet black eyes, except in Mrs Bramstone's face they still had the sparkle of youth, and looked positively bewitching.

"Was she that young when she was head here?" Josie asked.

"Oh yes," Miss Gordy replied. "My grandfather founded the school in 1890. But he died just a few years later, when my grandmother was only twenty-seven".

Josie thought of old Miss Willmott again. "Isn't that awfully young to be school head?" she asked uncertainly.

Miss Gordy smiled a little. "Yes, I suppose by today's standards, it is," she said. "But you know, in those days girls were often married with children while they were still only in their teens. Even Queen Victoria was only eighteen when she ascended the throne. My grandmother knew her three Rs, and she knew history, geography and French besides. Anyway, her school was for village children; I don't think they needed to know a lot".

Josie looked at another photograph. This one showed Mrs Bramstone seated in a chair, with a young boy standing beside her, and a little girl of about four years old perched on her knees. The little boy was bigger, perhaps about eight or nine, and had one arm around the little girl's waist. Both children were adorable, but had remarkably grave expressions, and their large doe eyes looked very sad. "Oh!" Josie exclaimed. "Is that – ?"

"Yes," Miss Gordy said softly, "That was my mother".

"She doesn't look very happy," Josie said hesitantly.

"No, she doesn't, does she?" Miss Gordy said, with her humourless laugh. "It was not… easy… for a child to be happy in this house".

"Who is the little boy?"

Miss Gordy seemed to hesitate. "That was my uncle – my mother's brother," she said shortly.

This was news. "The people in town said that Mrs Bramstone sent her little girl away to live somewhere else," Josie said, perplexed. "I don't remember anything about a boy".

Again Miss Gordy hesitated. "No," she said at last. "He died when he was only ten".

"Oh," Josie said. This was a puzzle. She had never heard of the boy before; he must have died even before his sister had been sent away. Josie badly wanted to ask more about him, but she thought it would somehow be in very bad taste. Instead, she asked, "Why did Mrs Bramstone send her little girl to live elsewhere?"

Miss Gordy looked at Josie keenly. "What do *you* think?" she asked.

Josie thought Miss Gordy sounded wary, and wondered if she had gone too far. "I don't know," she said slowly. "They said the people in the village here left too, so I guess something must have happened".

"Yes," Miss Gordy said. "I suppose then they told you that my grandmother closed the school at the same time?"

"Yes, they did," Josie admitted. "Some children went missing. Do you know what happened?"

"No," Miss Gordy answered shortly.

"Did Mrs Bramstone go with her little girl then?" Josie asked.

"No".

"Oh".

Josie didn't know what else to say. Miss Gordy didn't like her questions it seemed. Josie hurriedly turned her attention to another photograph.

This one showed Mrs Bramstone standing beside a man seated at a desk, with her hand on his shoulder. He too was dressed almost entirely in black, and in his hand was a curious metallic object that looked like two crescent moons stuck together. He was heavily bearded, but his thick slanting eyebrows and the soft expression of his eyes gave his face a gentle, puppy-like quality.

"Is that Mr Bramstone?" Josie asked. "I wonder what that thing is he's holding".

"Yes, that is Mr Bramstone," Miss Gordy replied. "He's holding a watchmaker's tool known as a balance truing caliper. His father was a clockmaker, you see, and it was from him that my grandfather learned to make the wheels and gears of his clockwork machines. You might say it was a kind of hobby of his. The works in that monkey automaton, for example, were made by him".

"Wow, he must have been really clever," Josie remarked admiringly. "He looks nice too".

"Yes, he does, doesn't he? I never heard my mother speak ill of him. But then he died quite suddenly, and left my grandmother to take care of everything… My mother said she never got over his death and I sometimes wonder how different things might have been if he had lived".

Looking at Mrs Bramstone's hard, chilly expression, Josie couldn't help thinking it wouldn't have made much difference at all, but then who could say…

Josie went over to the next photograph. Here, a large group of pupils stood together in rows, ranging in age from about eight to twelve, with the smaller girls in the front, and the taller ones in the back – all wore the same pinafore and dress Josie had seen in Margaret Helfrey's picture, and all had the same dismal, tight-lipped expression, as if they were sucking on lemons or something.

Josie thought of her own school, where the children were always in high spirits and the halls rang with boisterous screams and laughter. Mrs Bramstone's pupils looked very different; Josie couldn't imagine that they ever laughed about anything at all.

Miss Gordy seemed to read Josie's thoughts. "They look miserable don't they? Like they were attending a funeral, not a school".

Josie shivered. Closely scrutinising the shadowy faces, she suddenly spotted Margaret Helfrey with her light coronet of hair.

"You're very interested in that photograph, Josie," Miss Gordy remarked.

Josie started. She had been so absorbed in looking at the little faces that she had almost forgotten about the old lady.

"They're not at all jolly like the kids at my school," she said with a little laugh.

"No, I don't suppose they were," Miss Gordy agreed. "But I don't suppose you'd be jolly either if you had a ghost at your school".

Josie looked at Miss Gordy with wide eyes. A tingle ran up and down her spine. "A ghost?" she repeated. "There was a ghost?"

Miss Gordy smiled. "Indeed there was," she said. "Or at least, that's what my grandmother used to say. She said the ghost of Mr Bramstone walked the halls, making sure the school was running properly".

Josie stared. "Was it true?" she asked.

Miss Gordy shrugged. "Who knows?" she said. "I never saw it. But I'm sure it wasn't a nice thing to live with. Come now, it's getting late. You ought to be washing up and getting into your pyjamas. I'll come with you to turn out the lights".

"But she wouldn't have said that if it weren't true, would she?" Josie persisted, as she followed Miss Gordy into the hall.

"I really wouldn't know, my dear," Miss Gordy replied. "She told my mother this story before I was even born. And I myself didn't spend much time here until I grew too old to travel".

Miss Gordy stopped suddenly and turned. "Why do you ask?" There was a gleam of the same old eagerness in her jet bead eyes.

But Josie merely shrugged. "I was just wondering," she said.

"You're not afraid are you?" Miss Gordy asked, looking closely at her.

"Of course not!" Josie replied stoutly.

"Good," Miss Gordy nodded approvingly. "Come now, time for bed!"

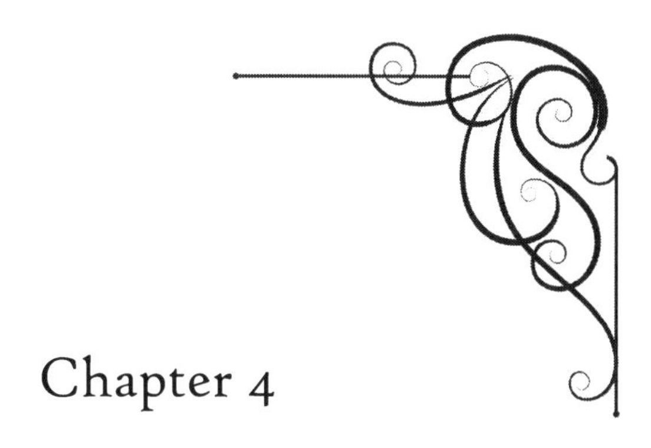

Chapter 4

Miss Gordy waited outside and chatted with Josie while she took her bath. She told Josie that in the "olden days", people only bathed about once a week; they generally used the washstands, she said, of which there had been two or three in the room before her mother had had them removed. As for the toilet, that was "a water closet out back" which sounded horrible. Josie was glad Miss Gordy believed in baths and modern plumbing.

After Josie had tucked herself into bed, Miss Gordy switched the room light off. Standing in the doorway, she said, "I shall be just two doors away; you can come over if you really need anything. Have a good night now".

Josie hugged her monkey tightly and tried to settle herself down. She had the vague feeling that Miss Gordy was trying to say something without actually saying it, but of course she couldn't tell what. Now she lay under her quilt, staring straight up at the ceiling, with Monkey lying on her chest, staring straight up as well. For a long time, she didn't move at all, while her eyes and ears strained to see and hear in the dark.

Then, just as she was finally starting to think that that horrible thing was not going to appear and she could at last relax a little, a strange scraping sound caught her attention.

CRRRR...

CRRRRRR... CRRRRRRK

All Josie's senses were alert in an instant – even the hairs on her arms seemed to be listening and trying to see. The scraping sound was very close by, too close for comfort in fact, and Josie felt herself growing colder and colder. *Scrape scrape scrape.* With a great shudder, Josie realised that the sound was coming from under her bed.

Holding her breath and clutching Monkey fast, Josie raised herself up and drew back against the wall as much as she could. There was a dull light coming from under her bed now, as though someone had turned on a small bulb there. As Josie stared, the little circle of light moved and the scraping sound became louder and more intense, as though whatever it was, was struggling earnestly.

In a moment, a small, ashy white hand appeared, its thin fingers scrabbling on the wooden floor like a crab. Then another hand appeared, and Josie realised that someone or something was trying to pull itself out from under the bed. The thought vaguely crossed her mind that perhaps she should help, give the hands a hand as it were, but she decided against it. It seemed better to wait and see what would happen.

In another moment, the rest of the body attached to the hands appeared. It was a little girl, and Josie recognised her immediately. It was Margaret Helfrey.

Dusting her plain nightdress with her small hands, Margaret sat down daintily on the edge of the bed.

"Hello," she whispered.

"Hello," Josie replied.

She wasn't afraid anymore. It was like she already knew Margaret from before. She saw now that the light was coming from Margaret's whole person, but it wasn't very bright, more like the glow from a dying fluorescent lamp, and it gave Margaret an unhealthy, pasty colour. Still, Josie could see Margaret's eyes were a very clear blue and her coronet of hair was silky white-gold.

"My name is Margaret," she said, "but you may call me Maggie".

"My name is Josie," Josie said, sitting up.

"I am pleased to meet you, Josie," Maggie said pleasantly. "I have been waiting a long time for you".

"For me?" Josie asked in surprise.

"Well, not for you exactly," Maggie said. "For another child. There haven't been any children here since Mrs Bramstone closed the school, and we do so need a child's help".

"Why?" Josie asked with interest.

"We would like our souls back," Maggie said sadly. "We are but wraiths now, trapped in this place and unable to leave for our real homes".

"Oh! Did someone take them?"

"Oh yes, Josie. The creature. Horatio".

Josie caught her breath. "Do you mean the one with the bedsheet on its head?" she asked excitedly, forgetting to keep her voice down.

"Hush," Maggie said, putting her finger to her lips. "Horatio doesn't like children speaking loudly. He doesn't like children at all really".

Josie remembered how she had raised her voice at Miss Gordy. "You mean he'll come if I make a noise?" she asked.

"Not only then," Maggie replied. "He'll come whenever you behave badly. That is what Mrs Bramstone told us. You haven't been here very long Josie, and yet you've already seen him. Are *you* very naughty?"

Josie couldn't help laughing. "Maybe a little," she said. "I should think Miss Gordy is tired of having me here already".

Maggie shook her head. "Ah no, not she – she wants you here too. We have given her no peace since she came to live here".

"Oh!" Josie said. "Are you very naughty then?"

Maggie paused, as though she were seriously considering this. "I don't think so," she said at last. "But Mrs Bramstone said I was, because I liked going on nature rambles and couldn't do some of my lessons properly. She said I was dirty and lazy and bad. But Josie, I did sincerely try my very best".

Josie nodded commiseratingly. "My teacher says I'm 'incorrigible', but I think maths is just stupid. I always do my drawings during maths".

Maggie looked a little puzzled. "Does your teacher not take away your soul then?" she asked.

Josie gave a snort. "I should like to see her try! She just calls my Daddy up and tells him, and then he has to do my homework with me. He isn't very good at maths either, so he doesn't get too mad". Then she frowned. "Why, does Mrs Bramstone really take away your soul when she thinks you're being lazy, Maggie?" she asked.

Maggie nodded solemnly. "She makes *him* come," she whispered. "The first time she told us, we didn't believe her. We thought she was just trying to frighten us. She told us that if we didn't do better, Mr Bramstone's ghost would come and take us away. She said bad children like us didn't deserve to be in her school; she said we were a waste of time and would never amount to anything. Ah, I can tell you Josie, it was most disheartening indeed to be told this with such unceasing regularity...

"Then one day, she became angry with Marianne Cook for biting her fingers. Marianne always did that when she was thinking, you know; she was a great poet, despite being such an imp. But Mrs Bramstone slapped her and called her a stupid, dirty girl, and told her that Mr Bramstone's ghost would come for her and put an end to her slatternly ways once and for all.

"And that night we saw a strange shape come into our bedroom. At first, we were afraid, because we were sure it was Mr Bramstone's ghost come for Marianne. But then Agnes Craig saw the thing had feet like Mrs Bramstone's coat stand in her drawing-room, and in a little while, we all saw that it was nothing more than a great sheet hanging on the old coat stand. So we began to laugh, which we very rarely did, and Marianne most of all, because she thought it so diverting that a coat stand was come to take her away.

"That was when Mrs Bramstone appeared. We never thought she was the one behind the thing. We thought it was Robert, her boy. He liked to play tricks on us sometimes, but this time it wasn't he. Oh Josie,

Mrs Bramstone was furious with us for laughing. She had thought to frighten us, and instead we had laughed and made such a noise. To be sure, we became quiet as mice as soon as we saw her, but it was no use. She was so angry, she said terrible things to us, and then, she took up the coat stand – "

The sound of footsteps on the stairs made both girls look towards the door. Maggie turned back to Josie in terror. "It is she! Lie down, pretend to sleep! Pray, pray, do not move or make a sound!"

Before Josie could say a word, Maggie had dissolved into a million tiny shards of silvery-blue light, like feathery snow falling on a grey winter's day. There was no sign at all that she had ever been there, save a faint coolness in the air. But Josie didn't have time to wonder about this. The footsteps had come closer, and were right outside her door.

Quick as a wink, Josie slid down under her covers and closed her eyes. She heard the door creak softly, and then a rustling, as the footsteps came into the room. They paused on the threshold. Even with her eyes closed, Josie knew the person was looking at her.

The rustling came closer and closer, till it was right beside Josie's bed. Josie knew from the swift footfalls that the person was not old Miss Gordy. It took all her willpower not to scream or open her eyes. She lay absolutely still, holding her blanket over her mouth. The rustling fell silent for a long while and Josie sensed that the person was standing just over her, staring at her intently. She kept her eyes squeezed shut and didn't move a muscle.

In a moment more, there came another rustling, and Josie suddenly felt the person's cold breath upon her cheek. Whoever it was had bent so close to her face that she hardly dared breathe. A sharp, hoarse whisper right at her ear made her almost jump out of her skin.

"I know you're awake! Open your eyes!"

Josie resolutely kept her eyes closed. She had had lots of practise pretending to be asleep at home.

"You wicked girl! Open your eyes! Get up!"

Now Josie began to feel a little annoyed. The person was clearly trying to catch her being awake when she should be asleep, but really, trying to *make* her naughty *in order* to catch her, was just a bit much. Josie kept her lips tightly pressed together so she wouldn't say something rude.

After a while, Josie heard the person inhale sharply with irritation, and draw back. The sound of rustling and receding footsteps told her that the person was leaving at last. Cautiously, she opened her eyes a fraction. She was just in time to see the back of a tall woman walking toward the door, dressed entirely in black. She was illuminated by the dull glow of a candlestick in her hand – Josie recognised the elegant figure as that of Mrs Bramstone. Within seconds, both the woman and her candle went right through the door and disappeared.

Although all was quiet the rest of the night, it was a long while before Josie finally fell asleep from exhaustion.

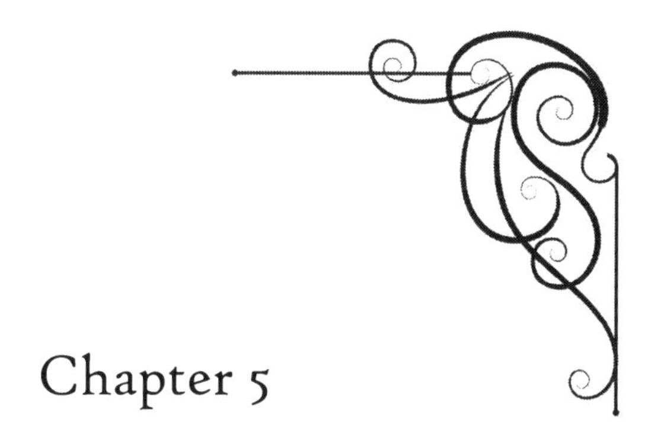

Chapter 5

The next morning Josie woke with a start. It was sunny, and for a moment she didn't quite know where she was. Then suddenly she remembered everything that had happened the night before. She sat up and bit her lip thoughtfully. She wished Maggie were around to help her, but there was no sign of her at all. She would have to go it alone for now.

The first thing, she decided then, was to confront Miss Gordy. She felt sure now that the old lady had nothing to do with the creature Horatio, but that she could at least tell her something about him.

Going downstairs, she was surprised to see Miss Gordy carrying a platter of toast, followed by a heavily freckled young man of about twenty with thick, curling red hair. He was very tall and sinewy, and his deep-set eyes and hard-angled brows gave him a hawkish appearance suggestive of keen observation and a continual silent analysis. He was carrying several jars of jam artfully balanced one upon the other, and Josie recognised him as the son of a man who ran a photography studio in the town; she often saw him out and about in awkward positions photographing things when she followed her father to the recording studio next door.

At the same time, a stout, middle-aged lady with a mass of grey hair piled up on the top of her head emerged from the drawing-room, carrying a feather duster and a pile of neatly-folded clothes. Her ruddy cheeks and bright blue eyes spoke of sprightly good humour, and she greeted Josie on the stairs as she passed her with a cheery "Good morning, miss!"

"Ah," Miss Gordy said, looking up, "you're just in time for breakfast. Say hello to Mrs Edmundson – she's here every morning to help me with the cooking and cleaning. And Casper here, he comes up three times a week to help me about the house". Casper paused a moment to nod his head at Josie before following Miss Gordy into the drawing room.

There, Josie found the table had been neatly laid; there were baked beans, toast, scrambled tofu and mugs of some kind of milk, as well as the jams Miss Gordy said Mrs Edmundson had "slaved to can".

"I'll see you again soon, miss," Casper said, tipping an imaginary hat at Josie. "I'll wait for Mrs Edmundson in the hall, Miss Gordy – she'd appreciate a lift back into town, no doubt".

"Thank you Casper, she surely would," Miss Gordy said. "We'll see you on Thursday".

In a few minutes, the housekeeper had come back down the stairs. No sooner had Josie heard the front door slam shut behind them than she dropped her jammy bread and turned to Miss Gordy.

"I want to know more about this house and the children who used to live here. You *can* tell me something about them, can't you?"

Miss Gordy grabbed Josie's wrist so tightly that she gasped. "What have you found?" the old lady whispered hoarsely, her black eyes flashing.

"I know about the girls here," Josie whispered back fiercely, "and I know about Mrs Bramstone and her horrid monster. Their ghosts still live here and they won't leave us alone until we help them!"

Miss Gordy had turned white. She was breathing rapidly and clutched at her chest as if she were having a heart attack. Josie remembered her father mentioning Miss Gordy's weak heart a long time ago, and felt a little anxious.

But a moment later, the old lady released Josie's hand. "You've seen them then," she murmured, almost to herself. She appeared to be thinking. "Remember that grey squirrel I was telling you about?" she suddenly asked. "Let's go for a walk and see if he's still out there". Her black eyes looked meaningfully at Josie.

"All right, let's!" Josie said eagerly, jumping up.

"Finish your milk first," Miss Gordy said firmly. "My mother used to say children who didn't drink their milk wouldn't have much backbone as adults".

Josie couldn't understand how Miss Gordy could think of the things her mother used to say even at such a time as this. She drank her milk down with a largely unnecessary amount of noise, then said pointedly, "That squirrel doesn't have all day".

Miss Gordy got slowly to her feet and gave Josie her arm. No one had ever given Josie their arm before. It was rather nice to feel needed.

The two of them made their way out the front door. Josie thought she heard something rustling upstairs but she refused to look. Again the sun had disappeared behind the clouds, and the house was shadowy and sad.

It was a relief to be outside. Josie couldn't help wondering how Miss Gordy could stand living there alone for so long and began to understand why she said the creepy things she did. The old lady led Josie along the crunchy gravel path that cut through the overgrown lawn. It ran close to the house and led toward the woods. Josie recognised the large windows of her dormitory.

"Keep close to the wall, so they can't see you," Miss Gordy said "I'm sure you wouldn't want them to suddenly appear right now".

It was the first time Miss Gordy had made any reference to what was happening in the house. Josie felt a grim satisfaction. They pressed closer to the wall, so that they were well under the long window ledges. Josie felt impatient, for Miss Gordy could not walk very fast, but she held her tongue.

It was a while before they finally walked the whole length of the house and reached the back of it. Here, there were no windows; indeed, the whole back wall appeared to have been plastered over, so that there were no openings of any sort at all.

"My grandmother had this side of the house completely blocked off," Miss Gordy said, "perhaps for the same reason I myself come here sometimes – it's the only part of the house where I don't feel like someone's continually watching and eavesdropping".

"But it must be tiring living like that," Josie remarked. "Why didn't you just move out?"

"I couldn't," Miss Gordy said regretfully. "I never married, and had no one to live with. We'd had a nice townhouse in the city, but after a while I couldn't afford to stay there on my own anymore. My grandmother had come from a wealthy family and in her will she had left provisions for my mother to be taken care of only for so long as she remained in the house and looked after it.

"Well, my mother *didn't* want to stay in the house of course, so that money just went to occasional maintenance – roof repairs and such – and it remained mostly untouched and came down to me. So you see, I *had* to come back here to the old homestead – I didn't have much choice. But it was really not something I wanted to do; I had terrible memories of it as a child, when my mother brought me to visit... I think you know why".

Josie nodded. "I do now. You've seen the creature then?"

"Only once. My father had gotten a new job in a different city and he couldn't bring us over right away. The lease on our apartment had expired and we needed somewhere to stay for a while, so we came to the house. It was dark when we arrived, and everything looked eerie and ghostly because they were covered in sheets, so I started crying. My mother seemed to become a different person – she looked tense and agitated – and she hissed at me to be quiet.

"But I didn't quiet down, so she lost her temper, and dragged me upstairs to my grandmother's bedroom. I went screaming all the way. And even after my mother locked me in, I still went on screaming. And that was when I saw something moving in the corner. It was the creature

– he was coming out of the wall! For a moment, I couldn't make a single sound. And then I screamed even louder than before, and banged and banged on the door with all my might".

"What happened then?" Josie asked breathlessly.

"I fainted dead away. The last thing I remembered was the thing coming toward me with his arms out, almost as though he wanted to hug me! My mother said later I must have been delirious, but I saw she was afraid too. I think she came and got me out of that room just in time".

"Didn't you ask your mum about the creature? She must have seen him too, when she was little".

"Perhaps she had, but she always denied it. Anyway, we had to stay on for a few days while my father settled our new home for us. My mother and I slept in the same room you are sleeping in now. After what had happened, I never dared raise my voice again, and my mother too told me to always whisper and do as I was told. She kept me close by her all the time.

"Then one night my mother didn't come to bed with me as she usually did. She was arguing with my father on the telephone, and told me to go to bed first. So I went alone, terrified. And that was the first time I learned about the girls".

"You saw Maggie?" Josie asked excitedly.

Miss Gordy looked puzzled. "Maggie? No," she said slowly, "the girl I saw was not named Maggie. It's been over eighty years but I can still remember her name as clear as yesterday. It was Hetty – Hetty Wright. She had long curling hair – light chestnut brown – and the sweetest dimples. It was her bed I was sleeping in.

"She told me that the creature's name was Horatio and that he had taken away her soul and the souls of other children who had misbehaved. I asked her what she had done, but she looked very troubled, and said she couldn't remember. Ah, I shall never forget her poor, pale face".

"Oh!" said Josie, remembering the names she had read on the beds. "She must be Harriet Wright. What happened then? Did she tell you more about Horatio?"

"No," Miss Gordy said regretfully. "My mother came up to bed then. Hetty was just telling me that they had been waiting so long for a chance to speak to me, because I was still a little girl then, about six or seven. She said that adults couldn't seem to see or hear them; it was as though they somehow lost or outgrew the ability. And then she heard my mother coming, and became absolutely terrified. I tried to assure her that it really was just my mother, but she seemed quite beside herself, poor thing, and she vanished before I could learn anything more.

"I didn't get another chance alone like that again; my mother took care to always keep me close by. In a few days more we left to join my father in the city. It was such a relief, I can tell you! We settled there, and when I was older, I went travelling and it was like the whole thing never happened. It was only much later, when my mother herself was very ill and her mind was wandering, that she said anything at all.

"But it was hard to understand her. Sometimes she talked about Robert, her brother; other times she would talk about their mother. Often, she seemed to confuse the two. She would say, 'Hush! Mother doesn't like noise!' or 'Robert is looking for me, he's always waiting for me'. It was horrible to hear her talk like that. Robert had died a long time ago, when she was still little, and my grandmother too. I don't know why she kept talking about them like that".

Josie was thoughtful. It certainly was disturbing that Mrs Gordy spoke of her mother and brother that way.

"Was Robert much older than your mum?" Josie asked.

"Yes, by about five years," Miss Gordy replied. "In the few pictures I've seen of them together as children, Robert is always standing over her; protectively, it seemed to me. She was a small thing, and always looked sorrowful and afraid; I liked to imagine he used his privilege as a boy to shield her from their mother whenever he could".

"Perhaps I shall ask Maggie about Robert," Josie said. "She might know what your mother meant". She went on to tell Miss Gordy about all that had happened to her since her arrival at the house. Miss Gordy sighed.

"Now you know the secret I've had to live with all these years. I knew it was not right letting you come here, knowing everything I did, but I could not help it – I didn't know when I'd ever have another opportunity to have a child come here to try to undo this – this – curse. I don't think that I could die in peace knowing that the souls of all those children are still trapped".

The old lady covered her face with her hands and Josie felt sorry for her. For the first time, she saw Miss Gordy as she really was – tired, tormented and sad, not crazy.

"I *will* try to help," Josie promised earnestly.

Miss Gordy looked up and took Josie's hands in both her own. "Will you?" she asked eagerly. "Oh, how lovely it would be to know peace and quiet again! My mother and I were both much older when we finally came back here again," she went on, "but though we never saw Horatio or the girls, we could always feel them somehow. Even now I still hear the footsteps and the whispers, and sometimes I'd see things out of the corner of my eye..."

The old lady paused. "But no – Josie, this is no place for children. It was selfish of me. I think I should call your father and ask him to take you away".

"*Nooooo!*" Josie cried.

She stopped, amazed at herself. She hadn't wanted to come, and now she didn't want to leave! No, she didn't – it was all too exciting really – and she couldn't abandon Maggie, of whom she had started to become really quite fond.

She *would* be much safer with her father of course, but then it would be just like all her other holidays, she thought – playing alone, and make-believing in the attic or out in the garden, while her father pottered about with his sewing machine and tape measure; it all just became rather dull after a while. Anyway, he was busy with her dying uncle now, and whatever *he* had might be even more dangerous than any number of ghosts.

"I *want* to help," she said firmly. "This is the most exciting school holiday I've *ever* had".

"But what if something happens?" Miss Gordy asked anxiously.

"Well, I hope something *does*!"

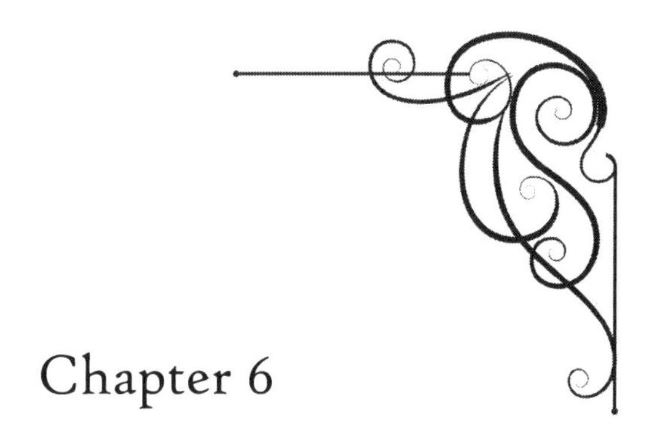

Chapter 6

Josie spent much of the morning in the dormitory, hoping that Maggie or one of the other girls might appear. But it seemed that that was not to be, and Josie finally decided she'd better turn her attention to getting some of her holiday homework done at least.

Then, Mr Harwood telephoned close to lunchtime and asked how she was doing.

"Daddy!" Josie squealed. "I'm doing great! I've been having so much fun!"

"Oh!" Mr Harwood replied with some surprise. "Well, um, that's good then; I'm glad to hear it. Uncle Eddie is really doing very badly; he could hardly say a thing when I arrived. But the doctors are saying now that there's a tiny chance he just might pull through – these next few days will be quite critical. If you need anything you must look for me here at St Jude's, not the hotel; they've given me a room here so I can be close by. Let me speak with Miss Gordy".

Josie passed the phone to the old lady, who told Mr Harwood his daughter was such a good girl, and took down his new room and contact details on a notepad. Josie hugged herself at the thought that Uncle Eddie seemed to be hanging on a little longer – she'd been a little worried he'd die too quickly and then her father would be home too soon.

After lunch, Miss Gordy settled down to her regular afternoon session of knitting random items for the house. She had lately decided to completely cover her grandmother's sofa in cable knit and this project was taking up a good deal of her time.

Josie helped her wind the blue-grey skein and watched her knit for a while; then, bored, she asked if she could explore the house.

"You may," Miss Gordy replied after a long pause. "But be sure not to go into anything that's locked, or open anything that's shut".

"Okay," Josie said, vaguely thinking that that was almost a surefire way to make anyone try to do those things.

"Remember, although the house has been wired for electricity, many of the rooms don't have bulbs or lamps plugged in – you'd be stumbling about in the dark. But all the rooms without light are locked anyway, so there's no chance of that happening".

Going out into the hall, Josie scanned her surroundings. Directly ahead of her, on either side of the main staircase, were two doors leading somewhere that ran under part of the gallery overhead. But the doors were closed, and when she tried them, she found them locked.

The door on her right shared one of its walls with the stairs, but the wall on the opposite side was set with two great stained glass windows featuring a floral geometric pattern in extended half round frames, very dirty and blackened with age. Josie went closer and tried to peer in.

All at once, something on the other side smacked against the glass, making Josie jump backward, almost out of her skin. Yet, in a trice, she was back at the glass again, rubbing the panes vehemently with the sleeves of her jumper. The grime was so thick she could barely get any of it off, but one pane in particular seemed to be a touch cleaner than the others, and in this she soon managed to scrub a circle just big enough for her to make out what appeared to be a small classroom, with a few school desks arranged haphazardly about, and a blackboard on one wall. In the middle was a large wooden table, on which were several long sticks, some slates and pencils, an inkwell and a thick, open book.

Everything was shrouded in dusty shadow, but the dismal obscurity was broken in the furthest corner by a softly glowing figure – it was a young girl, barely eleven or twelve years old, with coppery red hair streaming over her face and her bare legs covered in bloody stripes from knee to ankle. As her eyes met Josie's, she began scrambling to and fro, pressing her hands along the wall with a desperation more harrowing than anything Josie had ever seen.

"Wait, wait!" Josie cried, banging on the glass with her fists. "Don't be afraid! I want to help you! Don't go!"

But as soon as the words were out of her mouth, Josie was sorry. Had the creature heard her, or had Mrs Bramstone? She looked over her shoulder with apprehension. But neither appeared and now Josie's attention was entirely caught by the scrape-scrape-scraping of chalk being drawn across a blackboard with frantic energy.

Peering through the glass again, Josie was just in time to see the girl finish writing the last words in a series of apparently identical short sentences, written one after the other. Throwing the piece of chalk from her, the girl gave Josie one last anguished look before vanishing in a shower of iridescent dust.

"Wait, wait!" Josie hissed loudly under her breath, but the room was now empty and dark. I *have* to see what she wrote, Josie thought, but try as she might, all she could make out at that distance were vague shapes; they might have been Egyptian hieroglyphs for all she knew.

Still, she went back to the door and tried it again. It was decidedly locked, and in frustration, she kicked at it savagely with her Mary-Janed foot. Unexpectedly, there was a loud crack, as if something brittle had finally given way, and to her surprise, the door swung open.

As Josie cautiously took a step forward, she suddenly became aware of *both* the dampish, squelching sound that always marked Horatio's appearance, as well as the crisp rustling of Mrs Bramstone's long skirts. Coming through the wall ahead of her, with a curious heaving motion, the familiar shape of the creature Horatio began to materialise, while out of the corner of her eye, Josie saw the headmistress' forbidding black form gliding swiftly down the stairs.

For a moment, Josie stood between the two, looking in dread from one to the other. It seemed to her that they were both coming for her as fast as they could, almost as if they were in a race to see who would reach her first.

"Well, it's not going to be *either* of you!" Josie declared with conviction, and whirling about, she dashed madly across the hallway and into the drawing-room, almost tripping over her own feet and crashing right into Miss Gordy's upturned bottom, for the old lady had been busy measuring the underside of the sofa.

"Josie!! What on earth – ???"

"Oh Miss Gordy, I'm so sorry!" Josie exclaimed, bending over to pull the old lady up by both arms. "But you must come with me; quickly!"

Miss Gordy hurried after Josie as fast as her little feet could manage. Neither the creature nor Mrs Bramstone was anywhere in sight now, and the door of the room with stained glass stood wide open. Seeing it, Miss Gordy stopped short in astonishment.

"Why, how on earth did that – ?"

Quickly, Josie explained to her what had happened (though admittedly she did gloss over how she'd kicked the door and might have irreversibly damaged the valuable antique wood).

"We must find out what she wrote on the board – it might tell us something very important!" she cried. Impulsively, she took Miss Gordy's hand. "But I can't go alone – you need to come with me – I might need your help".

Miss Gordy nodded and squeezed Josie's hand. "Come on then; let's go see".

It was dark in the room; Josie wished she had brought her pocket torch with her and made a note to herself to always carry it from then on. Still, there was just enough light coming through the open door for her to see her way and make out the heavy layer of dust and cobwebs covering everything.

"I've never been in any of these locked rooms before," Miss Gordy said, looking around, her black eyes wide with wonder. She shuddered.

"I'm not relishing this at all".

"Nor I," Josie agreed. "What an awful place!"

Hurrying over to the board on the furthest wall, she let out a gasp as she read in amazement:

SHE KILLED THEM
SHE KILLED THEM
SHE KILLED THEM
SHE KILLED THEM

The lines of writing ran from top to bottom, and were written in large letters that curved extravagantly, as if the writer could barely control the chalk; now, as Josie stared at them, they began swiftly fading, as if an invisible hand were wiping the board clean.

"What is it?" Miss Gordy asked, coming up beside her.

Josie stared at the old lady in astonishment.

"The words!" she cried. "Can't you see them?"

"No!"

"They say she killed them," Josie said slowly. "*She* killed them". A chill sense of horror began to descend upon her.

"What on earth could it mean?" Miss Gordy breathed at last.

"I don't know!" Josie cried.

She fervently wished now the girl would reappear, but minutes passed and it was clearly not to be. Looking round the room, Josie tried to think what to do next.

The open book on the table caught her attention. Going closer, she was shocked to see that the pages had been filled with rows upon rows of names, dates and misdemeanours – it was apparently a methodical record of misdeeds and punishments, all written in a beautiful cursive hand:

May 10th, 1894
Eveline Clarke – Fidgeting – 6 strokes
Agnes Craig – Truancy – 10 strokes

Frances Shaw – Inattention – 100 lines
Hazel Phillips – Writing with left hand again – 6 strokes
Alma Thompson – Poor reading – Dunce hat till tea-time upon the stool

On and on it went, page after page after page. Josie glanced at the long sticks lying close by. "Oh!" she cried. "Are these – ?"

"Yes," Miss Gordy nodded. "These birch sticks were used to administer the strokes".

"How horrid!" Josie exclaimed, slamming the book shut and sending up a cloud of dirt and dust. "I wonder Mrs Bramstone had any energy left after all that!"

"She was not unusual in this," Miss Gordy remarked. "Such punishments were common in those days, and recording them was expected as well; future employers would sometimes ask to look at these logs".

Josie snorted in irritation. "I must ask Maggie about what that girl wrote," she said at last. "And I'm going to take this punishment book with me – it might tell us something".

Picking up the book, Josie and Miss Gordy left the room, carefully closing the door behind them.

"I'm going to stay in the dorm today and see if Maggie will come," Josie whispered. "And I'm going to go through this book and see if I can find out anything!"

"I think I'll stay with you while you look at the book at least," Miss Gordy said after a pause. "I have a feeling my grandmother will not be at all pleased if she sees you going through it".

"Good idea!" Josie replied. Miss Gordy took her arm again as they ascended the stairs and Josie smiled at her. She was beginning to feel rather fond of the old lady.

They reached the dormitory and sat down on Josie's bed. Balancing the book on her knees and dusting it off with delicate fingers, Josie lifted the cover.

Just inside, on the flyleaf, she read:

DISCIPLINE BOOK, 1894
J. BRAMSTONE

Carefully turning over the yellowed pages, Josie began reading down the neatly catalogued list of offences from the beginning of the year. As was to be expected, it was the same dreary repetition of barbarous punishments she'd read earlier, with most of them seeming far out of proportion to the purported offence. It was tedious work going through it all, week after week, month after month, but then suddenly, Josie stopped and frowned.

"What is it?" Miss Gordy asked.

"Look!" Josie pointed. "June 9th – Luella Davies, six strokes for ink blots; Tillie Robinson, a hundred lines for botching her homework or whatever..."

"Well, what then?" Miss Gordy asked, puzzled.

"Look!" Josie said, turning the page over to June the 10th.

Miss Gordy gasped. "Why, the handwriting! It's all – it's all *messy*! The letters are running into each other and goodness, there are even blots!"

"Right!" Josie said. "And the pen's pressed so hard into the paper you can see it's almost gone through in some parts... But that's not all – Just *look* at all the punishments that day! Agnes Craig, *thirty* strokes for truancy; Sarah Davenport, *two hundred* lines for speaking out of turn; Alma Thompson, *three* hours standing on the stool for being slothful... It goes on and on like this and then suddenly stops...

"Don't you see?" Josie cried, jumping up excitedly. "Something happened on the 10th, or maybe even the night of the 9th, that changed everything. Right up to the 9th, all the punishments *were* awful, but they weren't nearly as awful as what they became *after*. And then they all stop on the 10th – there's nothing else in this book after that.

"Now look at the dates on the beds here – June the 11th. It's like everything just suddenly changed, or stopped..."

Josie's breath caught in her throat as a new thought suddenly struck her.

"When did Mrs Bramstone close the school?" she asked slowly.

Miss Gordy's eye widened. "It was near the middle of June," she replied, almost in a whisper. "June the 13th. Lucky thirteen, as my mother used to say. You're right," she went on, taking up the book. "It's like – it's like – "

Josie nodded grimly. "Something happened to make Mrs Bramstone go *stark raving mad!*"

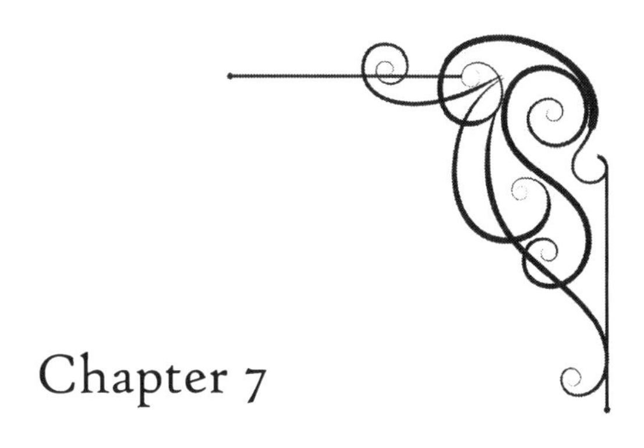

Chapter 7

It was already starting to get dark. Miss Gordy left to replace the book and start preparing dinner, while Josie stayed in the dorm, hoping Maggie might appear. It had already been quite an eventful day, but Josie felt in her bones that something more was to come.

Looking over at the bed next to hers, Josie recalled Miss Gordy's story about Hetty. She wondered if there might be anything of Hetty's in *her* chest of drawers, and went over to have a look.

But in this Josie was disappointed – the drawers were quite empty. She crouched down on all fours and peered under the bed. There was nothing there either, but as she raised her head, she had a sudden inspiration. Pulling down the blanket, she lifted the thin, moth-eaten pillow. Neatly folded underneath was a small square of ivory-coloured linen.

Opening it carefully, she saw that it was a handmade handkerchief, barely ten by ten inches, beautifully embroidered in all four corners with birds, leaves and flowers. In one corner, she read *December 1893*, and in the corner opposite, *For Hetty*. As she gently traced the fine stitching, a low voice suddenly spoke directly in her ear: "That belongs to me – pray have a care".

Josie whirled around with a squeal and came face to face with a young girl stooping down so closely that her long brown ringlets brushed against Josie's neck like down feathers. Deep dimples came into her cheeks as she spoke, and her small, sharp features and light green eyes lent her face a remarkably feline quality. Like Maggie, she wore a plain white nightdress, and she glowed softly too, as Maggie had – dimly, like a dying candle. Now, as Josie stared at her with wide eyes, she quickly held up her finger to Josie's lips.

"Hush!" she whispered. "My name is Harriet – Harriet Wright – Hetty, everyone calls me – and I mean you no harm. But please, I beg you, do not take my handkerchief from me. It was given me by my mother and is my most treasured possession in all the world. I was at home on Christmas Day and she gave it me then; I believe it was one of the happiest days of my life. After I came back here, I never saw her again".

Hetty began to cry, and Josie timidly touched her cold hand.

"My name is Josie," she said. "I lost my Mummy too. I know how awful it feels". She placed the handkerchief in Hetty's hand. "I wasn't going to keep your hankie," she said. "I was actually looking for clues. Here, keep it in your pocket or something".

"I cannot," Hetty said sorrowfully. "I am neither living nor dead. I can see your world – I can touch it and feel it and smell it, and I can hear and watch everything you do, but I cannot stay long or bring anything away with me… Here, I feel almost alive again, but where I go, everything disappears and I am in darkness; I become like air, a mere shadow, and the only path I can see always leads back here, to this place, this room – if I try to step beyond it, I fall right back into the darkness. But oh, I feel so much stronger when I hold my mother's handkerchief, even if only for a little while, so thank you kindly".

"You must tell me how I can help you," Josie urged her. "Tell me what to do".

"I know not," Hetty replied. "We have been trapped like this for so long; I fear one day we will no longer remember our names or where we came from, and we will never be able to leave or see our families again, to go to where they are... It will be like we never existed".

Josie shuddered. "Don't say that! I told you just now I was looking for clues – well, you can help me. Tell me what happened to you. Tell me what you remember that night Mrs Bramstone came in with the coat stand".

At this, Hetty trembled violently, and pressed her handkerchief so tightly in her fist that the knuckles gleamed white. "I forget myself when I think of it," she whispered fiercely. "I don't know that I can speak of it plainly".

"You *must*," Josie told her firmly. "We must piece together everything that happened that week in June. Maggie told me about the night Mrs Bramstone came in with an old coat stand covered in a sheet, pretending to be some sort of ghost or monster. Do you remember the date? You all laughed and she got angry – what happened then?"

"Yes," Hetty said slowly, "I remember. It was the night of June the 9th. I remember that tall, monstrous thing appearing at our doorway – I remember how it seemed to glide and then pause on the threshold and sway a little, and how we were all well-nigh sick with terror, when Agnes cried, 'Look! Look at its feet!'

"We looked, and we realised then that it was only the coat stand from downstairs, and we began to laugh, with relief mostly I do believe, and someone said, 'Oh Robert, you naughty boy! Come out at once!'

"But I think you know Josie, it wasn't Robert – it was Mrs Bramstone. She had been crouching behind, and now she rose up and screamed at us as I'd never heard her yet – she was that ashamed of having been discovered, I think.

"Oh Josie, I shall never, never forget what happened next. Mrs

Bramstone was accustomed to thrashing us whenever she felt we did wrong – all the teachers were, you know – so we knew to expect a beating. But what we *didn't* expect was that she would reach for the nearest thing she could lay her hands on right then, and that was the coat stand!

"She was big and strong, and she lifted it up, sheet and all, and swung it back… Ah Josie, I pray I shall never hear such a sound again as I did then – 'twas neither loud nor remarkable, a mere dull sort of thud, like that of an axe striking a tree, but 'twill forever and always be etched in my mind…

"Robert Bramstone had come up behind his mother, quite unbeknownst to her; I imagine it was to see what all the commotion was about. And one leg of the coat stand – 'twas made of cast iron – caught him squarely on the head, and he cried out a little, not loudly, but enough to make his mother whirl round… And she saw in an instant what she had done, for he tried to stand upright, but could not – his feet crossed one over the other, and he stepped forward and back for a moment, like a drunkard, then his knees buckled, and he fell upon the stand, which his mother still held…

"It fell with a clatter as she caught him, while we, all aghast, were up and kneeling upon our beds, some crying for their mammas and some saying to send for Matron or Dr Pryor at once. But Mrs Bramstone silenced us speedily with a look – 'Not a word more from any of you,' said she with bitter accent. 'It is your fault that this has happened. A little rest shall put him to rights in no time; all of you, however, may expect the birch tomorrow'.

"Ah Josie, Robert was a fine boy, only ten years old then and but a little older than ourselves, as thoughtful and affectionate as his mother was cold and hard; we were all very fond of him and many a tear was shed that night…"

Hetty paused. "Did you hear that?" she suddenly asked.

"What?" Josie replied, looking over her shoulders quickly. She had been too absorbed in Hetty's story to notice anything else.

"I thought I heard –"

"It was nothing," Josie said impatiently. "Tell me what happened next!"

"Listen!" Hetty hissed, tilting her head in a listening attitude. And now there could be no mistaking it, for a distinct scrape-scraping sound could be heard coming clearly from under Josie's bed. In a moment, a small white hand appeared, and Hetty let out a little scream.

"Shhh!!" Josie said, waving her hands at Hetty's face to quiet her. "It's only Maggie!"

"Maggie??" Hetty exclaimed. "She comes out from under the bed??"

"Yes!" Josie replied, nodding. "I guess it's her 'thing'".

"I beg your pardon?" Hetty asked. "Her 'thing'?"

Josie giggled. "It means it's the special way she does something. This is her special way of coming out into the real world. I'm not sure what your thing is; I missed that, sorry".

By this time Maggie had crawled out from under the bed and was, as usual, dusting her nightgown. "Hello Josie!" she said with a bright smile. "Oh! And Hetty! I didn't know you were here!"

"Yes I am!" Hetty replied. "Josie found my handkerchief; you know that always gets my attention".

"I wasn't trying to steal it," Josie quickly explained to Maggie. "I was looking for clues. And it was a good thing after all, because then I met Hetty, and she's told me more about what happened that night!"

"'Tis true," Hetty nodded. "And I do believe you could be the one who can help us! But Maggie, I did not know you come here from under your bed! My word, I should have had a fit if I'd seen you creeping out like that in the dark; I wonder Josie didn't!"

"Oh, I *am* sorry about that," Maggie said regretfully. "I couldn't help it – it's not my fault that that's where I was when *it* happened".

"Well, you could try to do it less ominously," Hetty admonished. "I well nigh stopped breathing when I heard you coming".

"We all stopped breathing a long time ago," Maggie observed drily. "Nevertheless, I shall try to do as you ask. I would not like to frighten

Josie needlessly".

"Oh, it's all right," Josie said, "I'm used to you already. And I'm so glad you're here; I have so many questions! Can either of you tell me what happened after Mrs Bramstone hit her boy that night? Did he die?"

"Well, that remained a mystery to us even then," Hetty replied, with a frown. "We heard and saw nothing of him afterward and thought he must be recuperating in the infirmary; we saw no fuss or to-do, and our hearts were therefore eased a little to think that he was mending, as his mamma said he would. But as we were not allowed in Matron's rooms, we actually never knew with certainty".

"Yes," Maggie agreed. "And no one else observed anything, for Robert was wont to shut himself up in the drawing-room, or ramble off in the woods alone. But we could tell Mrs Bramstone was sorely troubled, for she became as one stricken with some secret woe, and she vented her anger upon us, for she held that we were to blame for what had happened. The next day – 'twas a Sunday, a half day of lessons – she thrashed and punished us with a vengeance, ten times worse than she ever did before…

"'Twas a strange thing indeed, for the older girls had once told us she never used to be thus; that she had always been a kindly, gracious, warm-hearted body, and 'twas only in the past year that she had quite changed… perhaps 'twas after Mr Bramstone died, but that I cannot tell; for us younger ones, we never knew her any other way.

"That also was the day we first saw *him.* Mrs Bramstone ordered us out into the garden after morning lessons, to which we went with much pleasure, for certainly recent events had been distressing beyond measure. It was while we were out by the woods that Bessie took that photograph of me, the one you found in my drawer. Bessie's father had a photography studio in the town – 'twas a rare and marvellous thing to us then – and he had given her one of his old hand cameras at Christmastime. 'Twas then that I looked up at our bedroom windows and saw *him* looking down at us.

"He was standing at that middle window, and though I could not see his face, I knew he was watching and waiting for us. When Bessie took my picture I was all a-tremble and had turned quite white – she remarked on it and I told her what I had seen. But when she turned to look, he was no longer there. I remember she laughed at me then, but later, she didn't..."

"I don't remember the name 'Bessie' on any of the beds here," Josie remarked, looking puzzled.

"Ah, you wouldn't," Hetty replied. "Bessie was a little older than us and slept in the second form dormitory next door. She was our monitor; she taught us our lessons sometimes. Elizabeth Brasket, her name was".

"Brasket?" Josie repeated. The name sounded oddly familiar, but she couldn't think where she might have seen or heard it before. Suddenly, on a hunch, she asked, "What did Bessie look like?"

"Oh, she was a great beauty," Maggie replied, and Hetty nodded in agreement.

"The clearest blue-green eyes, and skin like peaches, with a splendid dusting of freckles," she said.

"And her hair – 'twas flaming red, and fell in marvellous profusion," Maggie added. "We used to call her Queen Elizabeth – in jest, you understand, for the real Queen was quite fearsome I do believe. Mrs Bramstone almost hated Bessie I think, for how lovely she was".

"I wonder what became of her," Hetty murmured thoughtfully. "She was a plucky one, she was, and a faithful friend – I hope she escaped and went home and lived a long, goodly life. I should like to think so, for 'twould be a crying shame otherwise. Our families sacrificed much to let us come here, to be educated almost as well as real ladies; ah, they little knew they were sending us to our doom".

Josie was in no doubt that the girl she had seen downstairs was Bessie Brasket and was about to sadly disabuse Hetty of her hope, when the sound of Miss Gordy's footsteps shuffling across the hallway caught her attention.

"Oh shoot, it's dinnertime," Josie said. "When can we speak together again?"

But neither Maggie nor Hetty had a chance to reply, for a familiar sound of damp linen being pressed and squeezed could be clearly heard coming through the last boarded window. The three girls exchanged anxious, wide-eyed glances, then –

"*Run!!*" Hetty cried, pushing Josie off the bed, while Maggie jumped up and disappeared like a dying pyrotechnic.

Josie didn't have to be told twice. But as she scrambled out the door, she suddenly remembered Hetty's handkerchief, which had been left open on the bed. Fearing it might get taken or damaged, she turned back, despite the precious seconds she knew this would cost her.

Wheeling around, she stopped short in amazement at the sight which met her eyes. Barely six feet away, Hetty stood facing the oncoming creature who descended upon her as swiftly as some bird of prey.

"Hetty!!" Josie exclaimed, quite forgetting her own fear.

At the sound of Hetty's name, the creature abruptly froze in its tracks. Seeing it with arms outstretched and blank face sniffing at the air, Josie was suddenly reminded of a blind dog she'd seen once at the local shelter and she felt an overwhelming pity now for this strange, faceless creature.

Hetty glanced over her shoulder at her. "It's all right, Josie," she said with a little smile. "Go!"

The creature reached forward with both its arms as if to embrace her, and at once she dissolved into a glittering shower of light that vanished as it fell toward the floor. Horatio's arms closed on the empty air and for a moment, he paused there, in an attitude of infinite sadness. Then he, too, sank down to the floor and disappeared.

Josie grabbed the handkerchief off the bed in a fit of trembling and ran out of the room. She had the feeling of one who had gotten a little more than they'd bargained for.

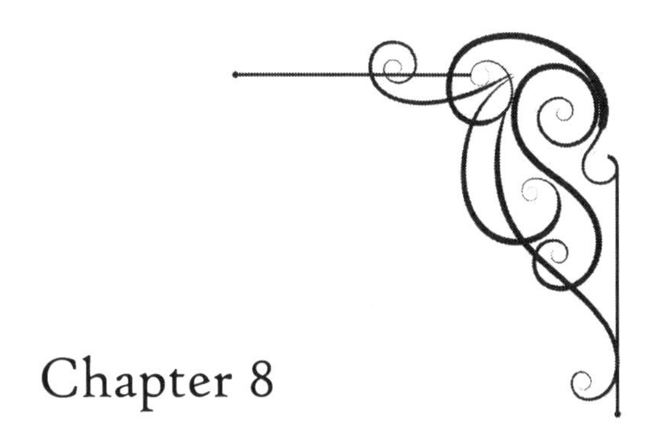

Chapter 8

"What say we go into town tomorrow Josie?" Miss Gordy asked over cauliflower steaks and a hearty tomato casserole. "I'd like to pick up some new wools and choose the fruits myself – Casper always gets them too ripe".

"Oh, I should like that very much!" Josie said eagerly, for she didn't often get to go out.

"Very well, then. I shall let Casper know and he'll pick us up tomorrow morning. Finish your tomatoes properly now; my mother used to say children who didn't eat their fruits and veggies didn't deserve to eat at all".

That night Josie was much too excited to close her eyes and sleep. After Miss Gordy left her, she replaced Hetty's handkerchief under her pillow and turned on her pocket torch to read. Perhaps Maggie or Hetty might come again, she thought, or even someone else, and she certainly didn't want to miss that.

The air was very still, and all Josie could hear was the choir of crickets out in the woods, which Mr Harwood used to say meant that baby crickets were on their way. Josie liked to imagine them having a party with lots of dancing, paper lanterns, and iced tea.

Now, as she turned another page, she suddenly became aware of an oddly muffled, clattering sound punctuating the crickets' chirruping.

She put her book down and cocked her ear to listen. At first, the singing of the crickets was all she could hear, but then again, in a moment, came the hurried clinking and bumping she'd heard previously. The sounds had a stifled, almost secretive, quality and seemed to be coming from somewhere outside her room.

In an instant, Josie had slipped out of bed and pulled on her cardigan over her pyjamas. Holding her torch tightly in one hand, she slipped Monkey into her cardigan pocket.

"Don't worry Monkey," she whispered, "this is no different from going to get a midnight snack. Let's go see who's making that noise!"

Monkey cast one anxious look at Josie before disappearing into her woolly pocket. Noiselessly, on socked feet, Josie crept out into the dark gallery. She had never seen the house all shut up for the night before – as quiet and still as a graveyard – and she shivered a little. A quick glance toward Miss Gordy's closed door told her it was not the old lady she had heard earlier; indeed, the faint creaking of Miss Gordy's bed told her the old lady had already turned in.

Leaning over the gallery banister, Josie looked down into the dark hall. She could hear the clinking more clearly now, and realised that it was coming from somewhere downstairs – then, a small moving light, like that from a single candle, caught her attention, and showed that the person making the sounds was in the kitchen directly below her.

For a moment Josie considered waking Miss Gordy, but then decided against it – the last thing she needed in the middle of the night was an old lady collapsing on her from all the excitement. Josie's own mother had had a weak heart, and she wasn't going to take any chances with *that*.

With bated breath, Josie descended the staircase as quietly as she could, holding her torch low so that only the step ahead of her was illuminated. She hadn't entirely discounted the fact that the person in the kitchen might be a *real* housebreaker; regardless, she thought it best not to announce her presence.

Reaching the bottom stair, she craned her neck out cautiously. In an instant, she saw that it was definitely *not* a burglar; indeed, there was no mistaking that dark, graceful silhouette, bathed in a soft, ghostly light, which now had its back to Josie and stood at the furthest counter where the pots hung – it was Mrs Bramstone.

Hardly daring to breathe, Josie snapped off her torch and edged closer to the kitchen doorway – she simply *had* to see what Mrs Bramstone was up to. But try as she might, she could not see past the tall figure, whose hands were busily occupied with an unknown number of invisible items that were intermittently lifted and replaced – these, Josie realised now, were the source of the knocking and tinkling.

As Josie stood there in some perplexity, she suddenly noticed an assortment of objects on the long wooden table in the middle of the room. Some she recognised immediately by their distinctive shapes – a large round mortar with a pestle resting within it; a stack of soup plates piled high.

Beside these, however, was a dark, unrecognisable mass, with bits and pieces sticking out of it every which way and smooth little inky blobs that occasionally caught the light. Josie could not even begin to guess what these were, but before she could decide what to do next, Mrs Bramstone suddenly turned around and looked her full in the face.

If ever there was a time Josie honestly felt that every single hair on her body was standing on end, this was probably it. Never had she felt her blood run ice-cold as she did just then, and never had time stood so still. While her brain frantically yelled a variety of crazed directives along the lines of *Run! Scream! Hide! Throw something!*, her feet remained rooted to the spot, and not even the tiniest squeak was she able to muster.

There by the light of the small, flickering candle, Mrs Bramstone's beautiful, austere features stood out in sharp relief. The dark hair looked darker than ever, the eyes enormous and sunken, the cheeks pale and hollow. In her gloved hands were large platters with mounds of steaming stuff on them.

Josie stood stock-still, almost as one mesmerised, staring with mouth agape. Then, with a shock, she suddenly realised that Mrs Bramstone was not in fact looking at her at all, but rather *through* her, as if she were not even there.

For another second or two Josie watched her with held breath, quite prepared now to scream or run or both, but the headmistress continued to look through her into space, as if she were absorbed in some elaborate calculation, before finally advancing to the oak table and laying down the dishes in her hands. At the same time, a ghostly blue fire flared up in the huge fireplace, lighting the room with an unnatural, eerie glow.

As Josie watched with increasing wonder, she began to feel as if some invisible, mystical curtain had been lifted between the present and the past, and that what she was about to witness was something quite momentous. Not wanting to miss a thing, she crept forward with thumping heart till she was standing right before the table. She was close enough now to reach out and touch Mrs Bramstone if she had so dared; indeed, an almost glacial air surrounded the headmistress, which made Josie shiver in her pyjamas and clutch Monkey tightly in her pocket.

Mrs Bramstone was now bent over the table, busily occupied with the rough, bushy mass Josie had noticed earlier. The candlelight revealed that they were a cluster of broken branches, with numerous oval leaves and purple bell-shaped flowers, out of which grew a quantity of berries at various intervals, all of a remarkably glossy blackness that Josie found most disquieting.

These Mrs Bramstone proceeded to pluck assiduously; in a few moments, she had the leaves and fruit separated into two neat little piles. While the latter were rolled off the table into a little drawstring pouch, the leaves were dropped into the stoneware mortar and soon completely crushed.

A cold hand seemed to grip Josie's heart as she watched the headmistress begin liberally sprinkling the ground leaves over the platters, which Josie now saw were heaped with different kinds of food. Satisfied, Mrs Bramstone turned to the huge fireplace and began throwing in the leftover leaves and branches. Though Josie could not feel any heat from the roaring flames, she could hear the twigs crackling as they slowly broke apart and disappeared.

As Mrs Bramstone stood over the fire, removing her gloves, Josie became aware of the approaching rustling of several skirts – in a few minutes more, two young women in long dresses and aprons, with hair neatly tucked under small white caps, appeared, carrying an assortment of pails, cloths and other cleaning implements. Somewhere in the distance Josie could now hear the sound of a bell ringing, of children whispering, and of beds being tidied and doors being opened, and footsteps scurrying along the gallery – all the sounds of the school over a hundred years ago.

"You may bring the first form tables their dinner now, Mary," Mrs Bramstone said.

The young women lit several candles and began arranging the plates and platters on large wooden trays; taking these up, they left the kitchen, sweeping past Josie in an icy gust, and leaving Mrs Bramstone alone again, thoughtfully regarding the cloth pouch in her hand.

Slowly, she opened it, and, emptying several of the inky-black berries into her palm, looked at them keenly. As she picked one up with her fingers, she smiled a little to herself, appearing for a moment almost unhinged, and causing a chill to run up and down Josie's spine.

Then, still with an air of deep contemplation, she began to fade, turning at once hazy and translucent; the whole scene, in fact, became gradually indistinct, and Josie realised that the curtain was being closed for now, and that this was all that would be shown here this night. In the next few moments, everything – Mrs Bramstone, the roaring fire, the chill evening light – misted over, and then was swallowed up entirely by the darkness. Somewhere in the house, a clock struck one.

Josie turned her torch back on and stood still for a second or two, trying to catch her breath and make sense of everything she'd just seen. It was evident that Mrs Bramstone had poisoned the girls' food; they had witnessed what had happened to Robert and must needs be silenced. Yet how she intended to get away with the murder of *twelve* children was quite beyond Josie – had she planned to kill herself after killing them? She would have to ask Maggie and Hetty what happened later that fateful night.

Reaching the top of the stairs, she was about to turn into her dormitory when she suddenly heard a sound coming from further down the gallery. Josie stopped in her tracks and peered into the thick darkness. At that distance, the sound was soft and muffled, but it was unmistakably that of a woman's voice.

Shivering, Josie looked down the long passageway, considering what she should do. A vague expectation of something suddenly jumping out at her was a most unpleasant thought to have at this time, and she shook herself.

"Get a grip, Josie," she told herself sternly. Taking a deep breath, she began inching forward on tiptoe, feeling her way with her hand along the wall.

As she got closer to the sound, she realised it was coming from a room at the very end of the gallery. An icy coldness permeated the air here; silently approaching, Josie raised her torch to see the single word that had been painted on the closed door: HEADMISTRESS

With a start, Josie realised that the sounds were those of a woman sobbing as if her heart would break – they were echoing eerily now in the quiet stillness of the house and Josie wondered that they did not wake Miss Gordy. Trembling, she leaned her ear against the door.

"Robert, oh Robert, my boy, my darling boy, come back to me;

don't leave me, don't leave me, Robert; don't leave your mamma..." On and on the voice went, wracked by the most heart-wrenching sobs Josie had ever heard.

But there was no reply to the sorrowful pleas, and after many minutes, Josie heard the sounds of much scuffling and rustling and then, finally, the rasp of a key being turned in a lock. A moment later, the rustle of skirts paused and then approached the door at which Josie was listening. Terrified, Josie stumbled away and ran back to her room at full speed, grazing her shoulder and arms along the wall as she went.

However, she soon realised her panic was quite unfounded – Mrs Bramstone's door did not open and no Mrs Bramstone emerged. Josie heaved an enormous sigh of relief and leaned against the wall, trying to catch her breath. An overwhelming curiosity now took hold of her and she looked back down the dark passageway thoughtfully.

"What say we try to get a look inside, Monkey?" she whispered.

Curiously, as the words came out of her mouth, she thought she heard an *actual* monkey chattering in reply, but after a pause, with no other sound breaking the silence, she shook her head. "Nerves," she said to herself, scornfully.

Holding her torch up again, Josie made her way back to the headmistress' room. Putting her ear against the door, she listened intently, but all was dead quiet now. Then, slowly, she grasped the doorknob and tried to turn it; but, as she'd mostly expected, it was locked. Stymied, she stared at the dark brass knob in vexation.

As she seriously considered kicking this door as she had done with so much success before, she suddenly became aware of that odd monkeyish chattering she thought she'd heard earlier.

Nervously, she clutched Monkey's round paw in her pocket. "That's not you is it, Monkey," she murmured.

Again, the chattering answered her, this time a little louder, and apparently coming from somewhere downstairs.

With thumping heart, Josie turned from Mrs Bramstone's room and peered over the banister into the darkness below. Nothing was astir. Reaching the hallway, Josie paused and looked around her. The kitchen was in complete darkness, as were all the other rooms, and for a moment, Josie stood there, uncertain what to do.

Then suddenly came that same chattering she had heard earlier, except it was now magnified ten times over till it sounded almost maniacal, and included a variety of grunts, hoots and screams at such a fever pitch of excitement that Josie was forced to cover her ears with her hands.

It was clear now that the frantic sounds were coming from the drawing-room, and with one hand still over her ear while the other brandished her torch, she inched forward with bated breath. She was largely comforted by the thought that it was probably *not* Mrs Bramstone gibbering, or even the creature Horatio, but nothing could have prepared her for the sight which met her eyes when, moments later, she was standing on the threshold.

Bathed in a dim amber glow, the monkey automaton who had graced every meal during Josie's stay at the house was now shaking frantically in the seat to which he had been attached, his previously dull, dead eyes now shining and alert, while his black fur stood on end and bristled in agitation.

Fashioned as a performing conjurer, the animal – a chimpanzee – was elaborately dressed in rosy silk pantaloons, an ivory canvas blouse, and a black velvet vest embroidered with magical symbols in bright gold. He had been seated on a high stool, at a little table covered in tasselled cloth.

Upon this table were an assortment of items – a crystal ball, a deck of cards, a wooden die, a melted candle stump – as well as two large silver cups, placed upside-down, which the monkey clasped tightly in each of his long hands. A white-and-gold crown, pointed like a bishop's mitre, had been perched on his head – this, too, was decorated with mysterious gold characters.

As Josie slowly drew closer, the chimpanzee shook up and down in his seat with even greater agitation than before, screaming with increasing vehemence as he showed his teeth in a broad smile. Josie knew from her voracious reading that this was a "fear grimace" and not a smile at all; and slipping her torch into her pocket, she showed the monkey her empty hands and tried to make herself appear smaller, keeping her own teeth as concealed as she could.

"Sshhhhh!" she said. "I can't help you if you keep screaming and shaking like that".

Unexpectedly, the chimp fell silent and cocked his head; then, shaking his hands, as if trying to signify that his arms were stuck, he looked at Josie with an expression of profound longing.

"Oh, you poor thing," Josie said, softly. "You want to get loose, don't you?"

The chimp shook himself and made gruff barking noises. Doubtfully, Josie drew another inch closer.

"You're not going to hurt me are you?" she asked.

Slowly, she edged forward with her palms open, till she was standing right in front of him. The chimp was still shaking and making disgruntled, gravelly noises, but much more gently now, and Josie finally took a deep breath, squeezed her eyes shut and put both her hands on his.

There was a moment of complete quiet, then a soft grunting, lip-smacking sort of sound. Still half-wincing in trepidation, Josie opened one eye cautiously. The monkey was looking down at her curiously, hopefully even, and was no longer showing his teeth.

"Oh good," Josie said, breathing a great sigh of relief. She stroked his hands gently. "Don't move now while I try to figure out how to get you free".

Slowly, she removed her torch from her pocket and showed it to him, making sure not to shine it in his face. As he continued to watch her with curiosity, she began examining his sleeves and arms. She was glad to find that the chimp himself was not permanently stuck to the board, but his clothes apparently were. For a few seconds, Josie tried pulling at the canvas with all her might, but it would not give.

"It's been glued on tight," Josie told the monkey crossly. "I don't understand why your arms were stuck down like this when you're obviously supposed to be doing the magic cup trick".

As she said this, a thought struck her and she looked more closely at the cups. "Is there something important under there?" she asked. "Is that what you're trying to tell me?"

Bouncing himself up and down excitedly, the monkey began making loud hooting sounds that echoed crazily round the room.

"Shhh!" Josie said. "I need to get a pair of scissors or something to cut you loose. I don't think I'll be able to get you free tonight".

The monkey seemed to sense that Josie was going to leave, and began to cry and whimper pitiably.

"Shhuush!" Josie hissed, putting her finger to her lips. "You'll have to be patient. I mean, I know you *have* been patient for a really long time already, but I need you to be patient a little longer okay? I'll come back soon. Try to sleep now or whatever it is you do".

As she stroked his hands comfortingly, the glow which had illuminated him began to fade, and the light in his eyes began to die too; in another moment, he was as still and silent as a statue and the room was plunged into darkness, save for the small beam from Josie's torch.

"I'll be back," Josie whispered, and turned to leave. A thousand sighs and whispers seemed to answer her in the stillness, but there was no more movement anywhere. Once back in the dormitory, she collapsed on her bed, wiping the cold sweat from her brow. From somewhere below came the melancholic notes of Chopin's *Nocturne*, weaving mournfully with the crickets, and lulling Josie into a strange, dreamless sleep.

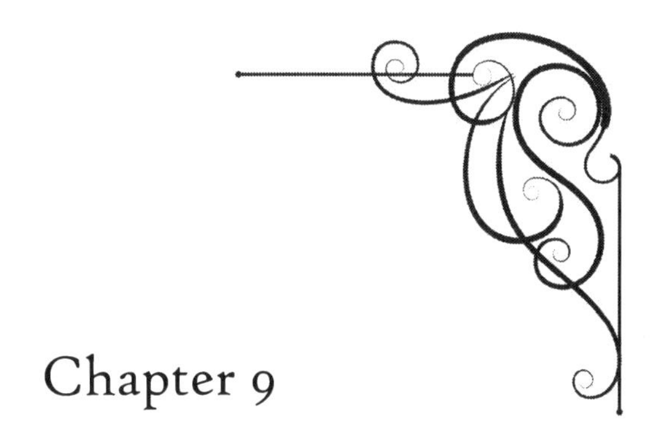

Chapter 9

The sun was well up by the time Josie awoke later that day, and Miss Gordy had to shake her several times to rouse her for breakfast.

"Did you have a bad night, Josie?" Miss Gordy asked, looking at her closely as she sat up in bed, stretching and yawning prodigiously.

"Rather!" Josie replied, rubbing her eyes. "But wait," she continued, after a pause, as she began recollecting everything that had happened. "No, no I didn't. I've learned ever so much and I wouldn't have missed it for the world, so I had a very good night really!"

"Oh my, what happened?" Miss Gordy asked with wide eyes.

"Didn't you hear anything last night?" Josie asked in surprise.

"No, nothing. It's always dead quiet here, pardon the expression. Well, except for the crickets; they're always there. Why, what happened??"

"Oh, I can't tell you everything just yet," Josie replied. "I'm still trying to put all the pieces together and I don't want you to start worrying and having trouble sleeping and all that".

Miss Gordy regarded Josie doubtfully. "If anything should happen to you – " she began.

"I'll be fine," Josie said firmly. "Don't worry. And I have friends too!"

"I see," Miss Gordy said hesitantly. "Very well, Josie; I won't ask any more for the present. But, I shall expect a full report by tomorrow. Your father would never approve of you creeping about in the dark and

I feel the same!"

As this largely described what *had* happened, Josie hastily changed the subject to the morning's outing.

"Yes," said Miss Gordy, "Casper will be picking us up after breakfast at ten. But mind, I want to hear about everything by tomorrow, Josie – I won't forget! Wash up now, and come help me lay the table".

Quickly brushing her teeth and pulling on her dress and cardigan, Josie hurried out into the gallery and looked to see if anyone was about. Then, hurrying down the passageway to Mrs Bramstone's room, she cautiously put her ear to the door. Everything was quiet.

"Let's get you open," Josie muttered and kicked at the door as hard as she could. But this door was far heavier and more solidly built than the one downstairs, and it refused to budge at all.

"Ow," she mumbled, wiggling her toes in her shoe. She would have to find another way.

On her way down to the drawing-room, the phone rang; it was Mr Harwood.

"Ah Josie, I've got excellent news," he told her. "Uncle Eddie's quite on the mend, it seems; if he keeps up like this for a couple more days, they'll likely discharge him and I'll be home before you know it".

"Oh," Josie said. "How nice".

"Yes, isn't it," Mr Harwood replied. "We've even been able to have a talk; not a lot, mind, but enough to know that he did remember us in his will, which I thought was very kind indeed".

"I see," Josie said. "Hm, so... I guess you'll be home by Tuesday then?"

"Yes! Or sooner even, if I'm not needed here anymore. Isn't that great news! I know things are probably rather dull over there with the old lady, but I'm very proud of you for being so good about it. I'll have a word with Miss Gordy now and just let her know what's happening".

Josie passed the phone to Miss Gordy and went to lay the table. She could hear the old lady telling Mr Harwood how they were intending to go shopping in a bit, and how Josie was really no trouble at all, and was so good at keeping herself entertained.

"Yes, I suppose that comes with being an only child; such a wonderful imagination," Mr Harwood agreed amiably. "But I should think you'll be glad to have her off your hands soon. I'll catch the first train back as soon as Eddie's discharged; it won't be long".

"Oh, no rush, Christopher, no rush at all," Miss Gordy reassured him. She was going to add something about the importance of bonding with one's siblings, when out of the corner of her eye she saw Josie scurrying from the kitchen to the drawing-room with something shiny in her hand.

"Um yes, as I was saying – "

Miss Gordy paused again as she now saw Josie scurry out from the drawing-room and return to the kitchen. Moments later, she saw Josie emerge from the kitchen again – this time holding a pair of gardening shears – and hurry back into the drawing-room.

"Yes um, I'm very sure Edward would love to have you around a little longer," Miss Gordy said hurriedly. "We'll wait to hear from you again then. I have to, um, see to something now. Goodbye!"

The old lady put the phone down before Mr Harwood could reply and hurried after Josie. She stopped short in astonishment to see Josie perched on a footstool before the monkey automaton, surrounded by a quantity of cutters and shears of sundry shapes and sizes.

"Josie!!" Miss Gordy exclaimed. "What on earth do you think you're doing??"

Josie turned and Miss Gordy was horrified to see a pair of long shears halfway through the chimpanzee's canvas sleeve.

"What – ??"

"I have to set him free Miss Gordy!" Josie cried. "He wants to show me something and he can't because he's all glued down, and the glue's made the cloth so thick, and I can't find proper scissors, and this thing just won't budge!!"

"Free him?" Miss Gordy repeated, wondering if she had heard right. "What on earth are you talking about?"

"He comes alive sometimes," Josie explained, as patiently as she could. "He came to life last night. And he's a magician, don't you see? He's supposed to do the magic cup trick. But he can't, because someone stuck his arms down so he can't move. But I really believe he wants to show me something important".

"But – but – he's a valuable antique! We've had him for over a hundred years!" Miss Gordy weakly protested.

"Well, he should never have been kept here at all, *I* think!" Josie said crossly. "Please can we just cut through the hard sticky part so he can at least move his arms again like he used to?"

Miss Gordy took a deep breath. "Very well Josie," she said at last. "I shall trust that you know what you are doing. Or at least that you are doing what you believe is best. I think a utility knife might do the trick, but I'm certainly not going to allow you to handle such a thing. We shall wait for Casper to arrive and ask him to help".

"Okay," Josie agreed, climbing off the stool. She patted the monkey's hand reassuringly. "Don't worry," she told him. "We'll get you free soon".

"Um right..." Miss Gordy said uncertainly. "Go wash your hands now and have your breakfast, for goodness' sake".

Josie was just finishing up her Marmite toast when the sound of Casper's estate car could be heard crunching up along the driveway gravel. She bounced up eagerly and hurried out to open the front door.

"Good morning, miss!" the young man called out as he parked his car. "You and Miss Gordy ready to go?"

"Not yet, Casper!" Josie replied. "You've got to come in and help with something please!"

Casper followed Josie into the drawing-room where Miss Gordy was standing beside the chimpanzee, knife in hand.

"What's this then?" he asked with a chuckle.

"Josie wants to free the monkey," Miss Gordy told him drily.

She handed Casper the knife and pointed out the areas that needed to be cut through.

"Don't hurt him!" Josie cried anxiously, as the young man set to sawing at the hardened fabric with a will.

It was a good many minutes before he finished with one arm, and a good many more before he finally finished with the other.

"How does he work then?" Casper asked, as he sat down on an ottoman to wipe his forehead with his handkerchief.

"I believe you have to wind him up," Miss Gordy said. "I never tried winding any of the automatons here, but I think I remember my mother doing it once; there was a sort of key somewhere in the back..."

Josie was already behind the chimp. "I think I feel something here!" she cried excitedly.

Casper went over to help her unlace the monkey's velvet vest. A hollowed-out space in the animal's broad back revealed a labyrinthine arrangement of miniature gears, cams, levers, springs and chains, each connected to the other in mind-boggling complexity. Toward the bottom, a large key attached to a crankshaft protruded invitingly.

"Will you do the honours, miss?" Casper grinned.

Josie grasped the silver key and began winding the monkey's intricate mechanism, which grated and creaked like a climbing roller coaster; and then – "I've reached the end!" she cried, her eyes shining with excitement.

"Let go then!" Casper exclaimed exuberantly.

Josie released the key and hurried over to the others, who were standing in front of the chimp. There was a pause; then, as they watched with bated breath, the cogs and chains began to move, and the monkey blinked his eyes and turned right and left, nodding and bowing as if welcoming his audience. A tinkling melody, at once sweet and haunting, began to play.

In the next instant, he lifted one silver cup, and then the other, and Josie gasped when she saw that a bunch of silver keys, tied with a quantity of string, had been hidden under the cup in his left hand. But as she reached out to grab them, the monkey suddenly brought the metal cup down with a forceful thud, and Josie drew her hand back with a little yelp.

"Be careful, Josie!" Miss Gordy cried. At the same moment, the monkey lifted his right hand, revealing that the silver keys were now under that cup; this too, however, he swiftly covered again in a few seconds. These movements were repeated several times more, with the keys moving back and forth between the cups, till finally the monkey lifted both cups to reveal that the keys had disappeared. Then, bringing both cups back down to rest upon the table, he bowed and was still once more.

"I must get those keys!" Josie declared.

Looking round the room for something that might serve her purpose, Josie's eyes lighted on one of Miss Gordy's long knitting needles (these could be found on various surfaces throughout the house since, Miss Gordy said, she always seemed to be misplacing them). Winding the chimp up again, Josie held the needle ready and, as the right cup was lifted, used it to swiftly swipe the keys onto the floor.

Pouncing on them, she held them up triumphantly. "See! I told you there was something important under there!" she said to Miss Gordy.

"A bunch of keys, miss?" Casper asked curiously.

"Aye, just more antiques," Miss Gordy said, looking at Josie meaningfully. Josie said no more, but cast her eyes rapidly over the heavy lot in her hand. There were some seven or eight keys of different sizes loosely held together by twine, all made of iron, and very rusty and heavy; each of these had a little label tied to its bow, with the name of the room to which it belonged written in a beautiful script: *Schoolroom, Pantry, Library, Infirmary, First Form*… and then – *Headmistress* and, even more tantalisingly, *X*.

Josie inhaled sharply, and glanced over quickly at Casper. He and Miss Gordy were now busy replacing the monkey's blouse and lacing up his vest. Placing the keys on a side table, Josie hurriedly untied them, separating the *Headmistress* and *X* keys from the others and slipping them into her pocket.

So this was what you wanted to show me, Josie thought, looking up at the monkey's inscrutable face.

"Satisfied, miss?" Casper asked, coming over to her and casting a quick glance at the keys left on the side table.

"Yes!" Josie said, feeling the two keys in her pocket. "Thank you so much for helping me; we can go now!"

The three of them were soon climbing into Casper's dark grey car. It was old – a restored Vauxhall Victor Estate, Casper told Josie proudly – but clean and very well-polished; behind the back seat was a sizeable boot, in which a quantity of camera equipment had been placed in cartons.

Josie looked over at them with interest. One in particular caught her attention – it was larger than any camera she'd ever seen before, rectangular in shape and very solidly built, with numerous round knobs and levers all attached to a thick black bar. But its most distinctive feature was an accordion-pleated bellows – this was very long, and covered at the end with a hood, and it immediately brought to Josie's mind the old photographs in Miss Gordy's drawing-room.

"That's a film camera, miss," Casper said, catching sight of Josie in the rear-view mirror.

"Wow, it's huge!" Josie exclaimed. "Is it an antique? It looks like one!"

"Oh, no!" Casper replied with a laugh. "It's modern all the way; digital lenses and everything. I *am* using it to work on something antique though – it's called tintype photography".

"Tintype?" Josie repeated.

"Yup," Casper said. "I'll bet you've seen quite a few tintypes in Miss Gordy's house. If you like, I can show you my pictures after I've dropped Miss Gordy off at the supermarket. I mean, if you want. And if it's ok with you, Miss Gordy?"

"Yes, please!" Josie replied with enthusiasm.

"That's fine," Miss Gordy said. "Just be sure you take good care of Josie, mind".

"No problem," Casper said. "I kinda guessed young Josie here had an interest in old things. We'll have lots to talk about".

After dropping Miss Gordy off at the supermarket – with a promise to be back in half an hour – Casper drove down the block to his father's studio. This was on the ground floor of one of the town's older, original buildings, which had been painted a muted greyish-green colour and was just three storeys high.

"Welcome home miss!" Casper said with a grin, as he opened the car door for Josie.

"Oh!" said Josie. "Do you live here too? How awesome!" She looked up in wonder at the tall display windows with their decorative wooden awnings, filled to the brim with cameras and tripods and black-and-white portraits, and above them, the large oriel window which jutted out from the second floor.

"Yup, four generations at least," Casper smiled. He led the way up the short flight of steps to the entrance. As he pushed the glass door open, Josie gasped in surprise. Printed in neat letters on the grey awning were the words – BRASKET & SONS.

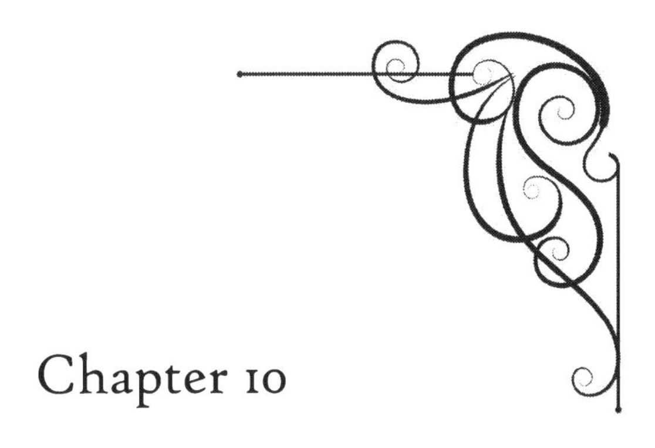

Chapter 10

"You recognise the name, miss?" Casper asked, looking Josie in the eye.

"I do," Josie admitted. "Is that your family name?"

"It is," Casper replied. Then, after a pause, "You've seen her then?"

Josie nodded. "Have *you*?"

"Yup, I have," Casper replied, sighing deeply.

A customer came in just then, and rang the bell on the counter. From behind a black curtain at the back of the shop, Casper's father appeared and came hurrying down the long passageway. Seeing Josie, he smiled at her amiably, then called out a greeting to his client, telling him that his picture was all packed and ready to be brought home. Like his son, he too had red hair.

"That red hair has been in our family for generations," Casper said, following Josie's gaze. "Come on, let's go up to the mud room; it'll be easier to talk there". He led the way down the narrow passage and Josie saw that the walls were filled with old photographs in frames of all shapes and sizes.

"We do love our pictures!" Casper laughed, as he lifted the black curtain at the end to reveal a flight of stairs.

The mud room was really a small open area at the top of the stairs, with a rustic black bench at a window, under which were shoes and boots and a few socks. There were large hooks on either side of the window for hanging one's coats, and more hooks on the walls, on which were hung several rackets, bags and hats. A small rug, a rocking chair and a quantity of cushions made the space have a very cosy feel, when otherwise it was actually really quite grubby.

"We take our boots and things off here before going into the rest of the house," Casper explained. "But it's nice for a quick chat too".

"I like it!" Josie said appreciatively, looking round. She seated herself cross-legged at the window. "Right," she said, becoming serious. "You know about Miss Gordy's house then, don't you?"

"A little, yes," Casper replied. "I kinda guessed you might too, because you're still pretty young and kids generally see 'things' a lot better than grown-ups do".

"You've seen 'things' then?" Josie asked.

"I used to, when I was younger; not anymore. My father used to go up there now and then with his cousin – that's Joshua Riley at Riley's bathroom supplies – to help with Miss Gordy's plumbing. Sometimes he'd bring me along and I'd wait for them downstairs, occasionally helping out with holding things or getting stuff from the car or whatever.

"Well, the first couple of times I went – I think I was maybe nine or ten – nothing really happened, probably 'cause I was mostly waiting with Miss Gordy and she was showing me things in her drawing room, or taking me for walks outside. I did keep hearing footsteps and whispering, but I didn't pay too much attention. The next time I went though, well, that's when it got interesting.

"Miss Gordy was upstairs with my dad and cousin Joshua, showing them this leaking pipe. I'd just finished some hot chocolate and was wandering around the hall, looking at random stuff. Then suddenly I heard this tapping sound, like tap-tap-tap against a window or something and I realised it was coming from that side room, the one with the stained glass. Someone was tapping on the window from inside.

"Let me tell you, my hair just stood on end then, and I literally just *froze* for a minute or two. But then the tapping became louder and more insistent, like they were using their whole palm now and not just the knuckles, and I felt like whoever it was, was *really* trying to get my attention. Well, I finally took my courage in both hands and went up to the glass. It was really dirty and I couldn't see inside. And then the tapping just stopped and it was all quiet.

"Well, now I *really* wanted to have a look inside, so I used a bit of spit on my sleeve and started cleaning one pane. And then just when I got a section clear enough to see through, this girl's face suddenly popped up right in front of mine, with both hands hitting the glass on either side and her mouth open, but no sound coming out.

"Well, *my* mouth opened and *lots* of sound came out! I went, 'aaaaaaaaaahh!!' and 'oh my gahhhdd!!' and 'sweet mother of all that's holy' and started calling for my dad at the top of my voice like a lunatic. I could hear him and cousin Josh hurrying down the gallery upstairs, but before they appeared, something else did, on the stairs! This thing, with a cloth over its head and these huge bird feet, was actually squeezing out through the wall!

"At the same time, my dad was shouting, asking what the matter was and if I was okay. I could tell he couldn't see the thing on the stairs at all. Well, I somehow thought I didn't want him to come running down the stairs right then and bump into it, so I yelled back that I was fine, and he said something about me being an ass and to stop playing the fool.

"But when he turned to leave, the thing started coming down the stairs towards me and I just stood there, petrified! It was literally just three or four feet away from me when that pounding on the glass started up again, but now really loud, as if the girl were beating on the window with all her might.

"The thing in the cloth stopped in its tracks, looked toward the sound for a moment, and then turned from me and went right through the window, right at that spot I was before. Well, I rushed after it and looked through the glass – I was just time to see that girl standing in the middle of the room, with her hands out, before that thing opened its arms and just swallowed her up! It was like… like she somehow – I don't know how else to describe it – *disappeared into him*…

"But there was something else too which really got me – that girl, her face and that red hair – they somehow just made me think of my grandfather. We have some old photographs of him as a child; I'll show them to you if we have time. He was a twin, you know, and there was a story from his childhood he used to share with our family – we called it granddad's ghost story".

"Tell me!" Josie said excitedly.

"Okay, well, at the time all that happened to me, I hadn't heard the story. I guess they thought I was too young or something, so I didn't know anything about it. When my dad and cousin Josh came downstairs a few minutes later, I was a wreck. I was just standing in the middle of the hallway, shivering, in a cold sweat.

"Miss Gordy asked if I was okay, and of course I said I was, but I could tell she knew something she wasn't saying. I couldn't even say goodbye properly and my dad got mad at me. All the way home in the car he kept going on about what an ass I'd been that day, and at the dinner table he brought it up again, telling the rest of the family.

"By that point I was so cheesed off, I told everyone what had happened and that they could believe what they liked, but it *did* happen, and I *wasn't* being an ass. Well, by all that's holy, you should've *seen* everyone's faces when I was done, my granddad especially. He'd gone totally white and looked like he was about to have a heart attack. I started to feel scared and was going, 'what, what?? what did I say??'

"And that was when they told me granddad's ghost story. Like I'd said, my granddad was a twin. By 1893, they'd made education compulsory for kids up to age eleven, so he and his sister got sent to separate schools. But soon after he turned eleven, he was brought home to help his father at work and learn the photography trade, while his sister stayed on at her boarding school. It was mostly to get her out of the way, but if she could get educated enough to be a lady's maid or even a governess, why not, right?

"My granddad had been close to his sister growing up, being twins and all, so it wasn't really a surprise to anyone that sometimes he'd voice his concern about her, just saying stuff out of the blue like, 'I hope they're feeding her right' or 'I hope they don't beat her too badly for reading that wrong again'. When the family asked him why he said these things, he said it was because she came to him in his dreams and told him. Everyone just wrote it off as some quirky kid twin thing.

"Then one day he came in crying his eyes out and of course everyone asked him what the matter was and all. He said things at his sister's school had gone really wrong and something bad was going to happen. He kept insisting they bring her home right away, but of course they didn't pay any attention to him since he was always acting weird anyway and there was so much work to be done, it being the summer and more customers coming in.

"Well, he was not to be comforted, and cried almost continuously all that day and the next, with the main result being that he got a whipping for his foolishness and missed a bunch of his meals. But the following night – June the 11th it was, he said – he went in to his parents' room, his face all drawn and white, and eyes red from weeping, and said to them, 'My sister is dead'".

Casper paused and heaved a great sigh. "You already know who his sister was, don't you?"

"Bessie Brasket," Josie breathed, eyes wide. "But how did your granddad know she was dead?"

"That's the ghost story," Casper replied. "He said he had been trying to sleep, when suddenly he felt the air in his room turn bitter cold, and he heard a strange, heavy sort of sound, like someone dragging themselves across the floor. Of course he sat up bolt upright in an instant, and that was when he saw Bessie standing at the foot of his bed, with her hands clasped together over her heart, and a trail of blood behind her, all the way out the door.

"Granddad said she just stood there and stared at him for what seemed like the longest time – though it was really probably only a minute or two – not moving, but looking at him with an expression of the most intense yearning; and he heard her voice calling his name, like an echo from far away – 'Lynton, Lynton, help me,' it said; then, as she reached out one hand to him, she began to disappear – to 'break apart' Granddad said. He called out her name and lunged forward to try to grab her, but his fingertips just brushed hers, and she was gone".

"How awful for him," Josie murmured. "And for her too".

"You're right there, miss," Casper nodded. "He never recovered from the shock. I mean, sure, he finally stopped crying, and he went back to helping his dad, and he grew up and got married and took over the shop and everything else, but you could tell he never got over it. The rest of the family grieved too of course, but not like him.

"Over the years, right up till he died at the ripe old age of ninety-five, he'd come downstairs some mornings and tell me Bessie had come to visit him again – not in the flesh, you understand, but in dreams and visions. He'd only tell me, because he said everyone else wouldn't understand, and might put him in a nursing home, or even a madhouse.

"So he'd tell me the things she'd said and I'd write them down in my diary so I wouldn't forget, 'cause I was thinking, one day, when I was older, I would go back to Bramstone Hall and see if I could get to the bottom of this whole thing. You see, after what had happened to me, my dad said he was *never* bringing me along again".

Casper rose to his feet. "Come on," he said, "I don't want to be late for Miss Gordy. I'll show you a picture downstairs of my granddad before we go".

As they re-entered the long passageway downstairs, Casper pointed out several large tintype portraits in black frames that had been hung on the wall. The dark metal plates looked old, and yet Josie could tell the sitters' clothing and hairstyles were modern – "Oh!" Josie exclaimed. "Did you make these?"

"I did!" Casper said with a grin. "What do you think?"

"They're amazing!" Josie replied. "I wish I could have a tinytype of me!"

"Well that's easily done, miss," Casper said. "You can come sit for me whenever you like. That black hair of yours will look stunning in tintype I'll warrant".

"Really?" Josie beamed. "Wow, thank you Casper; I should like that very much. And then maybe you can help me more with the Bramstone mystery!"

"I knew you'd think of that!" Casper laughed. "Here, quickly, come have a look at this one".

He beckoned her over and pointed to a much smaller tintype, in an ornate oval frame, of a young boy and girl who looked to be about the same age. The boy was seated, dressed in a black suit, with a little black hat perched jauntily on his head, while the girl wore a sweet pleated dress with puffed sleeves, and leaned against him, one arm affectionately in his. Josie recognised her immediately – it was the girl she had seen in the punishment room.

"That's her, isn't it?" Casper asked.

Josie nodded. "And the boy is your granddad, right? They do look rather alike; the same eyes and expression… They look like they loved each other a lot".

"Yup," Casper agreed, sighing dolefully. He led the way back out to the car. "Granddad was heartbroken about her till he died. It was terrible for the whole family, him especially, that she was never found to be brought home and given a proper burial. And not just for our family – all the families who lost children that day. That's why, even as a kid, I wanted to try to get to the bottom of what happened".

"All the families who lost children," Josie repeated thoughtfully, as Casper unlocked the car doors. She climbed into the back seat and put on her seat belt. "Do you know if any of those families are still at Gloam's End?"

"No, I don't think so," Casper replied. "They all eventually packed up and left after what happened. My granddad's folks wanted to leave too in fact, but my granddad wouldn't stand for it; just screamed bloody murder and said he couldn't leave Bessie all alone there like that. So they stayed on; it was the only thing they could do to comfort him I think."

"There was a great furore at first when it all came out of course," Casper continued, as they drove along. "Mrs Bramstone sent word that something bad had happened and the kids were to be fetched home immediately. When the relatives showed up at the school the next day, the cops were everywhere and they learned that all ten girls from the first form were missing, plus Bessie, who was in the second, as well as Mrs Bramstone's own son, Robert".

"What did they do then?" Josie asked breathlessly.

"Well, you know the rest," Casper said with a shrug. "They searched the woods, they searched the house, they questioned Mrs Bramstone and the staff – they never did find anything. The kids had literally vanished overnight. 'Course the general consensus was that they'd been kidnapped or something, and they figured maybe Bessie and Robert had surprised the perpetrators in the act. I wonder though…"

They had pulled to a stop at the intersection just before the supermarket, and Miss Gordy was sitting on a bench outside, surrounded by shopping bags. "Well, I'll help you any way I can if you're reopening the case now!" he said.

"Ask Miss Gordy if I can sit for a photograph!" Josie suggested excitedly. “But you’ll have to do it soon though – my Daddy said he’ll be home in a couple of days”.

“We’ll see,” Casper said, winking at her in the rearview mirror as the light turned green. “Mind you let me know what happens with those keys you took!”

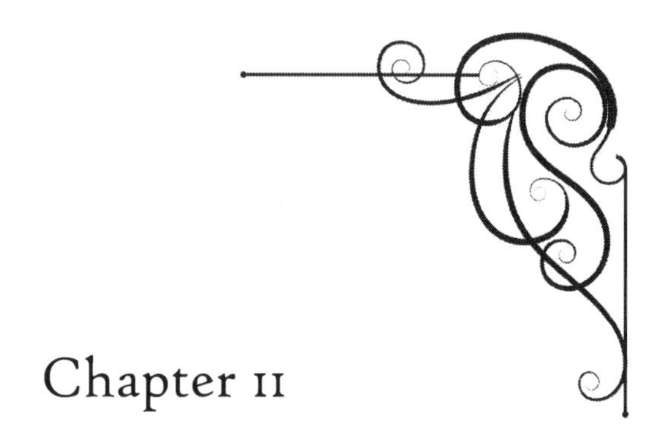

Chapter 11

The afternoon was looking to be a dreary one. Josie was impatient to try the keys still lurching about in her pocket, but Miss Gordy insisted Josie finish her holiday homework after lunch, which, she said, had been much neglected since her arrival.

"You can sit at the writing desk in the library," the old lady told her. "Perhaps you might even look at the books when you're done. I want to get started on knitting my tarantula floor pillow now that I've got my new wools".

The possibility of a bit of sleuthing was irresistible, and Josie obediently went to get her workbooks. She *did* have to finish her homework after all, but it also occurred to her that the library, probably much used by the Bramstones, might hold some valuable clues.

Entering it now with her homework in hand, Josie looked about her with interest. Like most of the other rooms in the house, this one was oppressively gloomy as well, but Miss Gordy soon pulled open the heavy drapes to reveal a large bay window, through which the cold light of the overcast day streamed in, and illuminated the oak shelves that lined the walls with books.

A sizable collection of specimens and fossils in cloches and frames had been arranged upon several side tables and a chest on stand, while in the middle of the room, an astronomical orrery encased in glass stood chest high on claw feet. There was a huge fireplace at one end, and close by it, a tall cabinet with a curiously rounded, sloping cover like that of a casket.

"Oh! Where's the desk?" Josie asked, looking around.

"That is it," Miss Gordy replied, walking over to the cabinet. She grasped the carved handles on its cover and rolled it up and back, uncovering a wide panel filled from end to end with little pigeonholes atop two miniature drawers.

"This part becomes the worktable," she explained, pulling out the narrow tabletop that sat above three larger drawers, till it had extended to double its original depth. "We call this a secretary desk. I'm told it comes from the Latin word for 'writer'. This one belonged to my grandparents".

"Oh wow, that's so cool!" Josie exclaimed. She cast her eye quickly over the pigeonholes – they all appeared empty. She'd have to look through the drawers later.

Miss Gordy pulled over an ornately carved chair upholstered in dark green velveteen, and Josie seated herself daintily, feeling quite the lady of the manor.

"Finish your homework and mind you don't get distracted," Miss Gordy told her drily. "My mother used to say not doing one's homework was the true mark of a clod".

Chafing at the delay, Josie nevertheless took up her pencil and set to work. It was nearly an hour before she was finally done, but at last, with held breath and a delicious sense of anticipation, she carefully opened the two little drawers beneath the pigeonholes. They were empty.

Then she remembered the three bigger drawers she had seen underneath the table. Putting her books and stationery on the floor, she cautiously pushed the tabletop back into the cabinet. She realised now that only two of the drawers had handles; the one in the centre was apparently just for show.

Excitedly, she opened the drawer on the right, only to find some blank sheets of paper, a quill and blotter, and a very dirty, dry inkwell.

The other drawer was no better – a gold-framed lorgnette lay on a blank piece of notepaper, a black velvet ribbon threaded through its handle. Josie stared at them for a moment, a little disconcerted; she had been so certain she would find something of importance. Then, as she began to shut them, she paused, cocking her ear – she had distinctly felt something move in the middle, the section she'd thought false.

Lowering her head to listen, she gently jiggled the drawer again. From within came the muffled sounds of sundry little objects rolling and sliding, bumping and thudding against each other. Josie ran her hands along the bottom and tried to slide the false section open, but try as she might, there was nothing for her to hold or get a grip on, and the drawer remained stuck fast; there was no help for it but to leave it for now.

She bit her lip and stared at the desk in perplexity. It struck her then that possibly something might be hidden far back in the numerous pigeonholes – shadowy and deep, and extending a good fourteen inches in, they gave a decidedly mysterious cast to the otherwise stolid façade of the cabinet, and stooping down, Josie peered into their depths, but it was too dark to see all the way in.

Quickly, she took her torch from her pencil box and directed its beam into the cubbies. Of these, there were two rows, varying in size and numbering twenty in total; while quite dusty and somewhat icky, it was soon clear that all the holes on the upper level were completely empty, and Josie began looking inside the lower ones next. The first was bare, but in the second, right at the very end against its back wall, Josie caught sight of a tiny square of paper that had been pasted up; a single letter had been written upon it – *M*.

There was something else too – almost directly in front of the pasted notepaper, a little round hole had been cut in the cubby's floor, its blackness suggesting significant depth. Josie quickly shone her torch into the next eight cubby holes. There were similar pieces of paper in all of them, and cut holes as well, of varying sizes. Taking up her notebook now, Josie carefully copied down the nine letters – Two *M*s, two *S*s, *N*, *V*, *E*, *U*, and *J*.

Well, that doesn't make a lot of sense, she thought, staring at the letters and trying to mentally rearrange them to form some sort of word. She was certain they were of some significance, but what? She tore the letters out into separate little scraps and tried arranging them in different orders. But after spelling random words like MUSS, MEN, JUNE, and the dreaded SUMS, she felt no closer to a solution than before.

Miss Gordy came in just then to check on her.

"Ooh, word games!" the old lady exclaimed. "How interesting!"

"Do *you* see anything that makes sense?" Josie asked, turning the scraps toward her.

Miss Gordy regarded them for moment. "Jesus?" she asked.

"Um, maybe," Josie said hesitantly.

"What about 'sun'?" Miss Gordy ventured. "Anyway," she continued, "I was wondering if you wanted a snack, perhaps some hot chocolate or biscuits?"

"Oh no, thank you," Josie replied, continuing to look at the letters.

"Well, I'm going upstairs to have a little nap," Miss Gordy said, turning to leave. "I'll put the biscuits in a tin on the kitchen counter for you in case you get peckish". Then – "Nevus?"

"That's a word?"

"Yes! Some sort of skin thing!" Miss Gordy replied over her shoulder.

"I really don't think so," Josie murmured, shuffling the little scraps again.

Then, as she considered if this was even a word puzzle at all to begin with, she was startled to see a dark, spindly form, at once bony and billowing, coming stealthily through the wall between the library and the drawing-room; it moved flat against the walls like a shadow, effortlessly following the corners and arrises, and gliding smoothly over the cornices and skirting boards like water, till at last, it reached the bay window.

For a moment it stood silhouetted against the paned glass, eerily beautiful in the chill autumnal light; then, as Josie watched with mouth hanging open, it stepped forward, gradually filling and assuming a three-dimensional aspect as it did so, till at last it stood in the centre of the room. It was a slender female figure dressed entirely in stately Victorian black mourning, and from its high collar rose the glossy black head of a carrion crow, with brilliant beady eyes and a heavy, pointed beak. Josie recognised the figure at once – it was the doll from the drawing room, except it was now at least six feet tall and very much alive.

Josie sprang to her feet, looking about her for a way to escape. But the crow did not move, and, after regarding Josie obliquely for a moment or two, silently raised one arm and pointed toward the brass orrery with the attenuated clump of black feathers emerging from its luxuriant bell sleeve.

Josie stared in amazement. "You're trying to tell me something, aren't you?" she asked. But the crow did not reply and only continued staring at Josie with its bright black eyes, before folding both arms over its full skirt, and turning away.

There was something so wretched and sorrowful about the figure's bowed head that Josie couldn't help crying "Wait!" and, rushing after it, she impulsively reached out and touched its sleeve.

Instantly, the crow turned and let out a piercing caw that made Josie clap her hands to her ears and stumble backward in fright. At the same moment, the crow raised its arms, apparently in a desperate attempt to fly; but this was in vain, for its wings had been cruelly pressed and squeezed into the tight sleeves in some grotesque semblance of human limbs.

Slowly backing away from Josie, its head snaking left and right, the crow continued to caw mournfully, impotently beating its clipped wings. As its bell sleeves rose and fell with its futile motions, Josie suddenly caught sight of a cut-steel chatelaine underneath, attached to the waistband of its dress. These devices, she knew, generally had a variety of objects attached to them, items which were held useful or dear by the wearer; and Josie was intrigued to see on this one a thimble, several buttons, a gold ring, and the bow of a broken key.

As Josie couldn't quite imagine Mrs Bramstone collecting these little things, she wondered if the crow itself had collected them, but this was puzzling, for she remembered that contrary to popular belief, crows did not steal or even like shiny things (and neither did magpies); they did, however, bring gifts to people they liked, and usually they were people who had somehow been kind or generous to them.

"Were these for someone?" she softly asked, pointing to the little trinkets.

The crow hunched down and cocked its head at the sound of her voice, and ceased its woeful cawing. Hesitantly, Josie reached out and gently touched its sleeve.

"Your poor wings," she murmured.

The crow cocked its head again and looked at her obliquely for a moment. Then suddenly, it shook itself, drawing itself up to its full height, and bringing both arms down over its bodice. Looking Josie directly in the eye with a disconcertingly cognizant expression, it opened its beak and said, "It's mine, it's mine; give it back, give it back".

Josie drew back with a gasp, a chill running up and down her spine. The crow had been unnervingly wooden in its delivery, yet the voice had been high-pitched and distinctly that of a young girl – the crow was evidently mimicking something it had heard in the past.

"Who said that? What happened??" Josie asked, but the crow did not say another word, and turned to leave.

Momentarily bathed in the light streaming in through the window, with its face turned up to the sun as if savouring the warmth it had so long lived without, the crow looked at once majestic and inexpressibly forlorn. In another instant, it had gracefully melded into the far wall, blending in with the shadows till it had quite disappeared.

Josie stood still, staring after it and feeling sorely troubled. Now, more than ever, she was determined to break the curse that hung over the house. Rousing herself, she walked over to the elaborate orrery.

"What were you trying to tell me?" she muttered, peering into the octagonal glass case, which stood nearly as tall as herself. Through its many panes and the intertwining rings of the stylised armillary sphere within, Josie could make out a large golden orb in the centre, connected, spider-like, to several smaller ones by long brass arms of different lengths. The smaller spheres varied in size and colouring, and a few of them had little offshoots of even tinier spheres attached to them. The entire thing was mounted on a black leather base atop an intricate arrangement of wheels, gears and bezels.

It's the larger planets of the solar system of course, Josie thought to herself, remembering her Space Atlas at home. That big one's the sun and those little teeny ones are the planets' moons. But what then?

Josie frowned and continued to gaze at the complex apparatus resting on its splendid mechanism. The sun, she repeated to herself, looking at the huge gold orb, and recalling how Miss Gordy had suggested *sun* when she'd asked her about the letters. Suddenly, Josie's eyes popped wide in astonishment. *Could it be?* she wondered excitedly.

She hurried to get the scraps of paper on the desk. Returning to the orrery, she looked at the planets and then at the little pieces laid out in a line on her palm – *M, M, S, S, N, E, V, U, J*. Of course! It *was* the sun, as Miss Gordy said, but not spelt out with the given letters; these were initials, Josie realised, corresponding to the planets – *Mercury, Mars, Saturn, Sun, Neptune, Earth, Venus, Uranus* and *Jupiter.*

The pigeonholes are somehow connected to the planets, Josie thought, but how? She gazed thoughtfully at the desk and decided to have another look in the cubbies. Swinging her torch between one pigeonhole and another, Josie compared the circles that had been cut into them. She wondered if she should try sticking her finger in to see if she could feel anything, but the thought of what she might touch was beyond even *her* venturesome spirit and she hastily dismissed the idea. She did however notice now that the circles were of different sizes – the circle in one of the *S* pigeonholes was the largest, she realised, while the other *S* was much smaller.

The sun and Saturn, Josie thought, looking at the two circular holes. Well, the sun *is* bigger than Saturn, that she knew; but why would someone cut holes in proportion to planetary size? And in a desk of all places? Josie mulled over this conundrum for some time, and then gradually it came to her – the reason a person would make *anything* a certain size was because they wanted something specific to fit into it.

Looking into the *S* pigeonhole again, answers rose swift and clear – that hole was the largest precisely because it was intended for the sun. And where would she get the sun? Josie looked at the orrery and smiled.

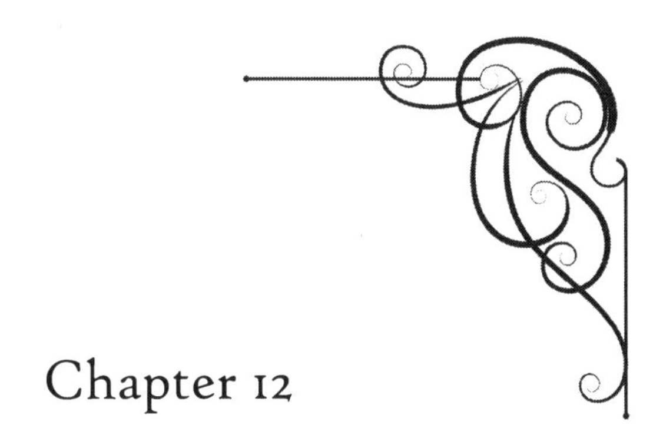

Chapter 12

The locked case of the orrery, however, quickly dampened Josie's excitement. Vehement shaking and jiggling of the large brass handle only risked breaking it off completely and Josie definitely didn't want to do that.

I need the key, Josie thought in vexation, looking at the little keyhole. She thought of the keys still in her pocket. Could this be what the *X* key was for?

Josie eagerly fished it out, but it was immediately apparent that it was far too big; its bit was very thick, and she noticed now that it also had a remarkably complicated series of maze-like cuts in it, as well as a curiously-shaped protrusion – it was obviously intended for an equally complicated lock. Suddenly, she remembered the other keys she'd left on the side table in the drawing-room. Oh, I do hope they're still there, she thought anxiously, as she hurried over.

To her relief, they were. But someone had obviously touched them, because they were no longer in the untidy pile she'd left them in, but had been arranged side by side in a row, from the smallest to the largest, with the *Library* key sticking out above the rest.

Josie glanced quickly at the bird dolls on the sideboard – it seemed to her that the crow was looking at her with a most knowing expression, but then, it seemed like all the birds were; indeed, *every* animal in the room seemed to be somehow bristling with expectancy, and there was an almost palpable electricity in the air.

"Thank you!" Josie whispered, as she grabbed all the keys and ran back to the orrery. Picking out the *Library* one, she inserted it into the keyhole. It was rusty and creaked stridently as she turned it, but in a moment there was a loud click, followed by another, and the top half of the case sprang open half an inch. Excitedly, Josie grasped the brass handle and lifted the lid.

But the gaps between the rings of the armillary sphere were too small for Josie to fit her hand through, and certainly there was no way she could fit the larger planets through anyway. She looked over the orrery again and caught sight of the intricate wheels and gears underneath. Of course, Josie thought. *It's an automaton!* She crouched down and looked for some crank or lever with which she could wind it up. But strangely, there was nothing at all.

There's nothing in the wood but the lock, Josie thought, puzzled. She looked at the key sticking out of it and had a sudden inspiration. It's not a lock, she thought; it's the mechanism itself! Grasping the key's bow, she turned it again; sure enough, it was a winding key. Eagerly, Josie wound up the works; then, reaching the end at last, she let go.

There was a momentary pause, then, with a loud groaning and grating, the rings of the armillary sphere began to turn, slowly joining and becoming level as they did so, till at last the planetary orrery itself was completely uncovered, its brass armatures rotating slowly and a little tremulously on the central shaft. After several revolutions, the orrery came to a grinding halt and Josie could easily reach for the nine orbs.

These, she found, had been held in place by tiny rods that extended upwards into little holes in the spheres, and it was fairly easy for Josie to pluck the sun and the planets off their stems. Carefully balancing them upon each other in both hands, she brought them back to the desk. Now to see if they'll fit, Josie thought excitedly.

Turning on her torch, Josie picked up the sun and pushed it into the *S* pigeonhole. To her delight, it rolled down the length of the cubby toward the hole and then dropped into it, in a fashion not unlike that of a pinball machine; from there she could hear it rolling heavily through some invisible tunnel in the cabinet's back section, before landing with a loud thud somewhere toward the bottom and causing something to very audibly click into place. Josie turned to the remaining spheres before her, and identifying them by their colour and size, soon had all eight planets traversing the cabinet in their respective tunnels.

As the last orb fell and triggered the device to which it was connected, Josie felt and heard the low rumbling of some hidden mechanism deep within the cabinet, a knocking and whirring as of countless cogs and gears set in motion, and she stood up in some alarm to see what would happen next.

In another moment, the false drawer in the middle of the cabinet slid slowly out with a loud rasping noise, revealing a rectangular compartment filled with a seemingly haphazard assortment of objects and papers.

Breathlessly, Josie began carefully removing all the drawer's contents: these comprised several photographs; a red leather ball; sheets of paper torn from some book; a pile of letters in envelopes, tied with black ribbon; three illustrated cardboard discs with strings attached; a bisque doll head, sans hair and eyes; a wooden spinning top, striped and worn; and two little porcelain animal figurines, dressed only in their underwear. As she laid them out on the desk, she heard Miss Gordy stirring upstairs, and hurried out to the hall to call her.

"You must see these!" Josie told Miss Gordy as she came down the stairs. She led the way to the library and showed the old lady what she had found.

"Oh my!" Miss Gordy exclaimed, looking at Josie's finds with wide eyes. "You *have* been busy!"

Almost reverently, she untied the black ribbon and spread out the envelopes and papers. "These are in my grandfather's handwriting!" she exclaimed, gently touching two of the envelopes. "And these," she went on, pointing to the torn sheets, "are in my grandmother's".

"We must read them," Josie said, pulling up another velveteen chair for the old lady to sit on. "They must be important to have been hidden in here like this. But I can't understand why these toys are in here too. Perhaps the letters will explain".

Miss Gordy picked up one of the envelopes addressed to Mrs Bramstone and took out the letter within. "It's from my grandfather," she said, her voice quivering a little. Opening up the folded sheet, now yellow and spotted with age, she read aloud –

My darling wife,

Ada is recovering well. Mother and I have been taking turns sitting up with her. The fever has quite abated and she eats now with relish, so that as she appears much easier, I can take up my pen to write a few words to you.

I was exceedingly glad to receive your report of our school's progress; indeed I can think of no one more fit to the task of headmistress than yourself, my dearest. Daily I give thanks for your conscientious devotion to the girls, motivated by such a spirit of charity and compassion as might have been seen in the saints of old. Only do not be too zealous in your exertions, my love, for overwork has driven many a person to collapse, however worthy the cause may be.

Be sure to give your mind and body their necessary rest, for the frequency of your headaches is troubling. I would suggest going to the shops or even a music hall or country ball, but that you find these amusements such a bore; perhaps you might instead give more time to your leisurely study of natural history or astronomy, in which you find so much enjoyment. By the by, with regard to this latter subject, have you worked out the puzzle I devised for your desk with the orrery I made? I am confident you have, given your cleverness! Give my beloved Robert and Grace a kiss each from their Papa; tell them I will be with them very soon, with sweets and presents from Grandmamma.

The letter was signed off "With love from your William" and dated April 9th, 1893. Miss Gordy put the paper down and her eyes met

Josie's. The same unspoken thought was clearly going through both their heads – the lady described in this letter seemed quite different from the Mrs Bramstone they both knew.

"She sounds like she was a very nice lady… once," Josie said hesitantly.

"Yes," Miss Gordy said slowly. "It makes one feel quite bewildered really. Eighteen ninety-three – that was the year my grandfather died".

"Who was Ada?" Josie asked.

"She was my grandfather's youngest sister," Miss Gordy replied. "She died of scarlet fever when she was only nine. She must have taken a turn for the worse after this letter was written".

Josie picked up another envelope addressed to Mrs Bramstone, but this time in a different handwriting. Unfolding the letter inside, Josie glanced down at the name of the writer. "Lucinda Bramstone – who is that?"

"My great-grandmother," Miss Gordy said, taking the letter. "Oh! It's addressed to Julia; that was my grandmother's given name". She began reading the letter aloud –

My dear Julia,

I am grieved to have still heard no word from you with regard to William. You must know I am daily racked with anxiety, not only on his account – for your last letter did nothing to assuage my fears about his condition – but on yours as well, for before William was laid low with the fever he told me of his disquiet about your increasing use of the tonics, which, it is true, provide relief of the headaches and nervousness; but this, I fear, is only temporary, and the effects of your ailments return with greater force than before.

How will you be able to care for our beloved William if you yourself are in such a sorry state that you even, as I hear, fall victim to hallucinations and fits of anger? Whether or not the contagion truly was from Ada only God knows, but William told me of his alarm at seeing your wrathfulness with the younger pupils and wondered if in some extraordinary way you have formed a resentment of all *children. Can it be so? Has the medicament become the illness?*

William is undoubtedly sorry now that he ever let you take his laudanum – I cannot imagine it mixes very well with your tonics! But now is not the time for censure or blame – I want only to hear of William's improved state and your recovered equanimity and self-possession. I shall await your answer in hope,

Lucinda Bramstone.

Miss Gordy laid the letter down. "What can it mean?" she murmured in dismay.

"I'm not sure," Josie replied musingly, "but it seems like Mrs Bramstone was not well, and her illness changed her…"

She took up a couple of other letters written by Mr Bramstone and quickly scanned them. "Oh wow, listen to this," Josie said.

I was grieved to hear of your suffering a headache so debilitating as to confine you to your bed for two entire days, my dearest, but was gratified to learn that Dr Pryor's coca tonic gave you so much relief that you were quite recovered enough to bring the girls not only for a walk and picnic in the woods, but foraging for mushrooms the very next day as well. Is it any wonder that the children sing your praises to their parents when they are home and I am the happy recipient of such glowing reports of your goodness when I chance to meet them in the street?

I congratulate you on discovering that poor badger's remains and giving him a second life, far more eternal than his first; I have always admired your tender sympathy for these defenceless creatures. I shall be helping Mother with her papers, but will return ere long.

Josie turned to the second letter in her hand. "And listen to this one!" she exclaimed.

My dear heart, do not be uneasy that my departure has been delayed – I was unaccountably struck with such a crippling headache the morning of my leave-taking that I was obliged to lie down – I must own to feeling quite enfeebled and wonder if this is like what you experience almost daily now?

Ada's doctor said that it is just a bit of cold and left me with some mustard plasters and catarrhal powder, though he did wonder in passing if I had not caught Ada's infection. However, as I am not feverish or showing any sign of rash, he was not much worried and neither am I. I shall be on the next coach as soon I have finished Mother's celebrated porridge.

Josie looked at the dates on the two letters – they were both written about a week or so before Lucinda Bramstone's. It was quite clear now what had happened – Mr Bramstone had fallen ill while visiting his sister; indeed, it seemed highly likely that he had been infected by her, though the severity of his illness was probably not apparent till days later, after he had gotten home.

"Scarlet fever is very contagious," Josie said, remembering Mr

Harwood's *Baby and Childcare* book that she'd read several times end to end. "Perhaps he did not think it was serious because he didn't feel or look too badly at first, but I guess he must have after a bit, and then Mrs Bramstone wrote and told his mum. And I guess then she got all busy looking after him or something, because she didn't write to his mum again afterward.

"But there's something else," she went on, with a frown. "Mr Bramstone mentioned that the tonics she'd been taking were made of coca – well, isn't coca what cocaine is made from? I think that's why his mum mentioned Mrs Bramstone's 'increasing use' of the stuff, because of course everyone knows cocaine is addictive, and although at first it might make you feel great, after a while you need more and more of it to get the same effect; and then, when you start having *too* much, well, you become… well, sort of crazy really!"

"Goodness Josie, how on earth do you know about cocaine??" Miss Gordy asked in astonishment.

"Oh, well, they had these anti-drug campaigns at school," Josie replied, "and there were these people who talked to us about drug abuse and addiction and things. Of course I wanted to know more, so I went and read books from the school library". Then, after a pause, she added, "I like to understand things".

"You certainly do!" Miss Gordy said. "I know this, at any rate – people in those days didn't quite understand the dangers of some of their 'medicines' – they were treating coughs and colds and all sorts of other ailments with things like opium and heroin and mercury – even arsenic! If my grandmother was actually addicted to cocaine – oh my, I can't even begin to imagine how bad things became for her when my grandfather died".

"Let's read the last letter!" Josie said excitedly.

"No," Miss Gordy retorted firmly, rising to her feet. "Time for a break". She began massaging her lower back with both hands.

"Come on," she said with a little smile. "Let's stretch our legs and take a breather. All this is really a lot for me to take in, you know. We can have some tea with those biscuits I left for you in the kitchen".

"Okay," Josie agreed, stretching her arms over her head as she stood up. She realised she actually was feeling quite peckish now.

"Perhaps you ought to put away your homework first," Miss Gordy suggested. "We don't want to mess up all your hard work by accident".

As Miss Gordy went to the kitchen to make some tea, Josie gathered her workbooks and went up to her room, thinking about how all this definitely beat Sophia Renford's visit to the Paris Catacombs last year.

But as she entered the doorway, she thought she heard a curious, soft scrabbling, like a rat scampering for cover, and she paused, looking around her cautiously. She could see nothing stirring, however, and the sound was not repeated. Then, just as she was packing her homework in her suitcase, she was startled to see her breath appear as white mist from her mouth – the air in the room had turned bitingly cold.

In the next instant, there came from behind her the loud rustling of voluminous skirts, and with a gasp, she swung round, just as the tall figure of Mrs Bramstone came sweeping into the room, her face dark with anger, and a long birch rod clenched tightly in her hand.

"Oh!" Josie cried out, turning her head and covering her face with both arms, but the headmistress neither stopped nor heeded her, passing right through Josie instead like a freezing gust of wind, knocking the breath out of her and leaving her in a fit of trembling.

"I've caught you now," Mrs Bramstone hissed, in a voice at once soft and blood-curdling that made Josie's hair stand on end.

The headmistress stopped and crouched down at each bed, seemingly possessed of a superhuman energy, and swung the rod with savage determination under every one of them. But no one was hiding underneath, and reaching the last bed, she stopped, her eyes darting back and forth angrily and her head cocked, as if listening intently for some noise that would give the fugitive away. For several nerve-racking seconds she stood absolutely still, then abruptly turned and glided directly to the bathroom, with Josie following hard upon her heels, speechless with apprehension.

At the bathroom doorway, Mrs Bramstone paused again and looked around with her cane held high, breathing heavily like some wild animal hunting. Then suddenly, she lunged forward, shrieking with almost maniacal fury – "I see you!!"

Simultaneously, several fingers appeared on the edge of the bathtub, and a small girl with a mass of short chestnut curls scrambled to her feet, a little red ball in one hand. But the tub was slippery and she lost her footing, so that she landed with a thump on her seat and the ball fell from her grasp. In an instant, Mrs Bramstone had scooped it up and slipped it into the chatelaine purse that hung at her waist.

"That's the end of that," she told the girl, with a suppressed elation most unpleasant to witness. She seized the girl by the arm and pulled her from the tub with ferocious strength. "Now let's see if you will dare play truant again, Agnes Craig".

"It's mine, it's mine; give it back, give it back!" Agnes sobbed, trying to reach for the headmistress' purse. "'Tis my brother's and he gave it me!"

But Mrs Bramstone held her easily at arm's length, and raising her cane, began raining down blows upon the girl's shoulders and back.

"Stop it, stop it!!" Josie cried, grabbing at Mrs Bramstone's sleeve. But her hands passed right through her and, at the same moment, both Mrs Bramstone and Agnes began to fade, while the frigid air around them slowly warmed and finally returned to normal.

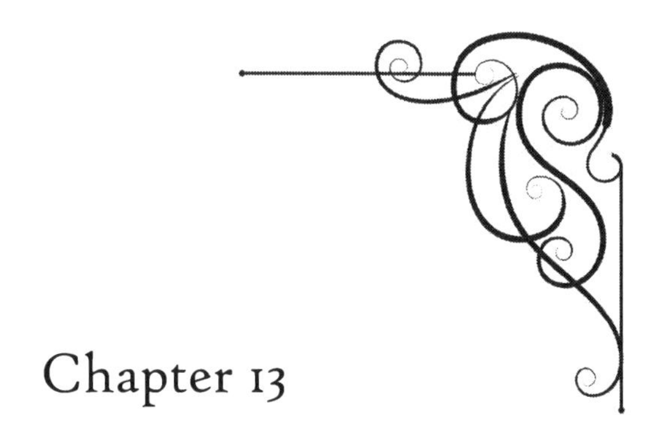

Chapter 13

It was with a wildly beating heart that Josie descended the staircase, horrified and shaken. Seeing the girl's white face as she entered the kitchen, Miss Gordy hurried over, guessing at once that something awful had happened.

"Are you all right?" she asked anxiously.

"I'm okay," Josie replied, "just a little wobbly". She told Miss Gordy about what had happened upstairs. "But don't worry," she added. "It's just a kind of vision of the past; I'm sure now her ghost can't hurt me or even see me".

"Josie, I really don't think it's a good idea that you stay on here," Miss Gordy said, looking distressed. "I'm sure your father – "

"No!" Josie exclaimed. "Please let me stay. I *will* get to the bottom of all this somehow". She took several gulps of her tepid tea to calm herself.

"You know," she said thoughtfully, taking a biscuit, "I think there was a reason all those things were kept away in the desk like that – I think whoever put them there *wanted* them to be found. They're sort of like the pieces of a puzzle, and now I'm going to try to put everything together".

"All right, Josie," Miss Gordy said reluctantly, after a pause. "Heaven knows I would like this sorted out once and for all. But you must promise to be careful!"

"I promise," Josie replied, taking another biscuit. "Can we go back and finish reading the papers now?"

"Eat some more first," Miss Gordy answered. "You need your energy. But don't talk with your mouth full – it's most unbecoming. My mother used to say – "

Just then the phone rang, and Miss Gordy went out into the hall to answer it. "Josie!" she called out a few moments later. "Casper is asking if you want to sit for a tintype photograph!"

"Oh yes!" Josie answered, as she ran out eagerly, her mouth full of crumbs. "I should like that very much!"

"Fine, tomorrow morning then," Miss Gordy told the young man.

"Can we go over the papers now?" Josie asked again, after she had hung up.

"You go," Miss Gordy answered, looking rather pale now. "I didn't have a chance to nap earlier and now I'm a little tired. This old heart isn't quite what it used to be. But will you be all right alone?"

"I will," Josie nodded. "Don't worry".

Going back to the library, Josie sat down and picked up the last unopened letter. Her heart beat a little faster when she realised it was from Lucinda Bramstone, and dated June 14th, 1894, the day after the school's closure.

Dear Julia (it read),

I am utterly devastated to learn of what has befallen you. How in God's name could all this have happened? By what evil contrivance could twelve children have been stolen, vanishing quite into thin air?

I hear the constables and detectives are everywhere at the house and in the town, but still they continue to say they have no evidence on which to base any conclusions – how could they not have uncovered a single clue to this unspeakable crime?

The teachers and servants apparently said they heard nothing save some muffled noises and scuffles, quite what they were accustomed to from the girls' usual mischief – yet, with most of them fast asleep – in sooth, how could they be sure? There was dreadful talk in London but recently of a number of young girls disappearing – sold or murdered, they said, and no trace of victim or perpetrator to be found. Yet while the criminal madmen roam free, you are slandered and maligned, and our name utterly ruined.

What will become of you, and my darling Gracie? She of course is welcome here as long as need be, but when will you join her? Surely she cannot be left an orphan? Her aunt has been consoling her as best she can, but it is heartrending to hear her crying for you, and to learn that, if truth be told, you forsook her long before the dreadful events of this past week.

Ah, Julia! But a year since my beloved William died, and now my precious Robert is gone too! I am entirely bereft of hope – Gracie alone comforts me under this loss, far too heavy for me to bear alone. Oh God, this has killed me quite – never more shall I know peace or joy.

So that's how Mrs Bramstone managed it, Josie thought to herself, as she replaced the letter in its envelope – she simply let everyone believe that the children had somehow gone missing, or been kidnapped or worse; and since the authorities could never find any trace of them… well, what could they do? What she actually *did* do with her son's body though, was still as much a mystery as what she did with the girls – they'd literally, as Lucinda Bramstone wrote, vanished into thin air.

Josie now turned her attention to the loose sheets. The papers, in Mrs Bramstone's handwriting, had evidently been ripped from a notebook or diary, for they were dated, and filled with the writer's private thoughts. There were three separate entries all told, and Josie began arranging them in order, reading the earliest one first –

April 16th, 1893. It has been three days since darling William's return, yet how changed he is – feverish and strangely agitated – I confess it has affected me quite, and I needed twice as much of my tonic to endure the day. I don't know what the matter is with me – my head throbs so, and I find the children intolerably tiresome; I can only think it is the strain of looking after William and worrying about him that has begun to tell on my nerves.

Dr Pryor confirms that it is indeed scarlet fever – doubtless my darling's exhaustion from tending to Ada predisposed him to the infection – though he cannot understand why William is so poorly. He has left me with ammonia etc and I am to give him broth and water only. Yet despite being so enervated, he startled me today by suddenly appearing at the door of the schoolroom in which I happened to step – presumably he had heard my voice, for in truth, the children's clamour had put me quite past my patience, and I was berating them more soundly than I had ever done hitherto, even employing the rod, which formerly I had but rarely touched.

I almost lost my temper with him *next for venturing out of his room, but – "I had no choice," said he. "You were screaming in such a passion that I had to see for myself what the matter was. I fear that you have become quite irritable, Julia; I have never known you to be so harsh or intemperate. That thrashing you gave Eveline was quite unconscionable!" Here he began coughing violently and no more was, or could be, said. But I own that his words troubled me, for indeed I had observed the change in myself as well – I fear that it stems from a sense of foreboding I have about the future – I will have none if William were to leave me.*

Josie turned to the next entry –

May 27th, 1893. It has been almost a month since my darling William left us, but the pain is still as keen as the day it was inflicted. Hourly I remember his dear face, conscious to the last, grasping my hands in such agony that I despair of ever forgetting it, or the anguish in his voice as he tried to wring from me a promise to have done with the laudanum and coca. What else could I do but give him my word, to make his mind easy as he crossed over into eternity?

"Love alters not with his brief hours and weeks, but bears it out even to the edge of doom," said he, before closing his eyes forever. 'Twas my favourite of Shakespeare's sonnets, but how bitterly the words sound now to my ears. How can I go on living like this, where all is cold and dark and blank?

The noise of the children drives a knife through my head; where before I delighted in their joy and ebullience, at once pure and untroubled, I now almost wish them away on the moon, silent and invisible. The younger ones especially bear too close a resemblance to Ada, whom once I loved, but who now, God forgive me! I loathe with all my soul, for it was she who took my William away from me. He is with her now, no doubt, but I – I am still here, all alone! Robert is my sole mainstay; Grace, I cannot abide, for her eyes are that same deep hazel-green William's were, and her solemn mien, like his too, reminds me too forcefully of my broken promise. I think I shall soon expel her from my room.

The rest had been torn out. Josie laid it aside and looked at the last entry – it was dated more than a year later – June 7th, 1894. Josie's eyes grew wide – it had been written only two days before the terrible events of June the 9th. With bated breath, Josie began reading –

It has been a day of lowering clouds and dark, forbidding skies, quite suited indeed to my disposition! Daily, hourly, I feel an anguish and despair that never leave me – oh William, how I miss you so – you would scarce recognise me now for I am changed, so changed, and, I suspect, not for the better. I scarcely even recognise myself – my cheeks have become gaunt and hollow, and my eyes have mournful dark rings around them from weeping through many a sleepless night.

My former diversions have long ceased to give me the same pleasures they once did. I try to read, but I cannot concentrate; the words jump off the pages like flies or a plague of locusts. I go on my customary walks, but I find the woods no longer hold the same beauteous charm for me as they did before; now I destroy the woodland creatures I once loved and cherished, and take an almost fiendish delight in transmuting their mangled bodies, as if I were another Osiris! Ah William, you once said I give them a second life – would that I had had the power to give you one as well!

My nerves have been in such a state that I have been taking more of my pills and tonics than ever – they endue me with an almost supernatural strength and vitality; but oh, how quickly it dissipates, and I am left dizzy and debilitated, my thoughts in disarray and my head throbbing a hundred times worse than before. Then it seems as if I am walking among shadows; sometimes it seems to me I feel light fingers touching my face, and on every side of me I can see nothing but desolation and darkness.

I can hardly bear the girls now – I have grown to positively abhor them and consequently I make them dread me. Indeed, I find they grow more and more provoking every day – what once I naively dismissed as childish folly or mischief, I now know to be vicious recalcitrance and insubordination. If I left them entirely in the care of their teachers, they would be in a tumult, and that I simply cannot abide. I have had some success with instilling terror in them of my darling William's ghost, but I feel I must devise something far more concrete. Ah, would that your ghost really were here, my love, to haunt me forever!

I have lately discovered that the little devils continue to defy my commands by keeping awake well beyond their appointed bed-time – this is utterly insufferable. When I retire to rest, I require absolute silence – to hear them whispering and giggling and fooling about when all should be still – it well-nigh drives me out of my mind. I have been thinking to invent an actual phantasm, one that I can produce as required, for fear is a marvellous disciplinarian…

There was no more. Josie put the page down slowly, dumbfounded and aghast. It was plain that over the year since her husband's death, Mrs Bramstone's health and state of mind had deteriorated considerably; her use of coca, and possibly other medications as well, had evidently exacerbated, rather than cured, the maladies from which she suffered, and markedly altered her personality and judgment.

Josie wondered if the crippling headaches of which she complained were actually indicative of something more sinister; if so, the coca would surely have had even more ominous effects. She was now no longer sure that Mrs Bramstone had poisoned the girls' food to silence them as witnesses; the revelations in the letters and diary entries showed something far more bizarre – a deep resentment that came to a head with the death of her son, for which she blamed the girls – it was, essentially, *vengeance*. The question now was, where did Horatio fit into all this?

And now there remained but one last, loose sheet of paper – this had apparently been hastily scribbled, for the letters were ragged and untidy, and the whole was dirty with inkblots, and much shorter than any of the other diary entries; despite its brevity, however, Josie soon found it was perhaps the most distressing of all:

I am forsaken. I am cursed. I am drowning drowning drowning and no one hears me. The ghosts are always watching me – is it their voices I hear continually in my head? Day after day the walls close in upon me; my room becomes smaller and smaller; I never leave it. I am like the fox whose leg is caught in a trap. How infinitely small I am! How empty life can be, and how bleak and desolate and hollow. Loving, and being loved – that is all that matters. I died long before this day.

Josie stared at the note, stupefied and horror-stricken. Was it a suicide note? It certainly seemed like it could be. Yet no mention had ever been made of Mrs Bramstone killing herself, which would surely have been memorable and newsworthy. After the disappearance of the children, her suicide would have likely confirmed her guilt, yet obviously that did not happen; indeed, not even Miss Gordy herself seemed aware of it.

Could the note have been written in some fit of madness perhaps, brought on by a combination of coca and goodness knows what else? Possibly, Josie thought, but she couldn't shake the feeling that it didn't sound entirely insane – in fact, she now thought it remarkably coherent, all things considered.

Then, suddenly, Josie thought of the glossy black berries she had seen the headmistress holding in the kitchen. She remembered Mrs. Bramstone's curious, unnerving smile at the time; knowing what she did now, Josie realised it had been a glimpse into the headmistress' state of mind. Thoughtfully gathering and arranging the loose sheets, Josie spotted the little stack of photographs underneath; laying the pages aside, she picked them up – there were four.

The first was a view of Bramstone Hall from the drive, but not as she knew it now – in this picture, the house looked bright and welcoming, with windows wide open, and a beautifully tended garden with large potted plants out front. This place used to be a happy one, it seemed to say – once upon a time. Josie turned the photograph over and saw the date had been written in Mrs Bramstone's hand – *July 28th, 1891.*

The next photograph showed a stout, older lady seated at a table, with two young girls about fourteen and eight years old standing beside her. Both girls were very pretty, though the younger was decidedly beautiful, and Josie thought she recognised her as Elizabeth Brasket. At the same time, all three were dressed sumptuously, with a quantity of lace and ribbons, which Josie felt certain was beyond the means of the Brasket family at the time; puzzled, she looked to see if there was anything written on the back. There was; it read – *Lucinda Bramstone with her two youngest - Sidney and Ada, 1893.*

Josie felt a curious thrill as she looked again at the younger girl. On closer inspection, this child might perhaps have been a little smaller, her mouth just a little wider or her eyes a tiny bit darker, but there was certainly an uncanny resemblance between Ada Bramstone and

Elizabeth Brasket, and Josie could well imagine how looking at Bessie might inspire feelings of antipathy in Mrs Bramstone, especially when she was under the influence of some hallucinogen.

Josie turned to the next photograph. This one was of another very lovely young girl, with soft, delicate features set in a perfectly oval face; she was dressed in white, with a great number of frills, and wore a wide, dark ribbon about her high collar. Casually leaning against a heavily-carved table, she looked directly at the viewer with the subtlest hint of a smile, and in the crook of her arm, she cradled a baby doll. Josie had never seen this girl before, but the bewitching black eyes were unmistakable – it was Mrs Bramstone as a child.

How sweet and innocent she looks, Josie thought to herself regretfully, as she gazed at the photograph for some moments, quite mesmerised. Just one wistful line was written on its back – *Remember me as I once was.*

There was just one photograph left. It was a close-up of an adorable little girl of about four or five, with very large, dark eyes and curling dark hair; she had a remarkably forlorn expression and there was something reproachful about it too – Josie recognised her at once as Miss Gordy's mother when she was a little girl. Turning the picture over, Josie read the poignant inscription –

Forgive me, my darling Grace, whom I cast away without cause – now as death looms over me, I wish so much to see you and hold you again – just once more – and to hear your dear voice calling to me with such sweet accent. One day perhaps you will see me again, and when you do, will you call me 'mamma' and embrace me as you once so lovingly did?

How awful, Josie thought sadly, looking at little Gracie's woeful, accusing eyes. She wondered now if Mrs Bramstone had left all these things, specially chosen, for her daughter, in the hope that Grace might one day return – was it her way of reaching out to her child from beyond the grave, a desperate attempt to explain herself and her actions?

Yes, maybe, Josie mused; maybe she gathered these things together for Grace in some moment of clarity – conscious that those moments were becoming increasingly fewer and far between – and hid them so that no one else would know and the Bramstone name might still be preserved. But she didn't know that Grace would never return to stay, and that now, she too was dead and gone, so that only her elderly daughter remained, and a stranger was uncovering the family's secrets.

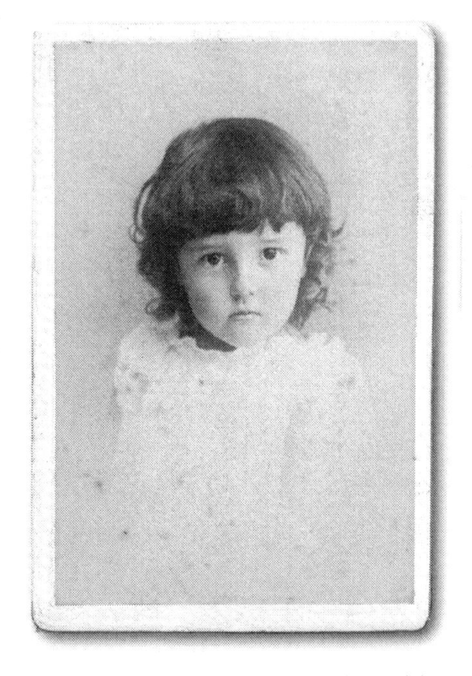

Why then, Josie wondered, did she also include the toys? Carefully stacking together all the papers and photographs, she glanced over at the red leather ball resting among the other old-fashioned playthings. With a start, she realised she had seen it before – why, that's Agnes Craig's ball, she thought to herself, holding it up – but what is it doing here?

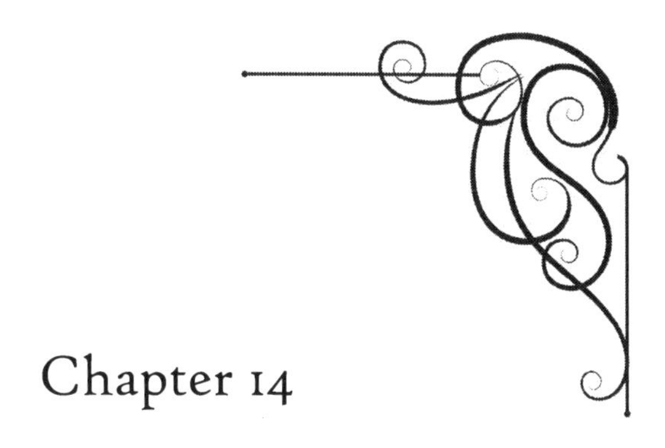

Chapter 14

Gently, Josie picked up the bisque doll head and examined it in the palm of her hand. It was just over an inch and a half, and had delicately drawn brows and eyelashes, with rounded, rosy cheeks, now worn and faded, perhaps with much loving. Josie smiled a little, imagining the girls playing with it in the dorm; then, turning it over, she was dismayed to see a long, deep crack in the back, the nature and position of which seeming to imply a forceful blow, possibly from a fall, or, more likely, from being deliberately thrown.

Frowning, Josie took up the little figurines next. The two had porcelain bear heads on stuffed cloth torsos and little black shoes painted on their porcelain feet. Josie imagined they probably had clothing once, but these had been removed and likely lost somewhere along the way, while the fissures running crazily across their heads suggested that they too had been roughly dealt with.

You poor things, Josie thought, wondering what had happened to them and to whom they belonged. The very fact that they were in the hidden compartment at all indicated that Mrs Bramstone had somehow gotten her hands on them and that usually did not bode well.

She recalled now how little Agnes had begged for her ball because it was a gift from her brother. It was evidently something she had treasured, and it somehow reminded Josie of Hetty's handkerchief. Hetty had treasured her handkerchief too, but she had had the wisdom to keep it hidden, as Maggie had done with her photograph.

As Josie thought about them, she was struck with a sudden inspiration. Gathering together all the toys, she hurriedly made her way up the stairs to her dormitory. There, she sat down on her bed and carefully lay the toys out on her blanket. Then, taking up the two bear figurines, she began moving them animatedly.

"I say, Mrs Bear, what shall we do today?" Josie asked, shaking the bear with the bigger head and making her voice low and gruff.

"Well, I think the very first thing we ought to do is go shopping for clothes!" Josie answered for the other bear, in a high, ladylike voice.

"And how do you expect us to pay for them, Mrs Bear?"

"'Pay for them', Mr Bear?"

Out of the corner of her eye, Josie saw a dark shape materialising at the open window and turned her head quickly to look; but just as quickly, the figure ducked out of sight, and there was nothing to be seen but the grey clouds against the evening sky. Josie's flesh crept to think of some unknown being standing behind her, but, taking a deep breath, she resolutely began again.

"Yes, pay for them, Mrs Bear," she said crustily. "You don't think they'll just give us the things for free do you? Perhaps we could do some sort of dancing bear act..."

The figure was back at the window again, Josie knew, for there was a curious chill in the air and at the same time now an odd, muffled sniffling. She tried to surprise it by turning more unexpectedly; yet again, though, it slipped out of sight into the wall, with a sudden, strangely jerking motion most disconcerting to see. There's no help for it, Josie thought; and taking a deep breath, she resumed her game, resisting the urge to turn around.

"I refuse to stoop to such indignity, Mr Bear! I am appalled that you even dare suggest such a thing to me!"

"Well, what do you propose doing then, Mrs Bear?"

"Isn't it obvious, Mr Bear?" Josie could feel the presence directly behind her now, and with heart beating madly, she roundly declared, "We can just eat the people up!"

At the same moment, two cold hands grasped her by the shoulders, causing her to leap up in a panic with a loud yelp. But the icy hands kept their hold on her and now the arms to which they belonged encircled her entirely, so that for several seconds she staggered about the room with the unknown figure on her back, waving her own arms about.

"Get off, get off, get off!" she yelled.

Simultaneously, Josie felt *another* set of hands grappling with the first.

"Stop it, Charlotte, for goodness' sake! Let go!"

"She's got my bears, she does!" an indignant voice replied. Josie felt a hand smack her squarely on her chest. "Give them back to me!"

"Ow!" Josie exclaimed. She held both bears out of reach and shook herself vigorously. She could feel the helpful fingers prying off the angry ones, and then suddenly she heard both figures fall with a thump to the floor. Finally pulling free, Josie whirled around breathlessly.

"Hetty! How – ? What – ?"

Hetty and the stranger had both fallen in a sprawl; now Hetty began dusting her nightgown crossly, while the other girl scrambled to her feet, still saying in an aggrieved voice, "She's got my bears, she does! Give them back to me, you!"

"Are these yours then?" Josie asked, holding the figurines out to her.

"They are," the girl said, taking them tearfully. "How did you come by them?" Dark-haired and dark-eyed, she was snub-nosed and gamine, and her full lower lip gave her a decidedly obstinate expression.

"Josie, this is Charlotte Mayhew," Hetty said, introducing her. "Lottie, she's known as. You must excuse her – she has always been rather an unruly little hoyden" – here she paused to give Charlotte a very pointed look – "but she has a heart of gold. We could always depend upon her for the most unladylike tasks, like rescuing the cat up in the tree, or evicting the mice from our property".

She turned to Lottie. "Josie is a friend," she said reprovingly. "She might be the one to save us".

"Oh. Oh, I see," Lottie said contritely. "Gosh, I *am* sorry, Josie. Are you very hurt?"

"It's okay; I'm all right now," Josie said kindly. "I felt certain these dollies meant a lot to you – well, to someone anyway – and this was the only way I could think of to make you appear. I found them in a drawer in Mrs Bramstone's desk. Can you tell me how they came to be there?"

Taking a ribbon from about her wrist, Lottie pulled back her smooth brown hair from her small pixie face.

"I was playing with them, just as you were," she said. "I was making them act out a story as the girls were wont to have me do, except their names are not Mr and Mrs Bear – they are Ira and Olive, and they are brother and sister. They live in the Underground Forest and only come out at night, because – "

"Because there everything is upside-down and backward," Hetty interrupted excitedly, "and the moon rises out of a hollow in the tree in the middle of the forest! Oh Lottie, how we loved your stories!"

"Yes, you certainly did," Lottie replied drily, "because that night you all made such a noise when I told you the Sorceror Fox had ensnared Ira in his trap, that Mrs Bramstone came bursting in upon us like a harpy; 'How dare you make such a noise?' she roared, swinging her birch rod about and striking us wherever she could.

"That was when she saw Olive and Ira in my hands and struck me so forcefully upon the face that my eyes watered in an instant; and before I could tell what was happening, she had taken them both from me and flung them out the door. I leapt up at once after them, but she thrust me back and struck me repeatedly till her hand was quite spent, and I could barely move for the pain.

"And that was the last I saw of 'em, for the next day she set me a hundred lines and would have nought to do with me. In truth, I myself wanted nought to do with *her*, for she seemed to me possessed of some sort of devil. But I lamented the loss of Ira and Olive greatly – indeed the whole class did – for many a time they had cheered and gladdened us, and they were a gift from my grandpapa besides. So I thank you kindly for restoring them to me now, even if it is only for a little while".

Lottie hugged the bears, and kissed them tenderly on their noses. "Ah, your poor, poor heads," she murmured dolefully.

"'Tis sad to see them so," Hetty said sympathetically, stroking Ira's cracked forehead. "Oh, but look here – Josie has brought a little heap of other valuables – is that not Penelope's Lumi? And there's Agnes' ball, the one she was crying about for days! Oh Josie, how lovely!"

"I worked out that it's these things that once belonged to you – that you once treasured – that have the power to bring you back," Josie explained. "Like Ira and Olive, or your handkerchief, or Maggie's photograph. It's like my Monkey, you see; Mummy gave him to me when I was a baby. I've always said I should like to have him buried with me – I should be homesick for him if I died and he was left behind. I'm not being morbid, mind; just practical – no one else would love him or take care of him as well as I do. And that's how I thought it must be with you; it's like a part of your heart always stayed with them".

"Oh, it's wonderful, Josie," Hetty cried, clapping her hands in delight. "I do believe you're right! But goodness, how did you find them?"

Josie told the girls how she had found the things in the secret drawer. "I really do think Mrs Bramstone put all your things there to be found," she said. "Do you know whose these are?"

"Well, this one is Lumi," Hetty replied, touching the doll head. "Or what's left of her. She belongs to Penelope Farwell. The spinning top belongs to Marianne Cook; the ball is Agnes Craig's; and the thaumatropes are Eveline Clarke's".

Hetty picked up one of the palm-sized discs and twirled the silk strings attached on either side. It featured the classic design of a bird and an empty cage, which appeared to merge into one as Hetty spun the disc.

"It's magic!" Lottie said, watching it in fascination.

"It certainly is," said Josie, picking up another disc, which showed a tiger attacking a man. "But the trouble is I only found these four, and there are ten of you – with Hetty's hankie, your bears and Maggie's picture, that makes seven – there's still three more not accounted for, plus Bessie too. And I believe I need all of you back again to help me lift the curse!"

"Bessie? Why, what happened to Bessie?"

Reluctantly, Josie told them what she had seen of Bessie in the room downstairs. "I'm afraid she didn't escape like the older girls," she said sadly. "She was your monitor, and I guess she somehow found out what had happened to you. It occurs to me now that there must be something of hers still left in the punishment room, because that's where she's trapped – I really ought to have a look in there again".

"But what did she mean by '*she* killed them'? Hetty asked with a frown.

"Well, don't you see?" Josie exclaimed. "She said '*she* killed them', and not '*he*' – it was Mrs Bramstone who did it, *not* Horatio! Tell me, do you remember feeling badly after having dinner at any time? Possibly on the 11th, or maybe the 10th?"

Lottie's eyes grew wide. "By Jove, I remember now," she said slowly. "Yes, 'twas the night of the 11th. We were summoned in to dinner – and we were given a bit of cold meat and potatoes and porridge – or was it pudding, I can't remember – which we gobbled in a hurry, for Mrs Bramstone could not abide wasted food or late bedtimes – and we were soon washing and undressing. 'Twas after everyone had lain down for the night that Maggie began to complain of pains in her middle, and crying that she was hot, and couldn't see clearly…

"We bade her lie down, but soon Agnes was saying she felt feverish too and so very tired on a sudden, and Hetty here had turned quite red and was all a-tremble; one by one we began to falter, feeling spasms when we tried to breathe, and seeing the strangest visions before our eyes.

"It seemed to me I was in the woods again, and a swarm of bees began to gather; I struck out with my hands and all at once they began to sting; I tried to run, but I was in agony, and I fell, and everything became dark…"

"Oh Lottie!" Hetty cried. "It was indeed just as you describe! I remember now how I shivered, and my fevered head, and my heart beating as if it would burst from my body… I remember Caroline Bishop in the middle bed, hanging over the side, heaving and retching, and Marianne Cook lying stiff as a corpse, her eyes starting from her head and her mouth working furiously… and it seemed to me then I was walking in the garden; the sun was setting and there were starlings in the sky, oh, so many of them, swooping and swelling, and I could not move for wonder.

"But they all seemed suddenly to turn upon me, so that they became as a large black cloud, surrounding me and smothering me quite – I strove to take breath, but found I could not – my chest hurt so – and then I saw Horatio…"

Josie bit her lip in perplexity. "Tell me," she said musingly, "how did you even know his name was Horatio to begin with?"

"Hush!" Lottie suddenly hissed. "Listen!"

"Wha– ?" Josie began, but Lottie squeezed her arm and held her finger to her lips. The three girls fell silent, eyes wide as they listened intently. Unquestionably now, there was a grinding, scratching sound that was becoming louder as it came closer – "Look!" Hetty whispered on a sudden, pointing upward.

In an instant, all three had looked upward and gasped collectively – directly above their heads, a thin, grimy hand, preternaturally pale, was reaching down through the ceiling, clawing and quivering as it did so. It was, however, apparently stuck halfway, for only the fingers could be seen, and it continued clutching at the air in a most unsettling manner.

"Lord save us!" Hetty breathed, staring in fear.

"What the blazes is that?" Lottie whispered, getting to her feet. "Here, help me pull the chest of drawers out!"

"Oh Lottie," Hetty remonstrated, "surely you're not – "

"I am!" Lottie declared testily, pulling at Josie's chest of drawers.

Josie slipped off her bed and went over to help Lottie position the chest as close as possible beneath the hand. Its fingers were now outstretched and taut, and, as Lottie clambered up toward them, began thrusting themselves forward in a peculiar stabbing fashion.

"Oy!" Lottie hissed, "Stop that, you!"

At the sound of her voice, the fingers became still, then suddenly, after a pause, a man's voice said, "The shadow you see in the mirror tonight is mine".

Lottie almost fell off the chest at this uncanny remark, and Josie felt the hairs on the back of her neck rise.

"Lottie! Come back down!" Hetty pleaded, pulling at Lottie's hem.

"The walls have ears," the voice continued, in a disconcertingly flat monotone. "Have you not felt the eyes that watch you behind the door? You should not have left that window open".

At the same time, the fingers began making a curious beckoning motion, which Josie found intensely unnerving.

"Oh tosh!" Lottie exclaimed. "Give me your pen," she said, gesturing impatiently at Josie.

"I only have pencils," Josie said, reaching for her box.

"Oh, hurry up!" Lottie said crossly. Josie selected one of her longer pencils and handed it to her.

"Did you see me on the stairs last night? There is a head in the drawer. Where the dark begins – *Ow!*"

Lottie had rapped the fingers smartly across the knuckles and the girls were amazed to hear the voice of a young girl cry out.

"Who are you?" Lottie asked.

"Eveline," answered the new voice, "Eveline Clarke!"

"Eveline??" Lottie and Hetty exclaimed together.

"Can't she get out?" Josie asked.

"I'm stuck!" the voice replied plaintively.

"Here, try to take my hand will you?" Lottie cried, standing on tiptoe.

Grasping the trembling fingers, she began pulling with all her might, as Josie and Hetty held the chest of drawers still. There was a loud groan, followed by the rapid clackety-clack of typewriter keys being struck all together in a passion; then, another hand appeared, grasping Lottie's hard; in a moment, the head and shoulders of a young girl with fluffy golden curls, framing her dainty face like a halo, appeared, dangling upside-down.

"Come on, can't ye!" Lottie cried, tugging at Eveline's arms, and visibly shaking in the effort.

"He won't let me go!" Eveline bawled, but just as the words left her mouth, there came the sound of something violently snapping; and all of a sudden Eveline slipped out completely with a little scream, landing in a heap on top of the girls and knocking over the chest of drawers with a resounding thud.

For a moment, the four of them simply sat there, stunned, and looking in some alarm toward the thumping sound of something rolling heavily overhead; then suddenly, all was still. As the girls looked about them, open-mouthed and wide-eyed, there came a soft whooshing sound like the beating of a small bird's wings, and snow began to fall within the room, in a flurry of the lightest, softest flakes, landing all over the floor and furniture, and the girls' heads and eyelashes.

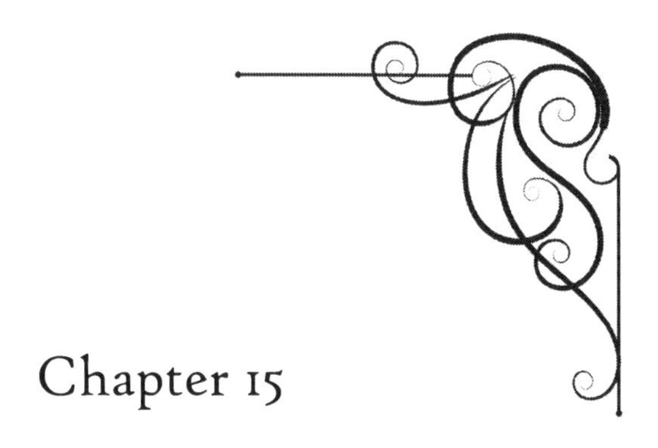

Chapter 15

"What the blazes –" Lottie began, but the sound of shuffling footsteps out in the gallery made her stop mid-sentence, and all three turned apprehensively toward the door.

It was Miss Gordy.

"Josie!" she exclaimed. "What on earth are you doing? Why has your chest of drawers fallen over?"

Josie stared at Miss Gordy in astonishment, realising with a start that the old lady could see nothing of what was actually happening, and the other three girls were as good as invisible to her.

"Oh, um, I'm sorry Miss Gordy," Josie replied, hastily fumbling with the chest. "I was just, um, trying to find something. I'll put it back right away!"

"Please do!" Miss Gordy said in some annoyance. "Those drawers are antiques, you know. And you made such a noise that you woke me up. Still," she went on, "I suppose now I can get a bit of knitting done before preparing dinner. It's rather chilly in here, isn't it? Put an extra cardigan on, and mind you come down at six to help lay the table".

The old lady turned to go, clearly oblivious to the snow that continued to descend like tiny white feathers the entire time she was speaking.

"It's what I've always suspected," Josie said, picking herself up after

Miss Gordy had left. "Grown-ups can't see anything properly! They definitely can't see you, so you needn't worry about *that* again. But really – what on earth is going on?"

"It's the man," Eveline said, getting up, and brushing the snowflakes off her yellow ringlets. "He's trapped too, you know".

"What?" Josie asked in amazement. "Horatio took his soul too? Who is this man?"

"No, I mean he's caught in the darkness too," Eveline replied, her blue eyes round with wonder. "I don't know who he is. But I think he's trapped because of what he did" – here Eveline lowered her voice to a tactful whisper – "I think he killed himself!"

"Oh! He told you that, did he?" Lottie asked, quite unsympathetically. She and Hetty were playing with the falling snow. "It's been ages since I've felt snow!" she cried gleefully.

"Och, don't talk so Lottie," Eveline said reprovingly. "You don't know anything about him. He said he'd done it to himself – those were his exact words. That's how he came to be there, and with his typewriter too!"

"How ever did he do that?" Hetty asked.

"Well, he killed himself with *something*, not the typewriter," Eveline explained, "but he held on to his machine to the last. It was a winter's day, it was; some time in November, or was it December, 1925. I think he was trying to make a point to his publishers".

"Rather silly, if you ask me," Lottie retorted. "Not much point if he's already dead, is there?"

"'Tis true," Eveline answered thoughtfully, "I didn't quite understand it myself. He could only speak – oh, what's the word – allegorically, so I could never get a plain answer from him. 'Twas most unfortunate that he fell upon me when he crossed over – I can't imagine he enjoyed being imprisoned with me in the dark like that, neither of us being able to get away from the other, and both of us having to listen to each other's tales of woe again and again. However, in justice to him I must say that some of his stories were really quite enthralling – they *did* make my flesh creep!"

"So it was him spouting all that nonsense then? About seeing him on the stairs and under the bed and behind the curtains and such?" Lottie asked. "It made *my* flesh creep too, horrid man! Why didn't you tell him to hold his tongue, Evie?"

She was sitting on Hetty's bed now, for the snow was finally tapering off, and only a few airy flakes were left gently floating down.

"I don't think he could help it," Eveline said generously, sitting down beside her. "I think 'twas the manner in which he crossed over. Or perhaps writers are always saying peculiar things. Whatever the case may be, I am much obliged to you for liberating me, and for restoring to me my dear papa's thaumatropes".

"You must meet Josie," Hetty said. "It is thanks to her that we are here at all, and have any hope of deliverance!"

"She is a favourite of mine already!" Lottie said exuberantly. "We ought to – oh, what the blazes now?"

From underneath Josie's bed came a familiar scrape-scrape-scraping. "Maggie!" Josie exclaimed. In a trice, she and Hetty were on all fours, waiting for Maggie to emerge. But after several seconds passed and there was still no sign of her, Josie and Hetty looked at each other in alarm.

"Maggie! Maggie!!" Hetty hissed at the floor.

"I'm here!"

The girls wheeled round to see Maggie sitting against the wall, on the bed's slatted headboard.

"Maggie!" Josie cried. "What are you doing up there?"

"Well, I remembered how Hetty said I oughtn't to frighten you by coming through the floor," Maggie explained, as she climbed down, "so I thought I'd try this instead. Hello, Evie! Hello, Lottie!"

"Oh," Josie replied, getting back on her bed, "how thoughtful of you! But I should think I'd be quite terrified if I were lying down here and you suddenly appeared above me – I think perhaps you can stick to coming through the floor like before; I'm really quite used to it now".

"Coming through the floor sounds ghastly to me," Lottie observed, as she tried to make the wooden top spin without a string. "I'd hate to be surprised by *anything* coming up through a floor".

"Well, 'tis a funny thing you should say that," Evie remarked, "because there's something coming up through the floor right now!"

Startled, the girls turned to follow Evie's gaze – it was directed toward the middle of the bare floor, through which they could now see the top of a dark head emerging; slowly, the figure rose straight up, revealing itself to be dressed in a white nightgown, with a profusion of black hair falling in long waves entirely over its face and down to its knees. As it found its footing, the figure began swaying uncannily, reciting in a high, singsong voice:

A ring, a ring o' roses,
A pocket full o' posies –
Atishoo atishoo we all fall down!

There was a moment of appalled silence before Lottie leapt up with an exasperated snort. Stomping over to the eerie figure, she unceremoniously parted the thick curtain of hair with both hands. A round, button-nosed face with mischievous blue eyes beamed out at her.

"*Marianne!*" Maggie shrieked. "Oh really! Have you still not outgrown this ridiculous trick?"

"Oh Marianne!" Hetty burst out laughing, falling backward on her bed. "Don't scold her Maggie; she has always been so diverting. But really Marianne, you oughtn't to do that to people you're just meeting".

"Marianne used always to do this to us," Evie explained to Josie, who was still staring at the newcomer with mouth agape. "It would frighten the wits out of me when she would suddenly appear like this behind the door or the bath; it was unfortunately not quite so amusing when she accidentally did it to Mrs Bramstone".

"Aye," Marianne agreed, throwing back her splendid hair, revealing a long, narrow scar that ran down her forehead and across one brow which added to her bold, cheeky air. "She swore to cut it off too, do you remember; but of course she quite forgot about it when *that* happened".

"Well, come meet Josie, you naughty girl," Hetty said. "She found your spinning top, she did".

"Ah, did she?" said Marianne, taking the little wooden toy from Lottie. "Then I am most truly obliged to you, Josie! When first it was taken from me, I was sorely grieved, for 'twas my brother made it for me; nor did I know how I should face him when I returned home. Little did I know I would never see him again".

"Ye shall see him again," Lottie said firmly. "Josie here will lift the curse!"

"Oh, I can't make any promises," Josie interjected quickly, "but I have found out a good many things!"

She was about to tell them everything she had learned, when a loud bang made all the girls jump – the bathroom door had slammed shut.

"How odd," Josie said, "I've never known that door to – "

She paused as a soft sloshing sound caught her attention – it was coming from inside the bathroom. For a few seconds, all the girls cocked their heads, listening to the unusual burble of running water.

"Why, the taps are on!" Josie suddenly exclaimed.

"What the blazes – " Lottie began, as Josie scrambled to her feet.

"The taps are running; I have to turn them off!"

In a few seconds, Josie was at the bathroom door; water was seeping out from under it and she was astonished to see that it was not clear, but a deep murky green, thick with algae and floating bits of pond weed. Reaching for the handle, Josie opened the door and cautiously looked in – the bathtub was filled to overflowing, complete with weeds, tiny fish and even pollywogs. Clambering in, Josie turned the slippery taps off; as she did so, two small hands appeared on the edge of the tub – Josie knew them at once.

"Oh, I *am* sorry!" a little voice exclaimed.

The person to whom it belonged stood up, and Josie hurried forward to grasp her arm, remembering how she had slipped before.

"Be careful," Josie said, helping the girl out.

Her brown curls and long nightdress were dripping wet, but even as she got to her feet, they began to dry, and the water in the room began to recede and disappear as well.

"I am sorry," she said again. She pointed to the taps, modern fittings that Miss Gordy had had installed. "I didn't know how those things work," she said ruefully. "But I've always loved water, you see, and I'd lie in the bath whenever I had the chance if I couldn't get away to the pond".

"Aye," Lottie said, coming up behind Josie with the other girls. "You must have been thrashed ten thousand times for playing truant, Agnes Craig!"

"I couldn't help it," Agnes replied piteously. "I hated this place. The pond was as close to being home as I could get; my brother John and I used to bathe there so often. And later, when I learned that he had died, I would go there to just sit and look into that deep, deep green, and imagine…"

"Och! Don't say such foolish things, Agnes," Evie said. "Look what Josie has found for you!"

Evie held out the red leather ball to her. Agnes' dark brown eyes grew large as she stared at it – "Is it really?" she breathed, hardly daring to touch it.

"It is, dear," Evie said kindly. "I remember how we used to play with it in the woods".

"Oh Josie," Agnes said with tears coming to her eyes, "thank you, thank you, a thousand times, thank you!"

"You're very welcome," Josie returned. "I was so glad to find it after seeing what happened that day Mrs Bramstone took it from you".

"You saw me – that day?" Agnes repeated, puzzled.

"Yes!" Josie replied. "I've been seeing quite a few things, really! And I must tell you – Oh wait, hang on – Penelope's dolly is still here – perhaps we ought to wait and see if *she* appears next!"

"Oh, if she does come, it shall be in some dark, medieval fashion, don't you think? She is such a romantic at heart," Maggie observed.

"I just wish she would hurry – " Hetty began.

"Oh, my word, look over there!" interrupted Marianne.

In the far corner, a black shape was pressing through the wall like a stain; in a few moments, it had assumed the form of a small person, though very irregular around the borders. As the girls cautiously drew closer, the whole shape suddenly heaved, as if taking a great breath, and then broke apart into a million tiny bits that scurried pell-mell over the walls and toward the girls with frightening speed.

"Spiders!" Maggie squealed, leaping up on to one of the beds.

"Don't squish them, Lottie!" Josie cried, pulling Lottie back.

"Oh, they're babies!" Agnes said, gently brushing them off her arms and legs. She looked up as she spoke, and saw that the stain on the wall had become a pale girl with drooping chocolate ringlets and remarkably dark circles around her light blue eyes. The girl remained pressed into the corner, at least half a foot off the floor, as if she were uncertain where she was, when on a sudden, she heaved again, and a quantity of exceedingly nasty-looking black liquid spewed forth from her mouth.

"Oh, what the blazes, Nell!" Lottie exclaimed, jumping up.

The black liquid smelt appalling and left a most unpleasant stain on the girl's front, but even as Lottie helped her down from the wall, the stain began gradually disappearing, and with it the noxious odour as well.

"I do beg your pardon," the girl said feebly.

"My word, was that the first time you've been sick since *that* happened, Penelope?" Maggie asked incredulously.

"It was," Penelope replied, still looking about her in a daze. "The last I remember I was shaking as if with ague, and my brow was burning hot… fleetingly I thought 'twas my consumption again, but no, 'twas far worse… I remember then seeing my mamma; we were walking in the courtyard of a great castle, and she led me toward the drawbridge… I remember we were crossing it when it began to rise, and mamma called to me from the other side to hurry, but I could not, and I fell back upon the ground… There were spiders everywhere and they made of me a silk cocoon, so that I could neither see nor speak, or breathe even; and then – and then I saw Horatio".

"Horatio again!" said Josie. "Okay, listen, you all *must* tell me how you even came to know his name to begin with".

"Oh, to be sure," Hetty said. "But first, do let's give Nell her Lumi".

The doll head was duly placed in Penelope's hands, who looked at it with great sorrow. "Ah dear," she said mournfully, tenderly touching the long fracture in the back, "she is quite hurt. I daresay this was all that could be saved after Mrs Bramstone threw her out the window. But I am exceedingly grateful to have even her head again".

"'Twas Josie here who found her," Maggie said. "She's the one who is going to set us free!"

"Oh, thank you ever so much, Josie," Penelope said. "And I think I can tell you how we learned the creature's name, for 'twas I who first saw him in this room, and 'twas I who told Mrs Bramstone".

"Oh!" said Josie excitedly. "What happened?"

"We were all out in the garden that day. Some of us decided to make a picnic of sorts with the scraps we had in our pockets from breakfast-time and I said I wished I'd brought Lumi so she could join us. Well, Evie said she'd come up with me to our room to get our blankets to sit upon and then I could get Lumi too, so both of us came back to the house.

"I came up the stairs and entered first, and what should I see but that most unnatural spectre standing by our window, no doubt watching us out upon the lawn and devising some fiendish scheme or other. 'Evie!' I cried, and 'Oh, merciful Heaven!' cried she; and at the sound of our voices, the creature turned towards us and seemed to consider us for a spell – I hurried then to my drawers and drew Lumi out – but my movement must have attracted the creature's attention because he suddenly swooped down upon me with his arms outstretched, feeling about as one who is blind... That was when Evie and I ran out of the room, screaming as if the devil himself was on our tails..."

"And we ran directly into Mrs Bramstone who had come out into the gallery when she heard our cries," Evie continued, "*not* because she felt any anxiety on our accounts, mind, but because she couldn't abide noise or commotion of any sort. But we had been frightened out of our wits, so that even though she pulled us both by the ears, we would not be silent, and we told her what we had seen…

"We saw then that she was troubled by what we'd said, and paid us much more attention than she cared to show; but 'How dare you make such a clamour?'" cried she, and still pulling us by the ears, she did drag us back into the room. But it was quite empty now and Horatio was nowhere in sight.

"'The creature has vanished, it seems,' said she, sarcastically. 'What have you to say for yourselves?' But we were quite overcome and could hardly answer her a word; we were crying so. And she, in a fury, took Lumi from Penelope and threw her out the window…"

"'Twas the last I saw of dear Lumi," said Penelope, tearfully. "The gardener found her in pieces, and gave them to Mrs Bramstone – I knew I couldn't hope to get her back again then. That day the other girls in our form caught glimpses of Horatio at different times – standing at our window again, or our empty beds, or in the corners – but we made certain to steer clear of him and only spoke of it to each other; no one dared say anything more to Mrs Bramstone.

"Then, as we kept talking about him in our beds that night, she herself suddenly came in upon us – 'I told you Mr Bramstone watches over this house still,' she declared. 'He has sent the creature Horatio to keep order here – hold your tongues or your very souls will be taken'.

"Needless to say, we all fell silent at once, and indeed, we were all so terrified that we remained quite mute the next day as well, being so subdued that even she could find no cause to punish us. Instead, however, she spent the entire day watching us with a most baleful countenance, so that we were quite worn out, but we thought we only had to bear it a few weeks till term's end when we would be fetched home".

"Well, little did we know we would never be fetched home," Agnes sighed.

"Ah, don't talk that way," Hetty said. "Look at us now – all together again! Well, *almost* all of us. Josie will find the others; you'll see. I have every confidence in her!"

"Aye, but what then?" Evie asked. "Horatio killed us – will he return us our souls now?"

"I've thought of that too," Josie admitted. "But I really do believe Mrs Bramstone collected your things together for a reason. The fact is, she was very, very ill; I think she was trying to make amends for what she did before she died. I must tell you – you have to know that it was *she* who killed you, *not* Horatio".

As the girls listened in amazement, Josie told them everything she had learnt over the past couple of days. "I still don't know how Horatio fits into all this," she said at last, "but I am certain he was *not* a murderer. Tell me, that plant – the one with the shiny black berries that she put in your food – do you know what it was?"

"Belladonna," Agnes said slowly, as the girls looked at each other in horror. "My brother used to point it out to me in the woods; every part of it is poisonous. Perhaps you know it by its other name – deadly nightshade".

"Mrs Bramstone kept the berries," Josie mused. "Could she have used them on herself? I must ask Miss Gordy if she knows what happened to her after the school closed. But the big question is – how did she manage to hide all of you, and Robert too?"

"Where *is* Horatio, by the by?" Maggie asked.

"You're right," Josie said. "I haven't seen him either, not since that day he came when I was talking to you and Hetty. Do you remember Hetty, how he tried to catch hold of you, and you just disappeared? He looked so sad then, I felt almost sorry for him. It seemed to me that he came to a sort of realisation when you did that; I'm not sure what exactly… He's not appeared again since".

"'Tis a curious thing, now as I think on it," Maggie remarked. "Girls, do you not think Horatio looked rather like the coat stand Mrs Bramstone brought in to our room that night?"

Evie's eyes opened wide. "I did think it!" she exclaimed. "But the coat stand was scraggy and spindly, and the sheet hung loose and empty –

Horatio had flesh and form…"

"And life," Lottie added.

"Yes," Marianne agreed, "'twas as if – why, 'twas as if Horatio somehow filled out the coat stand and made it alive…"

Josie threw a sharp glance at her. This was the first time a direct comparison had been made between the two and it certainly was an interesting thought. "It's rather a coincidence, isn't it?" she murmured. "I wonder what it could mean?"

Outside, a clock chimed six. "Ooh, I have to go for dinner," she said, hurriedly getting up. "Could you all wait for me to get back? You needn't always disappear, do you?"

"I'm afraid I cannot stay out here in the light for too long a time," Hetty replied sadly. "I grow faint and it is a fearful thing – I feel I might quite utterly vanish! It is a possibility I daren't contemplate".

"Yes," agreed Maggie. "I stayed out too long once, and saw my fingers become almost vaporous!" She shuddered at the recollection. "Something always makes me return to the darkness, even though it is quite against my will and I tremble at it! No, we'd best not tempt fate – for so long as we can control when we appear and disappear, there is still hope; when that is taken from us, then, I fear, all is over".

"Well, we won't let that happen," said Josie firmly. "Keep your things in my drawers then – I'll take them all out again as a signal for our next meeting. In the meantime, I'll try to find the things belonging to Bessie and the other three girls. Keep your chins up!"

The girls hugged and kissed each other on the cheeks; then, as Josie hurried downstairs to help Miss Gordy with dinner, they tenderly put away their treasures, and were soon gone in a shower of twinkling lights.

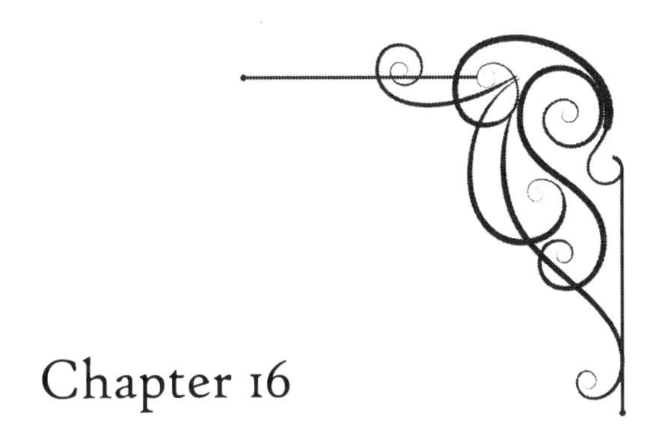

Chapter 16

Over a dinner of unexpectedly delectable vegan spaghetti and asparagus soup, Josie shared all her findings with Miss Gordy. The old lady was visibly shaken by the end of it, and spent several minutes staring into space and shaking her head.

"It's unbelievable," she said at last, "just unbelievable. To think – my grandmother was a – a *murderer*! There's really no other word for it, is there? Ah Josie, you're a godsend, you are. To think – living here, day in, day out, all these years – and not being able to see anything that could have helped them! I do believe the entire house is trying to help you, Josie – why, even Arthur the chimp here". She patted the monkey's hand. "I am sorry," she said to him contritely, "I didn't know".

"Do you know how Mrs Bramstone died?" Josie asked.

"Well, that has always been a mystery," Miss Gordy replied, frowning. "After the uproar following the children's disappearance finally died down, my grandmother withdrew from public life. She had most of the windows boarded up and, as you know, the entire back wall as well. She became very much a recluse – hardly going out, and getting anything she needed sent up from the town. The delivery people were told to just leave the things on the porch, and on the odd occasion they did see her, she apparently would say nothing – just stand there and stare at them till they left. They said she didn't look well either – you know, she was famous for her beauty – well, that had quite gone.

"And then one day, the orders for food stopped coming; a couple of months passed and finally the family lawyer paid her a visit. He found mail piled up at the front door and the garden quite overgrown; and of course when he knocked and hollered, no one answered him. They went in and searched – the house was empty. Of course she might very well have gone on holiday, but when years passed and there was still no sign of her, even after advertisements had been placed in the newspapers, she was finally presumed dead and the property was transferred to my mother.

"Well, as I'd told you before, *she* definitely didn't want to live in the house, so she merely oversaw some repairs and tidied the place up a bit. The police wanted to have a look about too, especially since the children's disappearance had always been a thorn in their sides, but nothing of them, or my grandmother, was ever found. And so that was it – the house remained empty until I finally moved in".

"And a good thing you did too!" Josie declared. Dinner being over, she had gotten up and was looking at the photographs on the mantel with renewed interest now that she knew more about the people in them.

As she moved along the wall, peering closely at each picture, she suddenly felt her foot strike something hard and heavy, and looking down, she was surprised to see a little white terrier dog standing alertly upon a red velvet cushion; it was gazing up at her from under a large glass dome with an extraordinarily winsome expression.

"Oh! What a cutie!" Josie exclaimed, kneeling down to get a better look.

"That was one of my great-grandfather's dogs," Miss Gordy said, looking up from her tea.

"She sure is sweet," Josie remarked, "or he. We had a dog once named Kenzie – he looked a lot like this, except he was brown".

As she looked at the dog's bright black eyes, she was startled to see its little pointed tail suddenly begin to wag; in the next moment, it had stretched out its front legs, and lowered its chest to the cushion – it was evidently inviting Josie to play.

She glanced over at Miss Gordy – the old lady was taking out her wools in anticipation of the morrow's knitting project.

Kneeling down, Josie carefully lifted the glass cover. The little dog immediately began doing its best to jump on her, but its legs had been securely attached to the cushion on which it was mounted, and it soon began whining piteously.

Josie stroked its head and tried to soothe it. "I'm afraid you can't come off – you've got pins or something in you holding you down".

The dog seemed to understand this, for it licked her fingers sadly and gradually resumed its former posture; as it did so, Josie caught sight of a little silver tag on its collar – crouching down, she parted the thick curling fur and read the fine inscription – *Horatio.*

"Oh!" Josie gasped.

"What is it?" Miss Gordy asked, looking up from her wools.

"This dog – his name! It's Horatio!"

"*What!!*" Throwing down her wools, Miss Gordy hurried over to have a look.

"Oh my, well I never!" she exclaimed. "My great-grandfather did have many dogs, but they were big hunting ones mostly; this little fellow was the only one he ever had mounted, I think because he was a favourite of my grandmother's – I believe there is a picture somewhere of her as a child with him on her lap. But gracious, what can it mean? This little fellow is surely not the creature who takes children's souls??"

Josie looked at the pup's adorable, smiling face and bit her lip.

"No-oo," she said slowly, "I really don't think so".

"Well, what then?"

"I think it's just a name Mrs Bramstone gave to the creature. Probably it was the best name she could come up with at the time, being an old pet of hers. Evie said that Mrs Bramstone looked troubled when the girls told her about him – it seems likely that Mrs Bramstone knew nothing at all. But seeing how frightened the girls were, she may have thought to use him to her advantage – she had once tried to create a creature; now here was one ready-made! The question now is, what part did he play in the disappearances?"

"Poor fellow," Miss Gordy murmured, patting the little dog's head.

"I should like to set him free," Josie said. "He does want to come out".

"What? But he's been preserved and mounted!"

"Well, please can I just try pulling him off?"

"Really, Josie, I don't think – oh, very well," Miss Gordy said. "I'll warrant you know what you're doing".

Josie grasped the dog's pudgy body with both hands and pulled him upward. But the nails holding him down were well wedged into the cushion, and he would not budge. "Hm, I shall have to ask Casper to help me tomorrow," Josie said at last, sitting back on her heels. "I'm sorry, Horatio; just wait a little longer".

Miss Gordy shook her head in disbelief. "Well, come on, then," she said. "Help me put the dishes in the sink; it's time for your bath".

That evening, the crickets were out again in full force. After getting into her pyjamas, Josie told Miss Gordy that she wanted to do a bit more sleuthing.

"Well, you know bedtime's at eight, Josie," Miss Gordy said, reprovingly. "My mother used to say – "

"Oh, but you know Daddy said he'll be home in a couple of days – that's not a lot of time," Josie pleaded.

"This is really most irregular," Miss Gordy said uncomfortably. "What if – "

"I'll be fine," Josie assured her, knowing the old lady would never approve of her going into Mrs Bramstone's room.

"Oh, very well," Miss Gordy said, after a pause. "But promise me you'll be careful! If anything – "

"Don't worry! I'll be *super duper* careful!"

As soon as she heard Miss Gordy's door close, Josie put on her cardigan and took out the *Headmistress* key still in her pocket. Now to see what's in there, she thought to herself. Slipping Monkey into her other pocket, she went out into the gallery. Miss Gordy was already preparing to retire for the night; soon, she switched off her lamp, and the house became completely dark and quiet.

Turning on her torch, Josie made her way towards the headmistress' room. The air had turned bitterly cold. With a thumping heart, she inserted the key. But before she could turn it, the key was pushed out forcefully from inside; as it fell with a heavy thud, the door suddenly swung open and Mrs Bramstone emerged, dressed entirely in black and with her thick raven hair flowing wildly about her face and over her shoulders. Illuminated by the moonlight streaming in through the tall stained glass windows above the staircase – their multicoloured panes now clear and unsullied as they were over a century ago – she looked as frighteningly beautiful as an avenging angel.

As the headmistress swept past her in a biting rush of wind, Josie grabbed the fallen key and hurried after her – the locked door could wait. It was clear that Mrs Bramstone was in the grip of some dangerous influence; there was something decidedly chilling about the purposeful way in which she was striding down the gallery, and now, with a sinking heart, Josie followed her as she turned into her dormitory.

For several minutes, the headmistress stood on the threshold, looking at the girls in their beds with a dreadful expression of bitter satisfaction. Several short candle stubs were burning on a few of the drawers, but even by their dim illumination, it was plain that the girls were all very ill indeed, for they were lying insensible, and the collective sound of their heavy, laboured breathing was more harrowing than anything Josie had ever heard in her life.

Then, as she watched, horror-stricken, Mrs Bramstone walked over to Maggie's bed and bent down close over her. The girl's hands were clutched over her chest and she was struggling to breathe.

"I know you're awake! Open your eyes!" Mrs Bramstone hissed.

But Maggie was too ill to respond or even move.

"You wicked girl! Open your eyes! Get up!"

"Stop it, stop it! Can't you see she's sick?" Josie cried, running forward and trying to pull the headmistress away.

But Mrs Bramstone neither saw nor heard Josie, and in the next instant, she had placed her hand over Maggie's nose and mouth.

"Stop it!" Josie screamed. "You're suffocating her; she can't breathe!"

Suddenly, Maggie's eyes snapped opened, and her little hands grabbed frantically at Mrs Bramstone as she heaved for breath. The headmistress began grappling with her, when, on a sudden, the girl apparently bit down on the hand that covered her mouth, for Mrs Bramstone drew back with an oath, and Maggie toppled to the floor with a thump. As she lay there in a faint, Josie felt a fresh gust of icy wind behind her and whirled around – it was Bessie Brasket.

The older girl took in the entire scene at a glance. "What have you done?" she cried.

As she stood there in her nightdress, with wide eyes and long coppery hair cascading down her back, Josie was struck by how much she resembled Ada Bramstone, and she shuddered now to see Mrs Bramstone turn slowly round, her black eyes flashing balefully. There was no mistaking the expression of extreme animosity on her face, but, undaunted, Bessie rushed fearlessly forward.

"Maggie, Maggie!" she cried, kneeling beside the stricken girl. But Maggie was barely breathing now, and Bessie stood up, tears streaming down her face. "What have you done?" she cried again. "I must get help!"

But as Bessie tried to pass Mrs Bramstone, the headmistress stepped before her, blocking her path; her face was darkly malevolent, and it was plain that Bessie suddenly realised then that she was in mortal danger, for she let out a little cry, and pushed against Mrs Bramstone with all her might. It was no use, however, for the headmistress seemed possessed of an almost superhuman strength; she seized Bessie by the arm, and dragged her out the door.

Horrified, Josie began to run after them, when she was startled to hear a familiar damp, squelching sound at the other end of the room – wheeling round, she was stunned to see the creature Horatio emerging through the furthest wall; for a moment, he hovered in the corner, seemingly sniffing at the air, then he turned and glided swiftly toward the bed closest to him at the end of the row.

Dumbfounded, Josie paused on the threshold, torn between the two – she desperately wanted to follow after Bessie and Mrs Bramstone, but, realising that this might likely be her only opportunity to discover Horatio's part in the entire mystery, she finally cast a last, anguished glance toward the door – the faint sound of Bessie's cries as she was pulled after Mrs Bramstone was heartrending beyond belief.

Steeling herself, Josie took a deep breath and approached Horatio, who was now bending over the inert form of Charlotte Mayhew in the last bed. Lottie's breathing was very irregular now – with only a few quick breaths between spaces of complete stillness; it was clear that she was very poorly indeed. As Josie watched in helpless despair, Horatio extended one sheet-covered arm over the girl's wet forehead.

In the next moment, she was staggered to see him softly stroke the fevered brow, and then whisper, in a very small voice, "Shhh, don't be afraid; everything will be all right". Then, as he carefully lifted Lottie in his arms, a brilliant light began to glow around them both, becoming so bright that Josie had to squint and avert her face; it lasted but a few seconds before it began to fade, and when next Josie looked, only Horatio remained – *Lottie had entirely vanished.*

In amazement, Josie watched Horatio make his way down the row of beds, gently comforting each girl before apparently spiriting her away, till at last he reached Maggie, who was still lying on the floor. She had clearly tried to move, for she was now partially under her bed, but her fingers were clenched stiffly and she was barely breathing.

Carefully, Horatio lowered himself beside her, his bird claws making a discordant rasping upon the floor; then, as he raised her up in his arms, Maggie's eyelids briefly fluttered and she murmured, very weakly, "Am I going home now?"

"Yes," Horatio whispered, and as he gently stroked her golden-white hair, the dazzling light enveloped them both – and then she too was gone. As Josie continued to stare with mouth agape, the creature stood up and for a few moments, hovered there, unmoving, with head bowed in an attitude of profound sorrow. Then, as if suddenly remembering Mrs Bramstone, he glided out at full tilt to the gallery and paused at the head of the stairs.

From somewhere below, Josie too could now hear indistinct cries; heartsick, she pressed past Horatio and ran down the staircase as fast as her feet would carry her. The house was dark and still, with doors tightly closed for the night – evidently no one else had heard anything. She reached the main hall in seconds, and a soft glow coming through the stained glass windows of the punishment room confirmed her worst fears – rushing in, Josie saw Mrs Bramstone thrashing Bessie with her heavy cane as the girl scrambled pell-mell against the far wall, striving vainly to avoid the blows, and banging her hands against the wall in desperation.

As she did so, there came a loud whooshing sound from within it, and it heaved as if it were alive; but Bessie's fear of Mrs Bramstone far outweighed any consternation she might have felt about that, for she beat her hands upon the wall even harder. "Lynton, Lynton," she cried, "help me!"

Josie started in astonishment to hear this, but she had no time to wonder about it, for now the shape of the creature Horatio was clearly outlined within the wall, and Mrs Bramstone stumbled several steps backward, petrified. For a moment, she stood open mouthed, her dark eyes almost bulging from their sockets; then, as the ghost-like figure seemed to billow against the wall, she gnashed her teeth in a fury, and lunged forward, brandishing her cane above her head.

But she was not to use it again, for before she could bring it down upon Bessie, Horatio stepped in between the two and raised his arms protectively over the young girl – in an instant, they were both engulfed in a blinding blaze of light; when it cleared, both of them were gone.

Letting out an almost inhuman cry, Mrs Bramstone looked about her wildly, swinging her cane savagely at the air. Then, evidently remembering the girls upstairs, she whirled round and rushed past Josie as if the very hounds of hell were upon her tail; reaching the empty dormitory, she screamed again, over and over, before suddenly sinking down upon the floor, with her face buried in her hands.

As Mrs Bramstone's body shook with long, racking sobs, Josie saw a small crowd of girls – evidently from the older girls' dormitories – slowly approaching from the gallery with candles in hand; the questioning, perplexed expressions on their pale, sleepy faces were quickly replaced by fear and alarm, but their dread was too strong to be soon overcome, and the entire scene began to close before any of them even dared step forward. In a minute more, all was dark again, and Josie was left alone with the crickets.

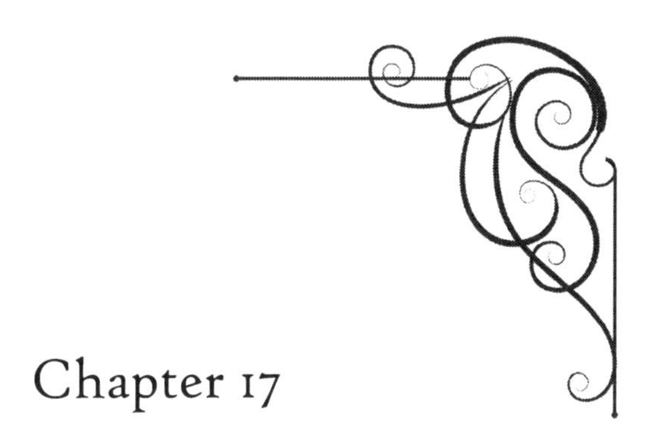

Chapter 17

"You could *absolutely* knock me down with a feather," Josie declared, as she sat on the edge of her bed with Monkey, trying to calm herself and collect her thoughts. She was still in a state of shock about Horatio's role in the girls' disappearance, and everything she had witnessed this night was replaying in her mind most unpleasantly.

The girls had literally *vanished*, she thought to herself incredulously, but where was Robert? He had not featured in the events of that night it seemed, yet he had certainly also disappeared at the time, as confirmed by Lucinda Bramstone's letter. Josie fingered the keys in her pocket thoughtfully – could the answer be in the headmistress' room?

"We'll have to go see," she told Monkey determinedly. Tucking him back into her pocket, Josie picked up her torch and valiantly ventured out once more. The dark and silence were almost palpable as she crept along, and seemed to press against her like something alive. Reaching Mrs Bramstone's room, Josie hesitantly placed her ear against the door, and was relieved to hear nothing stirring. Taking a deep breath, she inserted the key into the keyhole.

The lock was rusty, and the key grated harshly as Josie turned it with an effort, but soon there was a click, and the door swung open slowly. Stepping in cautiously, Josie shone her torch over the room. It was large, papered, carpeted, and well-furnished, but windowless and airless – a wardrobe, full-length mirror, dressing table and pedestal desk stood against the walls, while a heavy four-poster bed stood in the middle, flanked by a tall chest of drawers and a blue-and-white-tiled washstand.

Rows of bookshelves entirely lined the far wall, while a room divider with tapestry panels had been folded and propped against the fireplace. Indistinct zigzags and rectangular imprints in the thick dust suggested that the divider, and perhaps two smaller beds, once stood at the foot of the four-poster. Seen by the small light of her torch, the room seemed inexpressibly bleak to Josie; there was a mustiness in the air that smelt horribly of doom and decay, and was fast giving her a headache.

As she covered her nose and mouth with her hand, she suddenly paused, frowning – could there be something in the room's atmosphere that was making her head throb, and which may perhaps have made Mrs Bramstone ill as well over a century ago?

But now was not the time to consider this, for Josie did not want to stay any longer in the room than was necessary; quickly, she began shining her light over the furnishings, opening the cupboard and the drawers, and scanning the table surfaces. However, everything had been emptied and was quite bare; even the desk and dressing table drawers had been cleaned out – only the bookcase retained its collection of fusty, leather-bound tomes, which covered the wall from top to bottom. Disappointed, Josie turned from the wardrobe and then suddenly froze in her tracks – a dark, thin shape sat shrouded within the heavy drapes of the four-poster, its face turned directly toward her.

In a flash, Josie aimed her torch at the spectral form, lighting up a pale, sunken face with preternaturally large, dark eyes, covered entirely with a black mourning veil – it was Mrs Bramstone. Suppressing a scream, Josie staggered backward against the washstand, clutching at its edge to stop herself from falling; she could feel her heart pounding against her ribs and she was shivering uncontrollably now – the temperature in the room had dropped sharply.

However, Mrs Bramstone did not move, but only continued sitting upright and still as a statue on the edge of her bed, which was uncanny enough by itself; yet, as Josie slowly recovered her equanimity and warily drew closer, she was disconcerted to hear the headmistress murmuring unintelligibly to herself beneath her veil, sending chills up and down Josie's spine. All at once, the headmistress' white hand appeared on her lap; it was open, and in its palm Josie was startled to see a quantity of berries, glossy and inky black.

As Josie watched in horror, the headmistress slowly began eating the poisonous fruits, taking them up one by one within her veil and swallowing them resolutely till they had all disappeared; then, rising, she took a deep breath and began making her way to the bookcase that spanned the far wall from end to end. As she did so, she began to fade, and in a moment, Josie was left alone, staring breathlessly at the rows of dark volumes. She was now beginning to feel really quite overwhelmed by the stale, almost putrid, atmosphere, and deciding she would have to come back again another time, she turned and hurried out of the room.

As she stood in the gallery, taking in deep gulps of the comparatively fresher air, she suddenly became aware of the faint sound of a piano being played – as the plaintive notes continued, Josie realised it was coming from somewhere downstairs, and she recognised it as one of Chopin's nocturnes from the records her father liked to play. Creeping down the stairs with her torch held low, she hazily recalled hearing the same piece being played the night before.

Reaching the hallway, Josie now saw a dim glow emanating from the drawing-room – the pianist was evidently using the old upright there. Tiptoeing to the doorway, she peeped in cautiously – a lit kerosene lantern stood on the piano's lid, and seated with his back towards her was a man she had never seen before; he was dressed in a tweed ulster and dark wool trousers, and on the small table beside him were a stack of papers and a little black typewriter which were certainly not part of the Bramstone furniture. Outside the window, snow could be seen silently falling.

Overcome with curiosity, Josie crept round the piano and looked the pianist full in the face. His eyes were closed as he continued playing with great skill and feeling, and Josie saw now that he was a youngish man, not much more than twenty-five and very handsome, with small, regular features, and dark brown hair parted neatly down the middle. He wore a white shirt and striped necktie under a thick shawl-collared pullover, and Josie realised with a start that while he was certainly from a bygone era, he was not from Mrs Bramstone's time, but a few decades later – she had seen enough of Mr Harwood's vintage menswear magazines to know his clothes and hairstyle dated to somewhere between the twenties and thirties.

For some minutes more, Josie simply stood there, leaning against the upright and watching the young man play; he was doing it so beautifully that she felt quite moved, and indeed, the young man himself was evidently much affected by the hauntingly resonant tones of the antique instrument, which were quite unlike any of the modern pianos Josie had ever heard. Then, as he finished playing the last chords, he opened his eyes, and Josie saw that they were dark brown like his hair, and lent his face a very warm, charming quality that made Josie think unaccountably of otters.

With a deep sigh, the man rose from his seat, picking up a knit scarf he had laid beside him; pulling it on, he gently closed the piano, then turned to the table and picked up the stack of papers. Josie saw now that they were a mix of typed and handwritten notes, but before she could read anything of either, the young man had rolled the papers up and stuck them into the large pocket of his coat.

Hoisting the typewriter under his arm and taking up his lantern, he made his way toward the door; on reaching the threshold however, he suddenly paused and turned, and with a slight chuckle, bowed deeply, apparently to the stuffed and mounted inhabitants of the room. As he did so, there was a sudden surge of electricity in the air – every animal that could, turned its head in his direction and opened its mouth, bristling and shaking in palpable agitation.

But the young man was to all appearances oblivious to the anxiety he had provoked, and turned to leave, humming under his breath.

To Josie, however, there was no mistaking the intense apprehension in Arthur the chimp's eyes, and she now hurried after the man with growing misgiving. Out in the main hall, he stood looking about him, seemingly undecided; then, putting down his typewriter on the floor, he took out a little notebook and pencil from his inside breast pocket.

Standing on tiptoe by his elbow, Josie was shocked to see that it contained a list of the rooms in the house, with several of them – such as the kitchen, library and drawing-room – struck through, and it was with a cold thrill of horror that she saw the next room on the list was simply designated *Headmistress.*

"Don't go, don't go," Josie murmured, but the young man blithely drew a line through the name, and, picking up his typewriter again, began ascending the staircase.

Considerably disquieted, Josie followed him down the gallery toward Mrs Bramstone's room, feeling a momentary hope as she recalled that the door was locked. But to her dismay, the stranger produced a small ring from his trouser pocket, on which were hung several brass keys of varying sizes, with intricately-carved bows and bits. *Skeleton keys*, Josie thought to herself, watching him try each one of them in the keyhole.

In less than a minute, the door clicked open, and the young man entered slowly, with his lantern held high. The light threw the furnishings in the room into sharp relief, but it was to the walls that he went first, after setting his typewriter down on the headmistress' desk. Holding the lantern close to the wallpaper, he appeared to examine it closely, and then Josie heard him give a low whistle, and say to himself, "Well, well".

Pulling out his roll of papers, he spread them out on the desk; then, picking out a particular sheet, he began scribbling on it rapidly with his pencil. Leaning over the desk beside him, Josie's eyes opened wide as she read what he was writing:

Dec 5th 1925. Wallpaper in Headmistress' Room – Small blue florals and curling foliage against a dark green background, generously interspersed with large blades of seaweed – possibly Fields & Co – Arsenic?

Sticking his pencil behind his ear, the young man picked up his light and moved about the room, looking through the drawers and the wardrobe, and even flipping through a tattered book or two; but though he was there years before Josie ever was, everything had already been cleaned out and there was nothing to be found.

"Okay, time to go," Josie muttered, but the stranger brushed past her quite unconsciously, and seating himself at his typewriter, took up a blank sheet of paper and fed it through the machine's roller. She saw then that a name had been etched into the typewriter's front plate – *W. J. Fitzwater.*

For several minutes, she stood behind him, watching him type line after line with an almost hypnotic rhythm; he was evidently using the Bramstone house as a source of inspiration or research, or both. Reading his writing as it appeared on the page, Josie began to gather that he was telling the story of a certain Edith Wilkinson, who lived alone in a great mansion, where she was haunted not only by its previous occupants, but also a malevolent postman who took a fiendish delight in making cryptic remarks as he handed her her letters.

As Josie watched him struggle to think of yet another synonym for "evil", she couldn't help feeling that he did not seem suicidal as Eveline had said, but then of course it was so hard to tell sometimes… The young man was re-reading his last line of writing aloud with an air of great dissatisfaction, when he paused mid-sentence with a startled "Hallo!" and, grasping the central section of the desk at which he was sitting, began forcefully tugging.

Peering over his shoulder, Josie ran her eyes over the desk's frame – it was a dark English oak, elaborately carved with myriad flowers, leaves and vines, and Green Man handles on the stacked drawers in its pedestals. Bringing his lantern closer, the stranger scrutinised the desk's middle; there was no Green Man carved into it, but Josie was taken aback to now see an odd-shaped hole cleverly tucked into the curve of a twirling vine.

Quickly fumbling for the skeleton keys in his pocket, the stranger pulled them out and selected one. *It's a keyhole*, Josie gasped, as the man deftly inserted the bit, and with a delicate flick of his wrist, a click was heard, and a well-camouflaged drawer protruded about half an inch. Grasping both ends, the man pulled it out – a single torn sheet of paper lay inside. Carefully removing it, the young man closed the drawer, then sat back, studying the paper thoughtfully.

Standing behind him, Josie saw that it was a diagram of the solar system, showing the eight planets orbiting the sun. Beneath it, written in Mrs Bramstone's beautiful hand, was a list of the planets' names and, beside each, a number:

Mercury – 3
Venus – 7
Earth – 1
Mars – 5
Jupiter – 2
Saturn – 6
Uranus – 4
Neptune - 8

"Curiouser and curiouser," Josie heard the young man mutter to himself, as he examined the paper which was spotted and yellowed with age. It's some kind of code or cipher, Josie thought, as she and the young man stared at it in perplexity for some minutes. Finally, he set it aside and resumed his typing, and Josie, leaning against the bedpost behind him, wondered that the fetid atmosphere did not affect him as much as it did her; perhaps she was just sensitive, she thought with a frown.

The typewriter keys had recommenced their lively tapping, when suddenly, a thick, leather-bound volume fell off the bookcase with a thud, making Josie almost jump out of her skin.

The stranger stared at the wall of books for a moment – apparently disconcerted, but unafraid – then, rising, he calmly went over to it with his lantern, and moved his light over the rows of tall and tattered spines. As he looked into the space where the fallen book had been, Josie saw him pause and lean in closer; a second later, he had removed the books on either side of the gap, revealing the back wall of the shelf.

With bated breath, Josie watched him, expecting goodness-knows-what to materialise, but nothing untoward appeared, and now, looking in by the lantern's bright illumination, she was astonished to see what looked like a series of concentric circles carved into the wood – with the outermost not more than six or seven inches wide – and a little eight-pointed star in the very middle.

That's odd, Josie thought to herself, cocking her head. The man evidently thought so too, because *he* cocked *his* head also; then – "Well, well," he murmured, putting his hand in the space and feeling the curved edge of one of the circles. As he did so, the wooden ring moved slightly, pushing against the ring above it, and Josie saw now that there were tiny teeth cut into the edges at varying intervals, which allowed each circle to sit precisely within the next; suddenly it dawned on her – they're *gears!*

The stranger now tried shifting another circle, but although this one moved slightly as well, it soon jammed up against the next ring and wouldn't budge. However, he was not to be discouraged, and Josie watched him with increasing apprehension as he determinedly jiggled the curved pieces one after the other. As he did so, there came a whistling down the gallery outside, and a gust of icy wind suddenly blew into the room, making both him and Josie jerk their heads up in surprise; it caught up the planetary diagram on the desk, causing it to float momentarily in the air, before finally landing neatly at the young man's feet.

As he picked it up musingly, Josie's eyes slowly widened; *it's the solar system*, she thought to herself, looking back and forth between the paper and the shelf – the rings represent the planets' orbits round the sun, the eight-pointed star. She counted the carved rings – yes, there were eight. The stranger clearly realised this too, because he now stepped up to the shelf with the cipher in hand, and, after a moment's consideration, laid hold of the third ring from the centre, and turned it in an anti-clockwise direction.

Josie's mouth fell open as the gear now rotated gratingly but unimpeded, and began moving the other gears to which it was connected – *Of course!* Josie thought in amazement. The numbers in the diagram show the order in which the rings have to be turned, and the Earth is the third planet from the sun. The young man next gripped the fifth ring and turned that, then the first, innermost one – Jupiter and Mercury, thought Josie, watching breathlessly.

In less than a minute, he had rotated all the circles as far as they would go; now, as Neptune's outermost ring clicked into place, there came a grinding noise from somewhere within the shelves, and an entire section of the bookcase, hitherto camouflaged, creaked open an inch. *It was a combination lock*, thought Josie, staring in fear at the door – she realised now where Robert had been hidden.

She began making a note in her head of the number sequence, knowing she would need it in the future since the young man had pocketed the cipher; now, with a start, she saw that he intended to go into the secret room, for he was prising the weighty door open – "No, no, no," Josie said desperately, trying to pull him back. But of course, it was no use – her hands simply passed right through him – and in a moment more, an intensely foul odour assailed Josie's nostrils, and she clapped her hand over her nose and mouth.

The young man, however, was undeterred, and, lantern in hand, had disappeared into the other room for several seconds, when Josie heard him give a sudden exclamation; reappearing in Mrs Bramstone's room, he began hurriedly wrapping his scarf about his face. Then, collecting his papers and typewriter, he returned to the hidden chamber, apparently intending to continue his writing or note-taking there.

I have a real bad feeling about this, Josie thought, nervously clutching Monkey in her pocket, while the sound of the young man's footsteps and excited scribbling echoed through the room; as she continued standing undecided before the bookcase, she was alarmed to hear a sudden soft vibration from deep within the shelves – "The door is closing!" Josie cried, stumbling back, though she knew she could not be heard.

A split second later, the clockwork mechanism started to whirr ominously, and the heavy door began steadily creaking shut; the opening soon became too narrow for even Josie's small figure to fit into. Through the rapidly straitening gap, Josie saw the young man's handsome face become distorted with terror as he rushed to the door; it was plain that he already knew there was no way out from the other side – "I don't want to die, I don't want to die," he repeated in an anguished tone that cut Josie to the heart, but there was nothing she could do.

For a moment, his hands remained gripped on the edge of the bookcase; then, just before the door closed completely, they drew back and were gone.

Chapter 18

The night's events weighed on Josie so that she hardly slept a wink, and by the first light of dawn she was already up and brushing her teeth. Pulling on her dress and cardigan, she caught sight of the notebook she had left on her chest of drawers during the night; the last thing she had done before crawling into bed had been to write down the planetary number sequence before she forgot it, and now she put the notebook away with a woeful sense of foreboding.

Mrs Edmundson was just letting herself into the house and she smiled broadly when she saw Josie coming down the stairs.

"You're up early, miss," she said affably. "Hungry for breakfast, are we?"

"No, not really," Josie admitted ruefully. "I just thought I'd go for a walk".

"Well, mind you don't go too far," Mrs Edmundson replied, with a slight frown. "It's still early hours and you never know who's about. I'll come looking for you if you're not back in within twenty minutes".

Josie stepped out into the driveway and took a deep breath. The air was wonderfully fresh after the night before, and she relished the clean, earthy smell of approaching rain. Walking through the tall grass along the crunchy gravel path, Josie made her way to the back of the house, and looked up toward the corner where Mrs Bramstone's room was located.

She now understood why Mrs Bramstone had had the back wall cemented over – there was nothing at all in the plain exterior to indicate that there was a secret room hidden there, and no one would have been the wiser. Josie imagined that there probably had been rows of windows along the wall at one time, just as there were along the sides of the building, but Mrs Bramstone had taken care that the room was to be her grave – as it was her son's – and Josie shuddered to think of the young man trapped in the dark, airless space with them.

Sighing, she turned away, and was soon walking back to the front of the house, carelessly kicking at pebbles, when in the distance, she suddenly saw a young girl running towards her, waving. She was wearing the white school pinafore and dark green dress, and her short brown hair was combed straight back and tucked neatly behind her ears. Josie had never seen this girl before, but she waved back tentatively; as she did so, she felt a cold wind blow down her neck, and a second girl appeared, brushing past her so closely that Josie felt her stray white-gold hair tickle her ear – it was Maggie.

"Goodness, you have been a time!" the unknown girl exclaimed, coming up to them. "We've already laid out all the things; Hannah's mamma sent her a sponge cake and my word, it does look good. Do hurry; Brimstone was looking particularly off her nut today – one never knows now when she might appear and want to test us on our arithmetic, or French, or sense of smell!"

"Hush, you naughty girl," Maggie said, suppressing a giggle as she linked arms with her, "you never know where Mrs Bramstone might be hiding!"

The girls were cutting across the lawn, with Josie close behind; she saw now that the grass underfoot was verdant and neatly trimmed, and a profusion of pansies, snapdragons and other colourful flowers grew along the garden's borders. Several groups of girls were seated on blankets, evidently enjoying a recess or rest day on this fine spring day, and Maggie and her friend soon joined their party, the majority of whom Josie already knew.

"Do you know," Maggie continued, seating herself and producing several slices of buttered bread from her pocket, "she's put little Gracie in with Matron – imagine that! Sleeping in the infirmary with the sick girls!"

"She's going madder by the day, I tell you," Lottie said. "I say, I do hope you all don't mind my only having potatoes; I ate all the cheese".

"Well, Agnes and I saved some cheese," Hetty said, looking at Lottie reprovingly, "though really, the star of today's feast is surely Hannah's cake – just look at this beauty! Thank you ever so much, Hannah!"

The girls all took turns helping themselves to the little jammy cake, while Hannah – a pert-looking thing with wide-set grey eyes and black hair looped up in braids on both sides of her head – beamed amiably. "When did you see Gracie?" she asked Maggie, breaking up a hard-boiled egg.

"I didn't," Maggie replied, licking her fingers. "I saw Robert coming out from there, and asked what ailed him. 'Nothing,' said he, 'except to see my sister stuffed away in the infirmary as if she had the pox! Mamma said Gracie's noise goes through her head like a knife, but I have never found her to be especially loud, have you?' And when I agreed that little Gracie was certainly *not* especially loud, he sighed most woefully and said, 'She is a good deal paler than I remember – I fear she will catch some contagion just from being near Matron so much'.

"I commiserated with him, and said I was sorry Mrs Bramstone was feeling unwell. 'Mamma is much changed since Papa died,' he observed, and told me how he had come upon her thrashing Bessie for speaking out of turn; 'That's the third time this week I've seen her beating Bessie,' said he. 'It was all I could do to keep from stepping in between them! In the end, all I *could* do was offer her my handkerchief and some of my toffee, but that probably wasn't very useful, was it?' Oh, do look, it's Polly!"

Maggie began whistling and waving a bit of toast, and Josie turned to see a large black crow, with a single white feather in its right wing, regarding Maggie obliquely; as it hopped over towards her, Josie saw that it was holding something green in its beak.

"Oh, the dear thing, she's brought us a new present!" Agnes exclaimed, holding out a small piece of baked potato. The crow looked at it for a moment, before depositing the green item on the edge of the girls' picnic blanket; as it pecked at the bit of food, Lottie picked up the green object and held it up to the sunlight.

"I say, this *is* pretty, Poll!" she said appreciatively, handing it to the other girls to have a look. Josie saw then that it was a smooth piece of translucent sea glass.

"I'll put it in the box with the others!" Agnes said, pocketing it, as the other girls offered Polly their own scraps.

"You're sure old Brimstone won't get her hands on it?" Marianne asked.

"I hope not," said Maggie, making a face. "Well, she doesn't come much into the schoolroom now, so I think it is *quite* safe, especially since she doesn't really mind what she can't see; Agnes and I have it well covered with our slates and books".

She held out another bit of bread to Polly, who readily picked it from her fingers. It was evident that the girls had formed a special friendship with the crow and that it was in the habit of bringing them gifts in return for their feeding it; Josie felt certain now that this was the crow in the library, and she remembered the chatelaine she had seen dangling from its dress – I must have another look at it, she thought to herself excitedly.

A sudden drop of rain hit Josie on the nose, and she looked up in surprise. A storm's coming, she thought, looking at the lowering clouds. She glanced back at the girls – they were still enjoying the lovely spring sunshine with Polly the crow. As she watched them wistfully, they began to fade, and she heard Mrs Edmundson calling her name from the driveway. Rising, she started to run back to the house as a fork of lightning flashed vividly across the sky.

"Mercy!" exclaimed Mrs Edmundson, as Josie scurried under the portico. "You just made it, miss! What were you doing out there on the lawn? Look, you've made your knees all mucky".

"Just picnicking," Josie laughed. "Is Miss Gordy up?"

"Aye, she's in the drawing-room".

The old lady was already at work on her tarantula pillow as Josie hurried in. "Good morning, dear," she said. "I hear you went out for an early morning walk – did you see anything interesting?"

"Oh yes," Josie said, "and I have lots to tell you! But first, can I please have Casper's phone number so I can ask him to do something before he comes over?"

Miss Gordy looked surprised, but wrote the number down on a piece of note paper. "Mind your manners if it's his father who picks up the call," she warned.

But it was Casper who picked it up, after rather a long wait, and it was clear from his croaky voice that he had just woken up.

"Oh Casper, I am sorry," Josie said, "I thought you'd already be up!"

"Well, it is just 7am, miss," Casper replied with a yawn. "Why are you up so early?"

"I'm sorry; I couldn't sleep much," Josie answered apologetically. "Lots of things happened last night; I'll tell you all about them when you come over later. But I was wondering if you could help me with something before you do?"

"Sure, what is it?"

"Could you please help me look up a W. J. Fitzwater? Any information at all. I think he was a writer, and I believe he died in 1925".

Josie heard Casper take a deep breath. "The name sounds familiar," he said after a pause. "Sure, I'll have a look on the computer and maybe pop by the library too; I have to drop by there for my dad anyway".

"Thank you!" Josie said. "Oh, and Casper, could you please also help me look up something called Fields & Co? Find out if they made wallpaper, and if there was anything weird about it. See if they had a design of little blue flowers on a dark green background with lots of big seaweed-type leaves".

"Um, okay," Casper replied with a chuckle. "Never a dull moment with you, that's for sure. I'll see you at ten".

Putting down the receiver, Josie returned to the drawing-room. Miss Gordy's knitting needles were clicking away busily, but she looked up as Josie entered. "Did you get what you needed?" she asked.

"Yes," Josie nodded, walking toward the bird dolls. "I was really just trying to find out about wallpaper and someone named W. J. Fitzwater. I don't even know if that's his name. Casper said he'd help me look, but I don't know if he'll be able to actually find anything".

"W. J. Fitzwater?" Miss Gordy repeated, pausing in her knitting with furrowed brow. "How odd – I feel like I've heard that name before, a long time ago… Yes, that's right; Chopin – *Prelude in A Major, Opus twenty-eight, number seven*".

"What??" Josie exclaimed, stopping in her tracks and turning to Miss Gordy in astonishment.

"Yes, I remember my mother playing the record on the phonograph. It was the early 1920s, and I was still very young, maybe five or six; the piece is very short, but my mother used to say it was her favourite, and it was played by a W. J. Fitzwater. She told me the name so many times I guess it stuck in my head. I remember hearing him play on the radio sometimes too. And then later, when I was nine or ten, I remember policemen and detectives coming to the house; they wanted to talk to my parents about Mr Fitzwater.

"It seemed he had disappeared, and there was mention of his name in connection with this house. But I was too young to really understand what was going on, and my parents never explained. We were living in another city altogether at the time, so I think my parents didn't have anything really useful to contribute to the investigations. The police never found anything, I believe, and the whole thing eventually blew over. Why were you asking about him?"

Awful as it all was, Josie knew she had to tell Miss Gordy everything she'd learned the night before. When she had finished, the old lady covered her face with her hands. "My grandmother was surely not in her right mind," she murmured, shaking her head. "What a burden she carried! And that poor, poor young man – why on earth did he come to the house?"

"I don't know," Josie replied sadly. "It seemed to me he was very fascinated with it; it *is* an amazing house after all. Perhaps it was all a lark to him; he did seem a very jolly kind of fellow. Anyway, it was a good thing I saw him; I wouldn't have known otherwise about the door to the secret room or that it was designed to close like that. Now that we do, we can be sure to be extra careful when we go in, which I should think we will have to soon, now that we know where Robert Bramstone was hidden".

"To think, though," she went on thoughtfully, "your mum must have tidied up Mrs Bramstone's room because the books were all back in place when I first went in alone – she never guessed what was behind the bookshelf the entire time".

Miss Gordy shivered and laid her hand on her heart. "I don't know that I can take it," she said, her voice quavering with emotion. She looked very pale indeed.

Josie hurried to her side. "Are you okay?" she asked anxiously, thinking how terrible it would be if she were the cause of the old lady having a heart attack.

"I'm all right, dear," Miss Gordy answered weakly, patting Josie's hand. "I *had* wanted this mystery solved, and I still do, come what may. I told you once that I couldn't die in peace knowing that the children are all still trapped here, and I meant it. But learning the truth has been hard to bear, very hard indeed".

"It'll all work out, you'll see," Josie said reassuringly. "*How* it will, I don't know yet; but I'm certain it will. I just have to find a few more things first. And then when all the girls are back together again... well, I guess we'll see. I have a funny feeling in my tummy Horatio will be the one who shows us what to do".

Miss Gordy looked at Josie in surprise as she said this, but Mrs Edmundson came in just then, bearing a tray of tofu omelettes and beans on toast, and Josie had to stand up to help her clear a space on the coffee table before the sofa; in a few minutes, everything was nicely laid out, including mugs of tea and almond milk.

"Are you sure you won't join us, Mary?" Miss Gordy asked, unfolding her napkin.

"No, thank you, ma'am," Mrs Edmundson beamed. "I had breakfast before I came. I'd like to get the laundry going now; young Josie's pyjamas were looking quite grubby!"

She glanced quizzically at Josie as she picked up the breakfast tray and left, and Josie gave Miss Gordy a sheepish grin. "Some of the rooms are awfully dusty," she said.

"Well, I can imagine my grandmother's must have been," Miss Gordy replied drily. "You do know I would never have permitted you to go in there if I'd known – what if something had happened to you?"

"Well, nothing did," Josie answered soothingly. "And this really is the only way – the girls have always said they needed a kid to get to the bottom of all this – grown-ups just couldn't see what needed to be seen!"

She told Miss Gordy about what she had witnessed out on the lawn that morning. "I should like to have a quick look at the schoolroom to see if I can find that box Agnes mentioned," she went on, picking at the beans, "the one where they kept the gifts Polly brought them – I should think the girls would love to see it again! I'd also like to see where Mrs Bramstone made your mum sleep – perhaps I may find something there. The first thing I'd like to do though, is have a look at the treasures Polly is carrying right now!"

When breakfast was finally over, Josie brought Polly to the sofa. "Isn't she lovely!" she exclaimed, seating her on her lap. "Of course, I don't really know if this actually is Polly," she continued doubtfully, peering up the sumptuous lace sleeve. But though the wings had been well folded within, Josie could make out the single white feather tucked among the black.

"It *is* her," she declared, stroking the bird's iridescent head. "Poor Polly; I guess one day she came too close and Mrs Bramstone saw her..."

Carefully, Josie unhooked Polly's chatelaine. The doll was quite large, at least eighteen inches tall, and her chatelaine was quite large as well; it featured an enamel timepiece, from which hung seven chains – these held the ring, thimble, buttons and key that Josie had seen previously. Gently, Josie removed them from the miniature spring hooks and wrapped them in the flannel polishing cloth that Miss Gordy had laid out for her.

Tucking them into her pocket, she restored Polly to the sideboard. "Thank you," she whispered, as she set her down among the other dolls. She turned to Miss Gordy. "I'd like to do a bit of sleuthing before Casper gets here," she said. "I hope that's okay".

"I don't think I could say no!" Miss Gordy replied with a slight laugh. "The schoolroom's beside the library; the infirmary's upstairs. Mind you lock the doors after you leave, and be careful!"

As Josie went out into the hall, the phone rang and Mrs Edmundson came out of the kitchen, wiping her hands on her apron to answer it.

"Hello?" she said brightly. "Ah hello, Mr Harwood! Oh yes, I'm fine, thank you. Yes, Josie is right here".

"Hi, Daddy!"

"Hello, Josie; is everything okay over there?"

"Yes, Daddy! This has been one of the best holidays ever! What about you? When will you be back?"

"Josie, Uncle Eddie is dead".

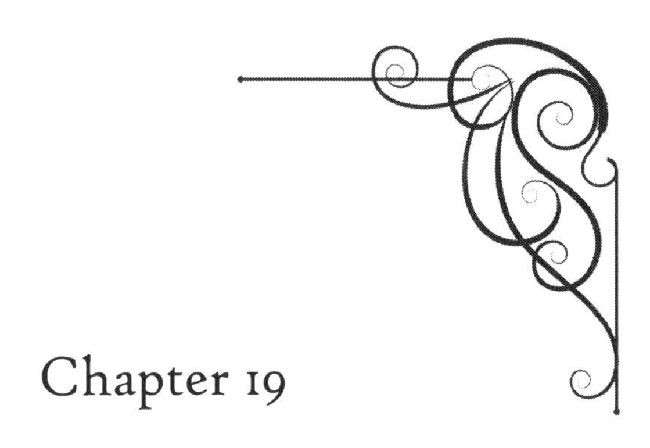

Chapter 19

Mr Harwood's news was admittedly rather dampening, but Josie hadn't known Uncle Eddie at all really, and she mainly felt sorry that her father was feeling so dejected. She assured him that she was fine staying on at Miss Gordy's for a few more days while Mr Harwood helped Uncle Eddie's estate lawyer with various grown-up details. Uncle Eddie had been very practical about his funeral arrangements, which was a good thing since Mr Harwood was too overcome with nostalgia looking through their childhood photo albums.

While Miss Gordy spoke with him about creative things people could do with a loved one's ashes, Josie went to the library, where she found the bunch of keys she had previously left on the open desk. Snatching up the ones labelled *Schoolroom* and *Infirmary*, she hurried over to the room next door.

This was directly across the hall from the punishment room, and was, to all appearances, equally small, being apparently a mirror image of the other, with the same single white door as its entrance. Yet Josie soon realised this was deceptive, for the door swung open into a room of very long and wide dimensions, and divided into four sections, each comprising ten iron-framed desks with benches attached.

Cautiously, she stepped in. The room was dark and shadowy, and smelt very musty too, for its three sash windows, though substantial in size, were all closed and tightly boarded up. Josie flicked on her torch and looked about her in wonder. There was a large table at the very front, beside which stood a lectern and standing globe, as well as a tall dunce's stool. A broad blackboard covered most of the wall behind this table, while a cupboard, two fireplaces, a pump organ and several bookcases lined the sides. A vast collection of specimens, globes, abacuses and miniature models were ranged along shelves on the back wall, and all were covered with a thick layer of dust and cobwebs.

Josie walked down the aisles between the desks, imagining the girls at their lessons, when all of a sudden, she had the distinct sense that she was being watched, and, stopping in her tracks, she looked around nervously. There was no one to be seen, but now, out of the corner of her eye, she saw something move stealthily and swiftly on the wall closest to her.

This wall had no windows, and was instead decorated with framed maps, natural history prints, and constellation charts, as well as portraits of Queen Victoria and other ostensibly important personages. These last Josie found especially interesting, for they were fine paintings of very stern and imposing ladies and gentlemen in empire dresses and stiff cravats; a quick glance at the name plates on their gilded frames identified them as members of Mrs Bramstone's family during the late 18th to early 19th centuries.

The sitters were painted from the waist up in kit-cat fashion, and as Josie drew closer and peered at them searchingly, she was startled to suddenly see the large eyes of a buxom lady in Regency costume move sharply to the left and right, and then turn to glare directly at her.

Letting out a little scream, Josie stumbled backward in a fright, landing with a crash on one of the benches, and scraping both her elbows in the process.

"Ow," she groaned under her breath, sitting up as quickly as she could and swinging her torch towards the painting, from which she was now greatly unnerved to hear a low laugh issuing.

As she stared at it in alarm, she was aghast to see the lady's stout form appear to swell and rise from the flat canvas as if she were about to emerge from it; but Josie soon realised this was illusory, for the lady's light, diaphanous draperies were soon replaced by crisp black silk, and something far more ominous began materialising – it was Mrs Bramstone.

For a moment, she hovered mid-air, before commencing a stately descent to the schoolroom floor, brushing so close to Josie's head that the hem of her skirt lifted the girl's hair with a chill wind; then, gliding down the centre aisle till she reached the third row from the front, she made her way purposefully to a desk under one of the great windows in the far wall. Breathlessly, Josie scrambled after her and was just in time to see her remove several small items from the purse hanging on her chatelaine.

Slowly, Josie crept closer and was taken aback to see that they were a collection of childish toys and knick-knacks – a frozen charlotte, pieces of glass and porcelain, a tiny horseshoe charm, a dirty marble, a broken toy soldier. Standing in the deep gloom, the headmistress glowed softly with an unearthly light as she regarded the little objects in her open hand. But before Josie could even guess at what these might be, she was chilled to hear the same low laugh she had heard earlier, at once sardonic and sad; then, on a sudden, Mrs Bramstone began speaking aloud.

"Ah William, look at these sweet treasures! Do you know, a little bird told me where to find them? No, I jest – it was far from little; it was a great black crow which I wanted as my own. It returned again and again to the house, you know, and I saw that it loved the girls, and the girls loved it, and I own that I was envious. I watched it for days – there was a ledge outside the girls' window where it would leave these wonderful gems, and I delighted in taking them for myself".

The headmistress' voice was low and wonderfully deep, and Josie felt a peculiar thrill to hear her speak in such calm, thoughtful tones, quite unlike any of the other times Josie had heard her. It was, however, disconcerting to hear her addressing her dead husband, and for a moment Josie glanced about apprehensively to see if he too might appear, but to her relief, he did not; evidently Mrs Bramstone was simply in the habit of talking to him as if he were still alive.

"How a few years in the world changes everything irrevocably," she now continued mournfully, gently caressing the tiny china doll in her palm. "We can never go back, can we, William? We can never change the past, or undo the hurts we have suffered – or caused. But I am not long for this world, and in that I take comfort. 'Tis a curious thing – I feel more lost and bewildered than I ever have, and the headaches are nigh unendurable, yet some thoughts seem to come to me very clearly now… They are fleeting though, so I must act while I can.

"I have lost Gracie forever, in this life at least, but I will speak to her from the grave. She has always been a bright child, and she will grow to be a clever woman; one day, when she comes home again, she will piece together everything that has happened here. There is no longer any hope for me – well, that is of my own doing and a just reward – but for the children whom I struck down, Gracie can still be their deliverance. I trust she will find them – they will not, they *must* not, be held here forever".

As she spoke, she lifted the wooden lid of the desk at which she was standing and removed from within it a long rectangular tin, decorated with red and gold scrollwork against a white ground; opening it, she stared at it broodingly, and Josie caught a glimpse of a jumbled assortment of odds and ends, before the headmistress dropped into it the items she had been holding. Replacing the box in the desk, she sighed deeply, and the large tears that had welled up in her eyes rolled down her cheeks.

"Oh William, how have I lived till now without you, and without my darling Robert too? His loss was too great a shock to me. Well, nothing can hurt him now, but for me, the wound is too deep; I cannot bear it. Will we meet again in that place where there are no more partings, no more pain? No; no, I think not. There is no room in Heaven for someone like me; 'twould be an insult to everyone who was there. It is enough that I cease to exist; with that I shall be content. Goodbye my darling," she said sadly; adding softly, under her breath, "*Love alters not with his brief hours and weeks, but bears it out even to the edge of doom*".

With bowed head, she turned away, and Josie watched the dark figure pass through the wall like mist and disappear entirely. She's going to her death, Josie thought to herself, shivering as she remembered the belladonna berries. She looked up at the painting from which she had seen Mrs Bramstone emerge. The sitter's eyes were static now and just imperceptibly outlined; *peepholes*, she thought, with a shudder – the girls would probably never have noticed or guessed that they were being observed.

Turning now to the wooden desk with hopeful expectancy, Josie eagerly lifted its thick, scratched lid and saw with a thrill the tin box still safely in place and looking remarkably well-preserved; with trembling fingers, she picked it up and read: *Peek, Frean & Co's Superior Biscuits*.

Shaking the box gently, Josie felt its contents move about with tantalising little clinks, but she had already decided she would only open it in the girls' presence, and, tucking it into her pocket, she hurried out of the schoolroom – the sense of grief and loneliness in the air was unbearably stifling.

"Now to find that infirmary," Josie muttered to herself resolutely, feeling the biscuit tin in her pocket with deep satisfaction as she climbed the stairs. She became aware of the same hushed whispers and footsteps she'd heard when she first arrived at the house; they seemed to be more restive now, as if bristling with anticipation.

Reaching the gallery, she began traversing its entire length, reading the painted titles on the closed doors as she passed – here were the second and third dormitories, as well as the bedroom of a Miss Thompson; then, turning the corner for the first time after Mrs Bramstone's room, she reached the opposite side, and passing the bedrooms of the Misses Denton and Bradshaw, as well as a Mlle Aubert, she found the infirmary almost directly across from her own room.

Inserting the rusty key, Josie slowly pushed the white door open. Almost immediately, a stale odour of age and antiseptic, mingling with an acrid, medicinal mustiness, wafted out and made her step back with a grimace; covering her nose with her sleeve, Josie snapped on her torch and stepped warily into the shadowy room.

It was long and wide, with five beds down each side facing each other, and two washstands in the middle. At the far wall was a small fireplace, and on either side, two closed doors. It was to these doors that Josie's attention was now directed, for the sound of a child crying could be distinctly heard coming from within, making all her hair stand on end; but plucking up her courage, she began walking past the rows of beds towards them.

As she drew closer, the crying stopped; Josie saw now that one door was marked DISPENSARY, and was in fact of the Dutch variety – split in half horizontally, so that the top section could be opened while the bottom remained shut. The upper half had not been secured and was open half an inch; as Josie hesitantly poked it with her torch, it swung creakily inward, releasing a pungent odour redolent of herbs and chemicals.

Peering in, Josie saw a tall wooden table, on which were arranged a pair of scales, a brass mortar and pestle, and a dry inkwell and pen, while against the far wall an enormous mahogany dispensary cabinet stood, with neatly labelled bottles and jars of all sizes ranged upon its shelves, beneath which were row upon row of little square drawers with faceted glass knobs. Everything was a dingy mustard-brown colour and looked very dirty.

Turning to the other door, Josie saw that it was marked MATRON – with bated breath, she grasped the handle and pushed it. The room was frigid as she entered, and smelt oddly of lavender and ginger; it was plainly furnished, with a chest of drawers between two beds, a desk and chair beside the small fireplace, and a three-panelled dressing screen in a corner. On one of the beds, a pair of small, ghostly figures sat together, glowing dimly in the gloom; Josie recognised the girl at once – it was Grace Bramstone.

Beside her sat a pale, slender boy, slightly older and bigger and very good-looking, with fine, dark eyes and dark hair neatly combed. He had his arm around the little girl's shoulders and was evidently comforting her, for her face was still wet and grubby with tears – "Robert," breathed Josie, gazing at him in wonderment.

She felt strangely moved now to see him thus with his sister, knowing that his young life would be cut short not very long after; she could see in his gentle face and conduct the kindness of which the girls spoke so warmly. He fumbled inside his trouser pocket for a handkerchief; then, suddenly – "*Shhh, don't cry; everything will be all right,*" he said softly.

Josie started as if she'd been shot.

"What did you say??" she gasped, rushing up to the two children, quite forgetting that they weren't really there. A rush of cold air left her shivering as her knees went right through theirs and hit the edge of the bed. "What did you say?" she muttered again, looking searchingly into his face.

"Shhh, don't cry," he repeated in a small, sorrowful voice that sent the chills racing up and down Josie's spine.

"Mamma doesn't love me anymore," Grace said desolately. "She doesn't come to see me at all, and when I called after her on the stairs yesterday, she looked at me for a moment, then clapped her hands over her ears and ran away! I think it's worse than when she used to beat me!"

"Mamma isn't well," Robert replied, holding his handkerchief under his sister's nose so she could blow into it. "She has *such* a lot of medicines now, you know – syrups and tonics and things – and she's *always* taking them! She hardly ever goes out; spends a good deal of time scribbling in her room and staring at nothing in particular and then suddenly going quite mad and screaming like a banshee at whoever is closest".

"Does mamma scream at *you*?"

"Not as much as she does the others, but that is only because I take care not to be near her if I can help it! I hide in the library or the drawing-room or wherever she is *not* when lessons are done – I don't think she even notices; she is only exacting about our mealtimes, where she expects me to sit and converse with her as Papa did, which of course I can't, and then she returns to moping and looking all gloomy and saying unaccountable things like, 'She killed him and now she is killing me'. It makes *my* head ache!"

"You will keep coming to see me and play with me, won't you?" Grace asked anxiously.

"Of course I will! Nothing will change between us, Gracie. You know I will talk to Mamma about you again, you may be sure of that – I don't care if she loses her temper with me or even if she strikes me; as long as she doesn't hurt you again! Matron is all right though, isn't she?"

"Oh yes, very. She is kind, and strokes my hair at night, almost like Papa used to. Oh Robert, I wish Papa were still here. I wish we were all together in the same room again, and playing by the fire after dinner, and going for picnics and rambles in the woods. Mamma never used to strike us then. I wish I could go to sleep and wake up and find that this is all a bad dream".

"Well, close your eyes," said Robert, "and I'll give you a magic hug".

Josie watched breathlessly as the little girl snuggled into her brother's open arms. "Where are we now?" she heard Gracie whisper.

"Well, we're standing on a long platform. There's a good deal of noise and people are hurrying about everywhere, with their boxes and trunks and carpet bags. Papa and Mamma are holding each of us by the hand, and in our other hands we're carrying our buckets and spades. Where do you think we are?"

"Oh!" squealed Grace, her eyes still closed. "Are we at the railway station? Are we going to the seaside?"

"Yes!" Robert replied. "And now there's a great black dragon flying down the tracks, huffing and puffing, and breathing white smoke into the air; there's a loud whistle, and Papa picks you up and Mamma says to mind your straw hat. Soon we'll be walking along the pier, eating ice-cream and watching *Punch and Judy*; the sky is wonderfully blue and Mamma points out a herring gull and a dark grey cormorant – can you see them?"

"Oh yes! Aren't they big! I do hope we have something for them to eat!"

"Of course we do. And now it's time for a paddle, and we'll race each other to the shore – "

There was a sudden cold draught as a tall woman in a long checked dress and full white apron entered the room and swept past Josie, bearing in her hands a tray which she set down on the table. She looked to be about thirty or so, and very warm and good-natured, with large blue eyes, and dark brown curls tucked into a white cap. Turning to the two children, she smiled, saying, "I've brought you your tea, Gracie; won't you have something to eat now, since you hardly ate anything at lunchtime? Robert can stay with you if you like, if Mrs Bramstone is finished with today's lessons".

"I can stay a while longer, Matron," Robert said, reaching for a sandwich.

"Mind you don't finish them all," Matron said to him with a twinkle in her eye. She picked up a stack of papers nearby and bustled out of the room, the many chains on her chatelaine clinking together noisily. As soon as the door swung shut behind her, Robert began digging about in his pockets.

"What are you looking for, Robert?" Grace asked, looking up from her sandwich. "Is it something for me?"

"Close your eyes, then," Robert told her, "and open your hand".

Grace did as she was told, and her brother placed something small and round in her palm. "All right, open your eyes," he said.

Grace opened them and squealed in delight. "Oh, Robert! Can I really keep it?"

"Yes, it's yours now," Robert said, beaming. "I know you've always liked it".

"Oh yes, thank you, Robert! I know how much you loved it. It is magic, isn't it? It's like a little rolled-up dragon!"

She held up the little brown object and Josie saw that it was a spiral-shaped shell, some two inches wide, and ribbed at regular intervals.

"It's a fossil," explained Robert, "which means it lived a very long time ago. This one is called an ammonite. Let's keep it in the magic box, shall we?"

"Ooh, yes, let's!" Grace exclaimed, jumping up. Both children got down on all fours, and Josie did too; she saw them squeeze their heads and shoulders under Grace's bed, and begin quietly knocking the wooden floorboards further in. Suddenly, one of them popped up half an inch, and a few seconds later, Robert had lifted several of the short planks surrounding it, revealing a seven to eight-inch square hollow in the floor, from which he extricated a small, rectangular container.

"The magic box," Robert intoned majestically, holding up what appeared to be a red and yellow tin of *Hillaby's Best Pontefract Cakes* as the children kneeled on the floor. "Keeper of all things extraordinary and mystical; custodian of that other world to which we may at any time escape – behold our new offering!"

He now proceeded to pry open the lid, and Josie saw that the box contained a number of curios and trinkets, evidently collected and prized by the siblings; to these Grace proudly added the little shell.

"Now let's do our promise, Robert," she said.

"All right," her brother agreed, fishing through the tin's contents. At last, he pulled out a dark fuzzy object shaped into a loop; as he laid it out on his palm, Josie saw that it was in fact made up of hair, tightly braided together and tied at the end with ribbon.

Grace now drew closer, and, placing her hand in Robert's so that the lock of hair was pressed between the two, the siblings solemnly declared in unison:

Come what may and come what might
In darkest dark and lightest light
Forever bound and never to part
Together always in soul and heart

Then, touching their foreheads together with great ceremony, they released hands and dropped the lock of hair back into the box.

"Now tell me more about the seaside, Robert," the little girl said.

"Well, first let's put the magic box back into our secret hidey-hole," Robert replied, closing the tin and crawling under the bed.

"You *are* clever to have found it, Robert," Grace remarked, as she watched him.

"Not really," Robert said, inching back out and dusting his front. "Papa showed it to me before they made it part of the infirmary. This used to be your nursery when you were a baby, Gracie, so really, you could think of it as coming back to your old room!"

As the children clambered back onto the bed and Robert resumed his story of their seaside expedition, the entire scene began to fade, and Josie was soon left alone again in the shadows.

For a moment she stood stock-still, staring, stunned and amazed; then, sinking down weakly on Gracie's bed, she shook her head in confusion. What did it all mean? Could Robert possibly be – ? But no, impossible! And then again, that voice – ! Josie had never forgotten Horatio's inexpressibly soft, sad accent, and to hear it again now – it was unmistakable, unbelievable!

All of a sudden she recalled how the girls had compared Horatio to the coat stand Mrs Bramstone had used to fashion her imaginary monster, that same coat stand which would ultimately be the inadvertent cause of her son's death – *it was as if Horatio had somehow filled it out and made it alive*, Marianne had said.

Perhaps that *was* exactly what happened, Josie thought, except it wasn't the fictitious Horatio, it was Robert – in some strange, inexplicable way, he had returned as the very creature his own mother had unwittingly created, though his spirit was clearly unchanged – still kind and gentle and caring, still wanting to comfort and help. He had obviously long been in the habit of protecting his sister from their mother, and that propensity hadn't ended with his death; but he didn't realise that in rescuing the girls, he had trapped them in the same soulless existence he himself endured.

Josie suddenly remembered now how he had halted in his tracks when he heard her scream Hetty's name, and how forlorn he had looked when Hetty slipped right through his grasp – Josie had not seen Horatio again after that time. It was almost as if he had been surprised, Josie thought, or even as if he had come to the realisation then that Hetty was actually no longer alive, and that perhaps all his efforts had been for nothing.

"But they *weren't* for nothing, Robert," Josie said out loud to the empty room, "you'll see!"

In the distance she could now hear Miss Gordy's voice shouting something, and she quickly rose and turned to leave, closing the door behind her. It was a relief to return to the significantly brighter, airier gallery, from which she could hear Miss Gordy downstairs, calling her name to tell her that Casper had at last arrived.

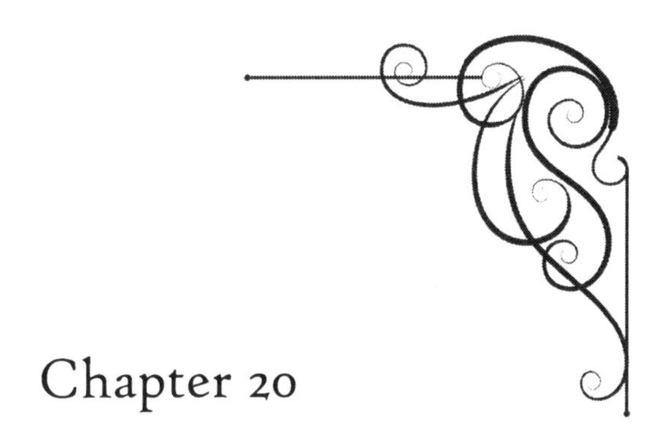

Chapter 20

Hurrying to her room, Josie carefully placed the girls' biscuit tin in her drawer, along with the trinkets she'd taken from Polly the crow. Quickly picking out a new dress and cardigan, she ran to the bathroom to wash her hands and face and change out of her grubby clothes. Slipping on her clean outfit, she giggled a little as she thought of what Mrs Edmundson would think when she went through the laundry.

Going downstairs, she found Casper and Miss Gordy sitting on the sofa in the drawing-room, having tea and sharing a joke about giraffes in a bar.

"Goodness, you have been a time!" Miss Gordy said, as Josie entered. "What on earth have you been up to?"

"Sorry, I had to change out of my mucky things," Josie explained. "The infirmary was awfully dirty".

Casper raised an eyebrow. "You went *into* the infirmary?" he asked, looking at Josie in surprise.

"She's been going into lots of places," Miss Gordy said drily. "You may as well tell Casper everything, Josie – you're probably going to need his help".

Taking a seat on one of the ottomans, Josie told Casper all about her discoveries – with frequent interruptions from both her listeners – right up to her most recent experiences in the schoolroom and Matron's.

Casper gave a long whistle. "You're a brave one, miss," he said to Josie admiringly, as Miss Gordy poured Josie some cold tea. "I don't know that I could've stomached half of the stuff that you've been through. You know," he continued thoughtfully, "I think those visions of the past you've been seeing are what they call 'residual hauntings'. It's like a recording or an old movie playing. Some people call them 'imprints' or 'imprint ghosts', and it's obvious this house has lots of those!

"They say many houses have them actually, but they usually go completely unnoticed. Sensitive people might feel funny or notice cold spots, but the *really* sensitive folk – like those with clairvoyant abilities, and lots of young kids and animals too – they can actually *see* them. Maybe you're psychic, miss!"

"Well, I'm definitely a kid at any rate!" Josie laughed.

"That you are," Casper chuckled, picking up his backpack and laying it on his lap. "Well, I think you'll be very interested in what I found out on the internet and at the library today".

"Ooh, do tell me Casper!" said Josie excitedly.

"Okay. First – that chap, W. J. Fitzwater. Well, it turns out that not only was he a first-rate pianist, he was an up-and-coming author as well; not all that cynical realism stuff which seems to define that period – you know, social classes and existential crises and all that – but good ol' spine-tingling mystery and horror. That's why he was visiting Bramstone Hall – he was apparently in the habit of exploring supposedly haunted houses, for – quote – 'ideas and inspiration'. Just listen to this!"

Here, Casper fished out a piece of paper from his bag and Josie saw that it was a photocopy of what appeared to be an old newspaper. "Miss Hertford at the library helped me make a copy of this," he said. "It's an article dated December 14th, 1925, and the headline reads *W. J. FITZWATER STILL MISSING.*

"'Detectives say they have turned up no new clues in the case of missing pianist and author Walter James Fitzwater, who was last seen by his friends more than a week ago at a party given by his publisher, John Chester Griffiths, of Griffiths & Sons. Nothing suspicious or untoward occurred at the time, and Mr Fitzwater was reported to have left in high spirits, saying he intended again to visit Harrowhead – otherwise known as Bramstone Hall – the old estate at Gloam's End some six miles away. Philip Lyme, the taxicab driver who brought him there, recalls Mr Fitzwater being very pleasant and giving him a generous tip, but nothing else of much importance. The public may remember the property as the infamous Bramstone School for Girls, from which twelve children went missing under mysterious circumstances thirty years prior.

"'Mr Fitzwater has garnered significant praise not only for his prowess on the piano, but his mystery novels as well, which incorporate elements of the supernatural and bizarre. The public will recall the sensational exploits of Frederick Wollerton the fishmonger in Mr Fitzwater's most recent work, *The Haunted Cove*, inspired by his visits to Whitby. Mr Fitzwater was reportedly working on his latest novel when he went missing – police detectives searched the Bramstone house and combed the woods surrounding it, but nothing was discovered to aid in furthering investigations.

"'Authorities have not entirely ruled out foul play, though associates of Mr Fitzwater said he was well-liked and had no known enemies. Said Chief Constable Willard Farquhar: 'This is perplexing indeed, but the public can be assured we shall leave no stone unturned. We expect to be reading Mr Fitzwater's riveting novels again in no time'. CC Farquhar said his officers had even gone so far as to pay a visit to Ms Grace Bramstone, the current owner of Bramstone Hall, though she and her family no longer reside at Gloam's End.

"'Ms Bramstone was reportedly much surprised to hear that someone had trespassed on the house, and that person no less than Mr Fitzwater, whose excellent renditions of Chopin's preludes she greatly admired; however, neither she nor her husband was able to shed any light on Mr Fitzwater's disappearance, not being in any way acquainted with him.

"'Mr Fitzwater's friends confirmed that the 'slightly eccentric' author frequently visited old and purportedly haunted properties for both research and inspiration, and routinely spent significant amounts of time in these places crafting his manuscripts. It is unknown whether Mr Fitzwater was aware that Bramstone Hall is not abandoned and that he was in fact trespassing; authorities surmise he made use of a bunch of antique skeleton keys which his friends said he had collected over the years.

"'It is also unknown whether Bramstone Hall is in actuality haunted. However, CC Farquhar has stated clearly that his men experienced nothing of a supernatural nature during their investigations and sternly warns the public against the very real dangers of trespassing on private property'.

"And I have this too," Casper continued, pulling out another piece of paper from his bag and handing it to Josie. She looked at it and inhaled sharply – it was a copy of an old black-and-white photograph, showing a handsome young man dressed in dark trousers and a white shirt under a sweater; he was leaning against a tree and smiling directly at the camera, with the same confident, jaunty insouciance Josie remembered.

"That's him, isn't it?" Casper asked.

"Yes," Josie nodded. How very jolly he looks here, she thought sadly; so self-assured and full of life. She thought she would have liked to have known him.

"He certainly looks very personable," Miss Gordy remarked. "I can imagine what a success he must have been in society. It's as my mother used to say – life can turn on a sixpence; you're going on your merry way, and then, bam! Like a clap of thunder on a sunny day, it all changes. You never know which way life will turn".

"Well, I'll bet Mrs Bramstone never guessed which way *her* life would turn," Casper said. "You asked me to look up Fields & Co, miss – see if you recognise any of these".

The young man handed Josie a small stack of coloured photocopies showing a selection of floral wallpapers.

"This one," Josie said in a few moments, pulling out one of the sheets. "This is the one Mrs Bramstone has on her bedroom walls".

"It's nowhere else in the house is it, Miss Gordy?" Casper asked. "Or anything like it?"

Miss Gordy shook her head. "I don't think so. None of the wallpapers in the rest of the house are like these – even the patterned ones are much plainer and simpler. This one might have been specially selected by my grandparents – or perhaps my great-grandparents – for their personal room".

"Well, good thing it was only used there then," Casper said, "because the paints used to create the greens in these wallpapers were a compound of arsenic and copper – and it wasn't just the greens; the other colours were arsenical as well. It seems there was about two grams of arsenic per square foot of paper. People began falling ill and even dying, and eventually, in the 1860s, doctors finally made the connection. But even if one doesn't believe that the pigments released a toxic gas when exposed to damp or heat, I should think that continually inhaling the toxic dust when the pigments flaked off was surely not the best for one's health in the long run.

"Fields & Co finally stopped using arsenic in their wallpapers in the late 1870s, so possibly the elder Bramstones installed the wallpaper before that. Or perhaps the younger Bramstones had some new old stock on hand. Whatever it is, they obviously hung it up and then never gave it another thought. Believe it or not, arsenic pigments were routinely used to colour lots of everyday things, not just wallpaper – the Victorians were using it in clothes, toys, paper, paints, cosmetics, medicines, even food!

"So it was probably a good thing Grace Bramstone was banished to the infirmary; however, I imagine both the children didn't spend much time in their mother's room anyway. But Mrs Bramstone was in there a lot presumably, especially after her husband's death – prolonged arsenic poisoning can cause headaches and neurological disorders in those who are susceptible, as well as a whole bunch of other very nasty things, so even if the arsenic wasn't the cause of her illness, it surely didn't help, and coupled with the cocaine and laudanum, well..." Casper shrugged ruefully.

"My poor grandmother," Miss Gordy said sorrowfully, "and the poor, poor children... If only they'd known then..."

"Unfortunately it's all past now," said Casper, "but at least we can try to set things right. Well, miss, what's next on your to-do list for today? I can't stay too long though, I'm afraid; my dad needs my help with some errands and deliveries".

"Well, first – please stop calling me 'miss', Casper," Josie said shyly. "I think we *are* friends now, and all my friends call me Josie!"

"Oh! Sorry about that – it's such a habit with us in the shop," Casper laughed. "Josie it is then, miss! What's next?"

"Well, there are a bunch of things on my to-do list, but I'll tell you the ones I need your help with first, since you need to leave in a bit".

Josie went to pick up the little white terrier on his red velvet cushion; bringing him to Casper, she placed him on the sofa beside the young man.

"Please help Horatio get unstuck".

Casper glanced at Josie in surprise, but didn't ask any questions. Grabbing Horatio's furry body with both hands, he pulled upward with a slight grunt. But, as before, the mounting nails kept a firm hold on the dog, and he didn't budge. Bending closer, Casper peered at the dog's little paws, and Josie took out her torch to help him see better.

"They're nails," Casper said. "They're embedded in his paws, and they're a little rusty. There might even be some glue in there as well. I'll need my pliers; I'll go get them from my car".

In a few minutes, the young man returned with a sturdy-looking pair of red-handled pliers and rubberised leather work gloves.

"I don't know what else you'll be having me handle," Casper said with a laugh, pulling the gloves on. "Shine the light here".

As Josie directed her torch at Horatio's paws, Casper wedged his pliers into the thick fur, gripping the dark nail shanks with the tool's pincer-like jaws; several seconds later, he had removed all the nails and Horatio was standing stiffly on the coffee-table.

"Is something supposed to happen?" Casper asked, looking in some perplexity at the dog's endearing face.

"Why, he's wagging his tail! Can't you see?" Josie cried, patting Horatio's head.

"He is??"

Casper and Miss Gordy stared at the dog, but Horatio was still standing stiffly as far as they could see, and eventually they gave the dog some tentative token back rubs.

"We'll take your word for it," Casper laughed, bending his face down to Horatio's. "He sure is cute anyway". As he looked closely at Horatio's bright black eyes, Josie was astonished to see the dog suddenly leap up excitedly toward Casper's neck – a small round pendant hanging on a chain had slipped out of the young man's shirt and was swinging back and forth at Horatio's nose.

"Gah! What was that?" Casper exclaimed, drawing back. "I thought I felt something push up against me – it was the weirdest thing!"

"It was Horatio," Josie said. "He saw that charm around your neck".

"Oh, this?" Casper asked, lifting up the fine silver chain. "It's not a charm; it's a locket. Well, one half of a locket, to be exact. It belonged to my granddad – when he and his sister learned that they would be going away to school, they asked that the locket be broken and made into two necklaces, one for each of them. Bessie took the one with Granddad's picture in it, and he took the one with hers. See?"

Here, Casper unhooked the chain from around his neck and handed it to Josie. Holding it gently in her open palm, Josie saw that it was one side of a silver locket, still in very fine condition and engraved on the back with little five-pointed stars; inside, a tiny daguerreotype had been placed under a glass pane. Josie looked at the photograph and recognised Bessie's face at once.

"How lovely she is," Miss Gordy remarked. "You do look rather like her, Casper".

"I'm not as pretty," Casper chuckled, "but I *am* told I look like my granddad. He gave this locket to me shortly before he passed away. We were pretty close so I wear it in memory of him, and also of the grandaunt I never knew. I wish I could find the other half, but she was probably wearing it when she disappeared".

Josie cast a startled glance at Casper. "Quick!" she cried, jumping up. "Come with me!"

"You two run along," Miss Gordy said, waving them away as Casper hesitated. "I'll be fine".

Josie was already running across the hallway toward the punishment room with Horatio at her heels; ahead of her, the room's door suddenly swung open, and Horatio ran inside, yipping excitedly.

"What is it boy? Do you see something?" Josie asked, as Horatio scampered to the far wall and began barking at it.

"Why are you staring at that wall?" Casper asked, coming up behind her.

"It's Horatio," Josie replied. "He senses something".

She crouched down beside the little terrier and tried to follow his line of vision, but couldn't see anything besides the wall. Calling the dog over to her, she held out Casper's necklace to him.

"Try and find the other half of this, boy," she whispered.

"What? Josie, that locket is over a hundred years old!" Casper exclaimed. "In fact, that dog is over a hundred years old too – he probably doesn't even remember how to do dog things anymore! There is no way he's going to be able to find it!"

"Shhh," Josie whispered, knowing he couldn't see Horatio scurrying hither and thither about the room, his nose alternately to the ground and lifted in the air. "Terriers were bred to hunt and track; I'm sure he hasn't forgotten how, and the house will help him too, you'll see. I have every confidence in Horatio's nose".

"This is crazy," Casper muttered, watching Josie swing around erratically as she followed the dog he couldn't see, while Horatio scampered about, enthusiastically sniffing at everything.

Suddenly, the little dog stopped in his tracks and looked sharply at the blackboard, causing Josie to turn and look at it sharply too – the hair on the back of her neck now rose and her eyes opened wide, for the wall was pulsating so that she could almost hear a heart beating within it, and a curious rippling movement could be seen across the slate board, as if something alive was crawling underneath.

"Horatio," she hissed loudly, "come here, come here!"

But Horatio would not come; instead, the little dog darted fearlessly forward and, standing on his hind legs, began barking lustily at the board. Josie saw the wall heaving beneath it, making the board knock repeatedly against the wall with a fearful clattering; to her great surprise, Casper now sprang to her side, and grasped the thick pine frame as it threatened to fall.

"What is going on?" he gasped, as the blackboard shook in his hands.

"I don't know!" Josie cried. "You can see this??"

"The blackboard?? *That*, yes! But what's happening?"

"I think Horatio's found something!" Josie exclaimed, as she reached forward to help the young man. But even as she did so, the board suddenly ceased its vehement banging and became completely still, and the only sound to be heard was Horatio's excited barking, as he pawed at the wall beneath the blackboard's ledge.

"What is it boy? Is there something here?" Josie scooped the terrier up in her arms. Almost immediately, she felt Horatio straining forward, and, bringing him closer, watched him sniff eagerly at the thick grey dust coating the narrow wooden frame. In a moment, the little dog began loudly whining and pawing unmistakably; quickly, Josie put him back down on the floor and called Casper over.

"Here – wipe that spot with your glove!" she said, pointing.

The young man began prodding at the ledge with his fingers; the dust and cobwebs were well caked on, but as he continued brushing at the dirt, Josie soon cried, "I see something!"

By the light of her torch, the two now saw the slight gleam of tarnished metal beneath the dark grime; excitedly, Casper scrubbed at it harder. Within seconds, a small silver object was revealed – it was the other half of Casper's locket.

"Oh my gosh," the young man said slowly, as Josie carefully picked up the dainty pendant with her fingertips. It was engraved with a series of little stars, and held the tiny portrait of a little boy; the chain, though broken, was still strung through its bail. With a big smile, Josie placed it in Casper's gloved hand, along with his own necklace, and stooped to rub Horatio's head – "Good boy," she cried, "good boy!"

"Oh wow," Casper said, looking at the two halves of the locket, slightly teary-eyed, "this is amazing. How did you know it was in this room?"

"It was just a guess, really," Josie answered honestly, "because of what you said about Bessie wearing her necklace when she disappeared. The things that the girls cared about when they were alive are what bring them back to the house; I figured Bessie must have left something special in here because this is where she keeps returning to. Perhaps it broke in the struggle when she was trying to escape… Anyway, it's a good thing Horatio was with us – I'd never have found it otherwise. Casper, would it be okay if I hang on to it a while longer? I think I'll need it when I try to get all the girls back together again".

"Oh sure," Casper replied, handing Bessie's necklace to her. He shook his head incredulously. "Man, what a story I have to tell my dad! My family never thought we'd see Bessie's half of the locket again – thanks a million, Josie! And thank you Horatio, wherever you are!"

"He's running around our ankles," Josie said with a laugh.

"Aw, I should like to be able to see him one day," Casper said wistfully.

"Who knows?" Josie said with a shrug. "This house is full of surprises and I have a funny feeling you just might be able to… But there's something we have to do first before that ever happens".

"What is it?" Casper asked warily, though deep down, he already knew.

"It's time to go into the secret room".

SHE

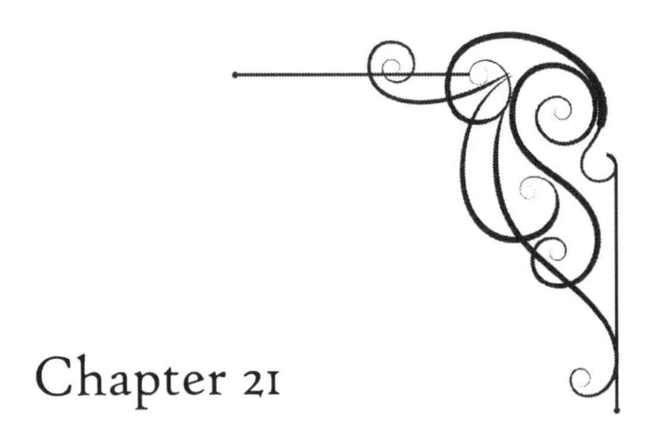

Chapter 21

"We'll need to have something fairly strong and sturdy to stick in there to keep the door from closing completely," Casper declared, looking around Mrs Bramstone's room. "I'm not taking any chances with that mechanism deciding to finally fail".

He was standing by the bookcase with Josie and Miss Gordy, and all three had scarves tied around their faces, while Horatio ran delightedly about their legs.

"What about this?" Miss Gordy asked, touching the walnut and leather desk chair beside her.

"That should do it, right Josie?" Casper asked.

"Yes, I think so," Josie replied. "I mean, I hope so anyway!"

Casper looked at her with an expression of great disquiet in his eyes. "Are you sure you'll be okay in there alone?"

"Yes," Josie said resolutely. "You're the biggest, strongest one of us here; you need to stay on the outside with the lock sequence – just in case. Even though all three of us have a copy of it; we can't leave it entirely to Miss Gordy".

"But we could just call the police!" Casper exclaimed. "There are dead bodies in there – we'd *have* to call them at some point anyway!"

"Yes, I know," Josie replied, "but please wait. They mustn't take Robert away, not yet – I daren't risk his disappearing for good. I'm certain he holds the key to freeing the girls' souls and I will need his help, just don't ask me how – and I couldn't explain all of this to the Chief Constable, not without him thinking I'm completely mad!"

"Okay, okay, fine," said Casper. "But you had better be out of there in twenty – no, fifteen – minutes, tops. I mean it, Josie – we'll definitely call the police and even the fire brigade immediately if we have to. I will be standing right here at the door; you yell immediately if you need me".

"I will," Josie nodded. She picked Horatio up and put him on the bed.

"You stay here, boy," she told him, patting his head. Taking a deep breath, she began removing the volumes nearest the spot where Walter Fitzwater had stood decades before, and soon uncovered the combination lock embedded within the shelf. Following Josie's directions, Casper now turned the rings one by one, his hand becoming red with the effort, for the gears were far stiffer now than they had once been.

As all three watched with bated breath, the clockwork mechanism began to whirr with what seemed to Josie an intensely sinister vibration, and, slowly, the hidden section creaked open. Swiftly, Casper grasped the door, pulling it open as wide as he could, before standing the heavy walnut chair against its frame. As the malodourous air in the hidden room seeped out, Josie took another deep breath and stepped in determinedly with her torch held out.

The room was narrow and very dark, with a low sloping ceiling and a carpet covering most of the wooden floorboards. By the beam of her torch, Josie could see that it was very simply furnished; a single bed had been placed against one wall, and a low bookcase filled with books and bric-a-brac stood beside it. Against the opposite wall stood a desk and chair, and in the corner, a little washstand and parlour stove.

It was all in all a very cosy room, apparently intended for one or two people at the most – that the mechanism automatically closed after just a few minutes indicated that it had been meant as a kind of snug hideaway, deliberately concealed from the rest of the school. As Josie continued to swing her torch about, she was startled to see an exceptionally wide keyhole with a curiously-shaped notch on the inner side of the door – she knew now what the *X* key was for.

As Josie took a few steps forward, her torch lit up a closed window at the far end, and as she looked at it, a black figure suddenly rose up fluidly within its frame – it was a man. Stifling a scream, Josie stumbled back, but the figure bounded towards her at full tilt, and caught her by the wrist.

"Shhh, don't be afraid; I won't hurt you," the man said, his face now illuminated by Josie's light. She knew him immediately.

"Walter!" she cried, her eyes wide.

The young man stared at her in surprise. "How did you know my name?"

"I was there – I saw – oh, it's too long to tell right now. But I do know a bit about you, and about what happened that night in December. The police were looking for you then, but they didn't know where to look. You've been trapped in here all this time, haven't you?"

"Yes! It feels like I've been in here an eternity. This is the first time I've been able to move and talk and by God, actually see light – the place has always been so damnably dark! Who are you, by the by?"

"I'm Josie," she replied, blushing. She had the feeling of one who'd finally gotten to meet their favourite celebrity, except this one was a spirit who'd been dead for some time already.

"Well hello, Josie – I'm Walter James Fitzwater," the young man said, shaking her hand. "W.J., my friends call me, but then, you already knew that, didn't you? I'd come here to do some writing, and then I found this room; I remember – " Abruptly glancing toward the open door, Walter suddenly seized Josie by the shoulders – "Get out; you have to get out!" he cried, pushing her. "The door will close and you'll be trapped inside!"

"No, no," Josie said, holding Walter's hands and trying to calm him. "I saw what happened to you that night; I know how the door closes. I have friends waiting for me outside right now, and we've even put a big chair in the doorway. Also, I've just realised that I have the key that unlocks the door from inside, though of course I don't really want to put *that* to the test. I came in here on purpose, you see – I needed to find – "

The ominous whirr of the bookcase's mechanism had started up, and both Josie and Walter now turned to look at the door breathlessly.

"Josie! Are you okay in there?" Casper yelled from outside, as the door began creaking shut.

"Yes!" Josie called back. "I'm talking to W.J.! Will the chair hold?"

"I think we're about to find out!" Casper replied.

As the door struck the heavy chair, there came a harsh grinding from within the bookcase, followed by series of loud clicks; in another minute, all was still.

"I think it's all right," said Casper, "for now, at any rate. Don't take too long in there".

"Well, you're a clever one," Walter said to Josie with a grin.

"It's only because I saw what happened to you," Josie admitted.

"Yes, that was damnably awful, I can tell you. I remember shouting and kicking and banging on everything I could – nothing worked. Even the damned window was blocked up! I knew that was it – the big one – and I just lost my grip; I literally went nuts. I think I started pounding some gibberish on my typewriter and then – and then – well, you won't believe me if I tell you".

"Trust me, I will".

"This – this – *thing* appeared; it looked like a – like a – "

"Like a sheet hanging over a coat stand?"

"Well, I'll be blowed – that just about describes it! It just appeared right in front of me, and I do believe I might have screamed. And then it actually started *talking* to me, telling me to 'hush' and 'calm myself', and 'no good ever came from being in a fury' – a whole bunch of poetic things. I was just too flabbergasted to do anything but stare, though I was in a cold sweat and shaking all over – and then, before I could even think what do, it came right up to me, and – brace yourself now – *hugged* me".

"Do you remember anything of what happened after?"

"No, everything just went black. It was like being asleep, and sometimes I even had dreams; strange ones, where I'd be reading my stories or writing again on my old typewriter. There was a girl in my dreams too; she had golden hair and kept crying… It seems like I've been asleep for as long as I can remember; you're the first person I've talked to in – in – well, forever! Hang on – how come I can talk to *you*? Am I all right again?"

"Um, no, not really," Josie replied hesitantly. "You're sort of trapped; I mean, your soul is. That's why I came in here; I'm looking for the creature you spoke with. I believe he can help free you, and the other girls whose souls are trapped too; like Evie, the girl you saw. Except he's not a creature really; he's a boy".

Walter's handsome face had turned white, and he now sank weakly into the chair. "I'm dead then, you mean?"

"Well, yes," Josie answered, "essentially. But honestly, I don't think you're meant to be imprisoned here, being all weird and ghosty – people aren't really supposed to linger in this world after they die, you know. I believe there's another place for you to go on to – a wonderful, bright place where your family and friends are, and all the things that you loved and made you happy, like the piano. But even if there weren't such a place, I don't believe you're meant to be stuck in this dark room forever".

"But *you* can see me – are you one of those clairvoyants or something? Wait – what year is it? How long have I been here?"

"It's – it's past the year 2000," Josie replied, unwilling to let him know the full extent of the time he'd lost.

"A new century," Walter murmured. "Everyone I knew must be dead and gone by now. Why did that creature do this to me?"

"He was trying to help you," Josie explained, distressed to hear the anguish in his voice. "You were suffering, and he was just trying to help. His name is Robert; he's always been a very kind boy".

"Robert, eh? Hm…Well, all right – I guess he *did* put me out of my misery. Frankly, I don't think I could have stood another five minutes in here without absolutely losing my mind, let alone a day or, jeez, a week – especially not with *those* two".

"What two?" Josie asked quickly.

"Why, those two," Walter answered, nodding towards the bed behind her. He lowered his voice to a tactful whisper. "I'm pretty sure they're dead".

Josie whirled around. The narrow beam of her torch barely lit the bed, but she discerned with a shiver that a dark shapeless form lay in a heap upon it, squeezed against the wall where it met the sloping ceiling.

"Don't go there," Walter said, holding her back. "You can take my word for it – it's not a pretty sight".

Josie looked uncertainly at the indistinct shadow on the bed; then, with a start, she realised that a tall, pale figure was standing in the far corner behind it, quietly regarding her – it wore a loose, flowing sheet over its head, and for its feet, were two fearful talons.

"Oh!" Josie cried. "*Robert!*"

"Oh for the love of – !!" Walter exclaimed, putting his hand to his heart. "JEEZ!! Don't just stand there scaring the living daylights out of us!"

At the sound of Walter's voice, the creature glided swiftly forward into the circle of Josie's light, bringing with it a curious aroma of ginger, lavender, chamomile, and even tea; the scent had an oddly calming, nostalgic effect, and Josie wondered that she had never noticed it before; but then she had never been face-to-face with the creature before either.

"I am awfully sorry," came Robert's small, soft voice from deep within the folds of his strange garment. "I can't help it – I was left like this for so long".

"'Left like this?'" Josie repeated. "What ever do you mean?"

"When my mamma found I no longer had the power to speak or move, she stood me upon the coat stand – she would not lay me down".

"But how?" Walter asked incredulously. "And why??"

"She propped me up like one of her mounted specimens," Robert replied ruefully. "I think she did wash and clean me, though thankfully, she did not try to coat me in arsenical paste. I fear she could not accept the fact that I was quite dead, you see. And when still I would not answer her, but began looking worse by the hour, she next covered me with the bedclothes – she simply would not lay me to rest".

"Oh! So… is your body still under there then?" Josie asked slowly, looking doubtfully at the dirty sheet, and shuddering a little at the thought of lifting it.

"Oh no," Robert answered, "she did at last remove it; a decaying corpse does become rather a mess. But I was never truly laid to rest and my spirit remained; nor could I get any peace, not when I realised what was happening to the other children – I *had* to aid them in some way; I had to rescue them from my mamma, just as I used to rescue my sister Grace".

"Then it's your body on the bed?" Walter asked. "And the other – ?"

"Is my mother," Robert replied sadly. "She came in on a sudden one night – I could not clearly see her, for everything appears to me misty and indistinct; but I knew 'twas her from the sound of her voice. I heard her sit upon the bed, and then I heard her talking, and I realised she was talking to me. I will not tell what she said, but it did break my heart, though I could no longer cry. I did not know she was dying then – 'twas only much later, when this gentleman came in – "

Here Robert gestured towards Walter, who looked at Robert in surprise. "I?" he asked.

"Yes," Robert said. "You came in, and as you shone your light about the room, I heard you say to yourself, 'Well, well, what have we here? *Two bodies on the bed* – an adult and a child – mummification in an airless environment – locked in an eternal embrace'. I understood then what had happened".

"Oh jeez," murmured Walter. "I am sorry, old boy; that *was* callous of me. And I *do* want to thank you for putting me out of my misery; I might have tried slitting my throat with my pencil otherwise, which would have been ghastly for sure, except unfortunately I'm now stuck in here unless we figure out how to get me my soul back. Josie here thinks you might know how".

"Josie," Robert repeated. "Then you are the girl recently come. I sensed the house stirring; there was someone new in it. And you could see me, so I knew you were a child too. In the beginning I was worried for you; I did not know how you would take the ghosts here – why, I even heard Arthur the monkey in the drawing-room!

"But then I perceived that you were different, for not only could you see them, you could converse with them, and even touch them too; and – and – I realised too that there were more ghosts here than I'd originally thought. Ah, I did not know that I hadn't saved the girls after all – I fear that I have instead imprisoned them, as I have done also to this gentleman here, and I fear I do not know how to remedy the situation".

"You realised it that day I was with Hetty, didn't you?" Josie asked.

"Yes," Robert replied sadly. "You cried out her name, and for a moment I could not understand why you were calling her when she had no business being here any longer – I thought I had already sent her safe away. I realised then that I hadn't; that she's trapped here, as I am, and as the others are too, I'm sure".

"Yes, they are," Josie admitted. "But you know, I don't actually think they're ghosts – at least, they're not like any ghosts I've ever heard of or read about. Tell me, how did you even know you had that power? I mean, that you could take people away, make them disappear?"

"'Twas the next day after my misfortune; I came upon some hares on the kitchen table that Mamma had snared – she meant to kill and stuff them, you know. The poor things were half-dead and crying so piteously that I could not bear it, and I tried to see if I could not free them.

"Well, as soon as I approached, they hushed most wonderfully, and I placed my hands upon them, trying to think what to do, and wishing them safe away and without pain; whereupon there was a most dazzling light; and when it cleared, they had utterly vanished! I was overjoyed – I was certain the light was from Heaven, and I had sent them straight there! When later I found my friends in that same grievous state, I thought I could save them too and send them directly to that safe eternal home, but alas! I fear my efforts were in vain".

"No, Robert," Josie said thoughtfully, "I don't think they were. Remember, the girls *were* murdered; I think their ghosts would have haunted this house regardless. But you helped them pass on as peacefully as they could under the circumstances – same as for Walter – and I think because of that, they didn't become all horrid and disembodied. They were able to return – why, almost as they were before! And then, they could tell their stories – we would never have learned the truth if not for you. Do you know, I don't even think that they're ghosts – I believe you saved their souls and we just have to find them".

"Then that is a comfort," Robert replied, "for which I am eternally grateful to you, Josie".

"Even Arthur," said Josie. "And Polly the crow, and Horatio – you somehow made them able to come back too, didn't you?"

"Ah, with them, I do not know," Robert answered. "They were already dead; they had been dead a long time, in fact. But I had talked with them and played with them in the lonely hours, and they moved and answered me…"

"It is a marvellous gift you have, Robert," said Josie.

"It sure is," said Walter, "but what do we do now? I don't think I could stand going back to the dark and silence again!"

Josie bit her lip in perplexity. "Robert," she said at last, "you'd wanted to send everyone somewhere safe – and you did – but the trouble now is, we don't know where that is. All we know is that the girls, and Walter here, refer to it as some place very dark which they can't seem to get out of. Now, I know this is going to sound strange, but do you think *you* created that place? And that *you're* the one keeping them there somehow?"

"If that is so, I do not mean to," said Robert in some distress.

"I know, I know. I'm just trying to figure out where their souls might be. And then of course, you're trapped too. What is it that's keeping you here? Is it because you weren't properly buried? Or because the murders weren't solved? What do you think?"

"In truth, I do not think it is either," Robert answered. "I'm waiting. I have been waiting, for a very long time – "

"Josie!" It was Casper. "I think you'd better come out A-S-A-P! This thing is starting to rumble and you've been in that noxious air long enough. Time to finish up – for now, at any rate!"

"Okay, okay, I'm coming!" Josie called back. She turned to Walter. "Please," she said quickly, "can I take your typewriter with me? I'd like to try something, and I'll need something of yours that meant a lot to you, that you cared about. I promise I'll take real good care of it, Walter, and I'll definitely bring it back if what I'm trying doesn't work".

"All right," he nodded. "You're a smart kid; I trust you. You stay put and I'll get it for you; I don't want you seeing me in that miserable state".

As he headed towards the window, Josie turned to Robert next. "We must talk more," she said. "Please come out again; I promise I won't scream. And I'm going to tell the girls about you – I know they'd love to see you again, even if you are wearing a bedsheet. You can hear where I am, can't you? If I call your name, will you come?"

"Very well, Josie," Robert replied, "I will appear again; that is, if you're certain I can be of use".

"Oh, you surely can," Josie said eagerly. "Listen for me!"

"Here you go," Walter said, coming up to them with his typewriter. "Old Faithful, I call him. He's been with me on lots of adventures, but this is definitely the biggest one yet". He gave Josie's hand a squeeze as she carefully took the typewriter from him.

"I'll be listening for you too, kiddo," he said with a little smile.

"Good," Josie replied. "I'll be seeing you again soon!"

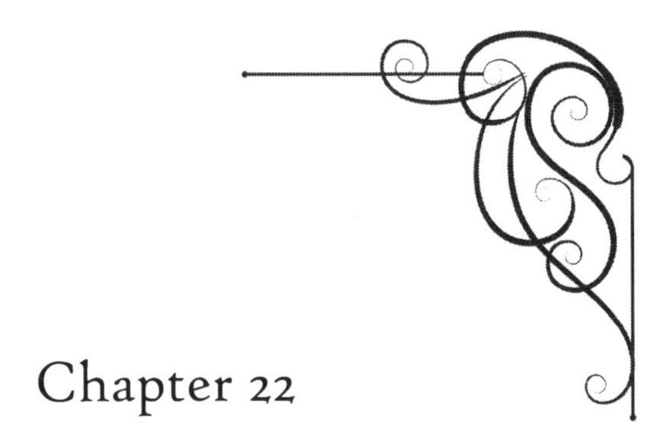

Chapter 22

Casper was running late now and had to leave soon after they closed the secret door. But before he left, he helped Josie carry Walter's typewriter to the drawing-room.

"I'm hoping this will bring poor Walter out of that horrible space," she declared, as Casper laid the machine gently beside the old piano. "I think he left quite a strong – what did you call it – oh yes, 'imprint' – in this room!"

"You still owe me a tintype," Casper laughed as Josie saw him off.

"Oh yes, I know!" Josie replied. "You will be back again soon though, won't you?"

"Sure thing. I've got some assignments to work on after my dad's deliveries, but I'll call you as soon as I'm free. I'm dying to know what you saw in there".

"I'll definitely tell you all about it! Talk to you later!"

Josie hurried back into the house to help Mrs Edmundson bring out the lunch things. Miss Gordy had said she was feeling tired and was now lying on the sofa with her feet up.

"You do look peaked, ma'am," Mrs Edmundson said, as she and Josie laid out the cabbage and potatoes. "P'raps you oughtn't to have lunch so late. Here, have some of this hot tea".

"Oh, I didn't sleep very well, that's all," Miss Gordy said weakly, sitting up and taking the tea. "Does Horatio want some cabbage, do you think?"

"I beg your pardon, ma'am?" asked Mrs Edmundson in surprise, as Josie glanced at Miss Gordy sharply.

"Oh," Miss Gordy replied, shaking her head and looking momentarily confused. "I, um, I was thinking of something. It was nothing, Mrs Edmundson; don't mind me".

"Ahem, yes, well, all right, ma'am," Mrs Edmundson said doubtfully. "I'm just finishing up the ironing. I'll clear the plates before I go".

"Can you see Horatio, Miss Gordy?" Josie asked, as soon as the housekeeper had left. "I mean, running around?"

"I thought I did," Miss Gordy answered, still looking confused. "It seemed to me he ran up to the table when the food was brought in, and stood up on his hind legs… But when I looked again, he wasn't there; I must have been imagining things".

"No," Josie said, puzzled. "That *is* exactly what he did – he ran up when we came in, and got up on his hind legs to sniff at the plates we laid out… what can it mean?"

But neither of them had a ready answer to this, and the meal commenced in a somewhat uneasy silence, till at last Josie decided to tell the old lady about everything she had discovered in the secret room.

"There's no doubt that that's where Robert had been hidden all this while," said Josie in conclusion. "Walter wouldn't let me go near the bodies, but I saw enough. Casper's right; you will have to call the police at some point".

"Do you think if Robert were properly laid to rest, he and the girls would be free at last? Don't they say ghosts haunt a place because they weren't given a decent burial?"

"Yes, but somehow I don't think that that's what's holding Robert here; even he himself didn't think so. I mean, of course we could try, but then I guess once the news got out, the house would be filled with investigators and reporters and sightseers and everything – you know, like how you see on TV – I mean, if you had one – and then, if it *didn't* work, I don't know that I'd ever be able to talk to Robert or Walter or any of the girls ever again – the nature of the house would have changed. Why, it might even become a tourist attraction or something!"

"I'll wait," Miss Gordy said without hesitation. "I am *not* up to dealing with another – another – *circus* at this house. I do believe Robert should be laid to rest properly of course – and certainly Walter and my grandmother, as well – but *after* you've left, not before, and not right now. I really don't want you and your father, and goodness, even the Braskets, dragged into this if I can help it. Robert has already waited this long; waiting a little longer isn't going to make much difference, I don't think".

"No, I suppose not. But I must find out what he meant when he said he was waiting. If we could help him find what he's been waiting for..."

Josie gobbled down the rest of her cabbage. "I'm going to try bringing all the girls back together again – I think we can somehow figure it out together. Will you be okay here by yourself? Mrs Edmundson was right; you do look a little pale".

"I'm fine," Miss Gordy replied, "really I am. Just a little tired, that's all. I think I'll go read in bed for a bit. You run along, but be sure to call me if you need anything. Better yet, I think I'll give Casper a call and ask him to come over when he's free. He can help keep an eye on you!"

It was still raining when lunch was over and Josie finally ran back up to her room with Horatio. Excitedly, she went to the chests of drawers and took out the belongings of all the girls she knew, calling their names as she did so. One by one, they now appeared, materialising with broad smiles, though seeming to glow less brightly than they did before.

"Oh!" Josie exclaimed, regarding them with some concern. "Are you not feeling well?"

"Just a bit of chill," said Maggie, giving Josie a kiss with her cold lips.

"Aye, it does feel a bit frostier," said Marianne, twirling her top as she perched on Josie's bed frame. "In fact, we all look a wee bit wispier, don't you think? I wonder how much longer we can last like this?"

"Long enough," replied Maggie firmly. "Let's say no more about it for the present. Who is this precious little one?"

She knelt down to pat Horatio, who was jumping about everyone's legs with wagging tail and yips of joy.

"Say hello to the real Horatio," Josie said with a laugh, trying to quell her uneasiness about the girls. She told them how she had found the little dog, and how helpful he had been. But she was sorely troubled by how pale the girls looked, and somehow more delicate; it was evident that time was taking its toll on them, and she too wondered how much longer they could last.

"Oh, he *is* darling!" Agnes cried. "Here, do let me pat him!"

"How extraordinary you are, Josie!" said Hetty, clapping her hands in delight. Then she paused, her brow furrowing. "But I'm muddled," she said. "If this little chap is Horatio, who is the creature then?"

"Well, the creature is actually someone you know," Josie replied. "It's Robert".

There was a stunned silence.

"I beg your pardon?" Evie said at last.

"The creature – it's Robert," Josie repeated. "I know, it seems crazy, but it's true – I've even spoken with him. His mother couldn't accept what had happened, and she tried to – to – keep him – like one of her preserved specimens I suppose – and he became like one of those strange monsters she created in the drawing-room. But he's still the same boy at heart – I think his goodness, his kindness, they're what gave him this amazing power. He tried to use it to save all of you, and unfortunately it didn't quite work out the way he'd hoped; but I think it might be what could save all of you now".

"Oh Josie!" Maggie cried. "To think of poor Robert like that, and all of us not knowing and terrified of him!"

"It *was* awful," Lottie agreed. "Josie, you must tell us everything that's happened since last we met. Have you discovered how we may leave this place?"

"No, not exactly," Josie replied, "but I do have an idea. First, let's try to find the remaining girls. Look what I've got!"

Here, Josie carefully opened the flannel polishing cloth on her bed, uncovering the buttons, ring, thimble and key. "Polly found them," she said, as the girls gathered round her. "Do you recognise anything?"

"Polly!" Maggie exclaimed. "You found Polly?"

"Yes, I believe so. I'm afraid she wasn't in… quite the best condition though. I mean, Mrs Bramstone stuffed her".

"Ugh!! That vile, miserable, wretched…" Agnes began.

"Hush," Evie said. "It's done with now. Come, look here, isn't this Hannah's thimble?"

"Oh yes, it is!" cried Penelope. "Why, I remember her using it when she helped me mend my pinafore. See here, it's inscribed 'Victoria' – it had belonged to her older sister".

"And this," said Hetty, picking up the tarnished gold ring. It was tiny, and featured a dainty floral carving with a turquoise stone in the middle. "I do believe this is Bridget Mulligan's! Mrs Bramstone forbade her wearing it, so she took to carrying it about with her in her pocket. I told her time and time again she'd be bound to drop it somewhere and she finally did".

"That's two, then," Josie said, "plus Bessie's locket here, which Horatio helped me to find. That leaves one more still unaccounted for – who's left out?"

"That would be Caroline, wouldn't it," Marianne said, "Caroline Bishop. But how will we – "

"Oh, my word," Maggie interrupted, "do you all see that thing on Bridget's bed?"

Turning, the girls saw a peculiar form taking shape and slowly rising beneath the blanket of a bed near the far wall; it soon became clear that a small figure was outstretched underneath, with its arms crossed over its chest like a medieval effigy. The girls could hear it making a distressing raspy sound with each breath as it rose several feet by the minute; then, in the next moment, it suddenly began clawing frantically at the sheet as if it were being suffocated.

"This is what comes of reading too much Tennyson," Marianne

declared crossly, getting up.

Agnes rose and joined her at the foot of Bridget's bed. "Shall we?" she asked, giggling as she grasped one corner of the blanket.

Taking hold of the other, Marianne nodded. "We'd better, before she hits the ceiling," she answered grimly.

With a hard tug, the girls pulled the sheet off with a flourish, causing it to billow for an instant like a full sail, and revealing a slight young girl floating on her back with eyes wide open, her long auburn hair wrapped around her neck like a scarf. As she sat up in alarm, the girls rushed forward, but too late – with a squeal, she plummeted down, as if an invisible carpet had been pulled out from under her, and landed flat on her bed in a cloud of dust.

"What *can* you mean – ??" she sputtered indignantly, as the girls broke into shouts of laughter.

"Oh Biddy," said Hetty, "are you still playing the Lady of Shalott?"

"I am," Bridget replied loftily, unloosing her magnificent hair so that it lay spread out over her shoulders like a cloak. "I'll have you know – " She paused mid-sentence on a sudden and stared straight ahead in dismay.

"Oh, I say, you're not about to be sick, are you?" asked Lottie, crinkling her nose.

"Oh, just let it out, Bridget," said Evie, "you'll feel better for it".

There was a long pause as Bridget took several deep breaths and gulped determinedly.

"No," she declared at last, "I refuse. That would be too demeaning for words; I shall keep it all in. Oh!" she suddenly cried, her amber eyes widening. "Is that my ring? Oh, it is, isn't it? I'd recognise it anywhere!"

She took the little ring from Hetty's open palm. "Oh Hetty, thank you ever so much!" she cried.

"You must thank Josie," Hetty replied, "'twas she who found it!"

"It was Polly really," Josie said with a smile.

"Oh, thank you, Josie," said Bridget, turning to her with the tears coming to her eyes. "This tiny thing belonged to my baby sister, who left us when she was barely three; she took ill with cholera and died in my arms".

"I am sorry," Josie said. "I hope you shall be able to see her again".

"I hope so too," Bridget replied wistfully. She looked about her now in some bewilderment. "But how is it that we are all here together like this? For the last I remember I was lying in a boat and floating down a river, and before long a throng of people had quite surrounded me; they covered me with a winding sheet and I tried to rise, but could not..."

"Well, you're here with us now," said Maggie, putting an arm around Bridget's shoulders. "You needn't think on that anymore". She turned to Josie. "Robert spared us the worst of that horror, didn't he? Dear boy – I should so love to see him again".

"And you shall!" said Josie. "In fact, it's what I wanted to talk about with all of you. I was thinking that – "

A cold hand on her arm made her pause and look around in surprise. Penelope, pale and trembling, was pointing to the wall behind one of the beds. Above its slatted headboard, a strange figure hung suspended, entirely coated from head to toe in what appeared to be a viscous black ink. For several seconds, the girls gazed open-mouthed at the extraordinary sight, while the figure remained still as a statue, black goo dripping off its bowed head and making dark pools on the blanket below.

"What the blazes – " muttered Lottie, inching slowly forward.

"Oh Lottie," whispered Evie, "do you really think you ought to – "

But Lottie had already climbed on to the bed; now, as she cautiously leaned closer, with one finger tentatively extended, the figure suddenly lurched forward with a sharp inhalation.

"Ahhhhh!!" yelled Lottie, as she fell backward on the bed with an expression of intense revulsion, flailing wildly as the figure clutched at her with slippery hands and retched convulsively. "Get it off, get it off!!" she wailed.

"Look!" cried Bridget. "The ink! It's – it's *rising*!"

As the girls stared in astonishment, the black liquid gathered into tiny rivulets that floated gently upwards, before gradually disappearing; bit by bit, the little heart-shaped face of a young girl was revealed, wearing an unexpectedly sweet expression under the circumstances. Josie gasped as she remembered the wide-set grey eyes.

"It's Hannah!" the other girls cried in unison.

"Stop gawking and pull this thing off!" roared Lottie.

At this, Hannah sat up, and looked about her in confusion; then, clapping her hand to her mouth, she began heaving ominously.

"Not on me, not on me!!" cried Lottie, kicking at the girl in a passion.

She was not a moment too soon. Hannah flung herself over the side of the bed and there began vomiting mightily, causing everyone to turn away with a good deal of vicarious embarrassment. It was several minutes before she could at last catch her breath, while the offensive black liquid pooled at her feet, then slowly shrank and disappeared.

"Are you quite done?" Hetty asked, advancing warily.

"Yes; yes, I think so," Hannah replied, clearing her throat a little, and looking quite mortified. "I *do* beg your pardon".

"You always did eat too much," said Lottie testily, wiping at her arms with a shudder and smoothing down her hair and dress.

"Here, this should help you feel *much* better," Penelope said soothingly, holding out Hannah's thimble.

The girl stared at it speechlessly. "Vicky's thimble," she breathed at last. "Where ever did you find it?"

"Josie found it," Penelope replied, "with Polly's help. Do come meet her".

"Ah Josie, please accept my gratitude," said Hannah, as she shook Josie's hand. "I cherish this thimble because it was given me by my sister before she was taken ill. I remember so clearly the day I lost it. I used to sew in the garden, you know, close by the woods, and I'd get lost in my daydreams… One day Mrs Bramstone came upon me thus and she struck at my hand with her cane. I'd quite forgotten to go in to dinner, you see – I was so deep in my thoughts I hadn't even heard the bell – but she would allow of no excuses.

"I lost the thimble that day; it rolled away under the leaves and I was forced to go in with Mrs Bramstone. The loss of it was a cause of much sorrow to me, for but three days later, Vicky was dead. So I am much indebted to you, Josie, and to dear Polly too – ah, wouldn't it be lovely to see her again!"

"Perhaps you shall!" Josie said. "But now we must find something of Caroline's. Look girls – do you remember this?"

She brought out the white biscuit tin and laid it gently on her bed. A hush fell over the girls as they drew close.

"Oh Josie," murmured Maggie at last. "You found our box!"

"How ever did you know where to find it?" asked Evie, with wide eyes.

"Oh, let's open it!" Lottie exclaimed, picking it up.

"Yes, do!" said Josie. "I'm hoping we'll find something of Caroline's in there!" She told the girls how Mrs Bramstone had led her to the desk. "Whose desk was it?" she asked.

"'Twas mine!" Agnes replied. "But my word, to think – she was watching us all the time!"

"And to think she stole Polly's gifts to us!" added Bridget indignantly.

Lottie had managed to pry open the rusty lid by this time, and she now proceeded to pour the contents out on Josie's blanket. "Look girls!" she cried, holding up the piece of green sea glass. "Remember this?"

"Aye, 'twas the last thing we got from poor Polly," said Penelope, picking up a little grey pebble with a white line through the middle.

Josie gazed at the odds and ends in fascination – broken bits of porcelain, an assortment of beads and cogs, torn scraps of paper, a piece of cork, an earring.

"Oh, wasn't this a lovely one," said Hetty, holding up a blue enamel pin with the word *Baby* inscribed in silver.

"Aye, this one too," said Hannah, picking out a tiny reverse intaglio of a boxer dog.

"Look here!" Marianne exclaimed suddenly. "Isn't this Caroline's?"

She held out her hand, and Josie saw a large glass marble in her palm, well worn and pockmarked, and filled with swirls of blue, red, green, yellow and white.

"Why, that's one of the things I saw Mrs Bramstone put in the box!" said Josie.

"Well, no wonder we never saw it then!" said Lottie, making a face. "Dear old Polly must have spotted it in the shrubbery somewhere; I remember Caroline being quite downcast at the loss of it".

"Well, it's found now," said Josie gleefully, holding the marble up to the light and marvelling at the lovely ribbons of colour. "We've found everybody!"

"Where's Caroline then?" asked Evie, as the girls looked around expectantly.

"Here," said Josie, in a whisper. As the girls glanced at her in surprise, Josie's eyes fell shut and her fingers closed tightly about the marble.

"Josie?" Maggie asked hesitantly, approaching her with a puzzled frown; in the next instant, she reeled back with a scream, for Josie had begun to shake convulsively and now her eyes suddenly shot open – they were completely black.

"Lord have mercy!" cried Penelope, as she and the other girls scrambled to their feet in a panic.

"What *are* all of you doing?" a voice asked at the doorway.

The girls turned, electrified.

"*Bessie!!*" they cried, all at once; for indeed, it was their redheaded monitor of old, looking in on them as she was wont to do over a hundred years ago, except now she was glimmering with a soft glow that lit up her whole being with an otherworldly luminosity.

Shouting with excitement, the girls rushed to her, and amid a clamourous cascade of delighted hugs and kisses, they dragged her by the hands to Josie, who was now sitting rigidly upright and staring straight ahead unblinkingly.

"Oh my," said Bessie, gazing at Josie in consternation. "What ever is the matter with her?"

"She looks a fright," declared Lottie, with a grimace. "*That's* what's the matter with her!"

"Oh Lottie," Hetty chided her. She turned to Bessie. "Josie was just looking at Caroline's old marble, when she suddenly became like that," she said. "But girls, do you remember – when Evie asked where Caroline was, Josie answered, 'Here' – do you think she might have meant – "

But before Hetty could finish, Bessie had marched up to Josie and taken her firmly by the arm.

"See here now," she said, in her very stern, monitor-ish voice. "This simply will not do – we can't be taking over people's bodies just because we feel like it. You come out at once, Caroline Bishop – you can have your marble back after you do".

As Bessie pronounced the missing girl's name, Josie shuddered again as if she were being shaken hard by the shoulders; in the next minute, she began heaving violently, and the girls watched in astonishment as a pale, nebulous form gradually pulled away from her like a mist.

"Good Lord, she's giving up her ghost!" Hannah exclaimed.

"Giving up *Caroline's* ghost, more like," said Bessie, as the airy figure separated itself from Josie entirely and became increasingly solid and distinct, showing itself to be an elfin-faced young girl with thick brown hair and light hazel eyes, and a quantity of freckles concentrated on her nose. For a second or two, she looked about her in confusion before giving way to a very phlegmy-sounding cough, while Josie seemed to rouse herself, as if from a deep sleep, and blinked several times in rapid succession, her eyes dark blue once more.

"What an odd dream I had," she murmured. "This house… but pitch black…"

"Yes, yes," said Maggie soothingly. "You gave us a bit of a turn, but you're back here now, and so is Caroline – look!"

"Oh, I am sorry," the girl said woefully, as soon as she could draw breath, and she clasped Josie's hands in both her own. "'Twas the deepest darkness where I was and all I could see was my marble and I reached for it… somehow I passed into you… I do beg your pardon".

"It's quite all right," replied Josie, squeezing Caroline's hands. She recognised her as the girl whom she'd thought was waving to her on the day of the picnic. "You're here at last and that's the main thing, and I'm glad you've got your marble back too – it certainly is pretty!"

"Aye, it is," said Caroline gratefully, looking at the marble between her fingers. "Thank you so very much for finding it. My brothers and I were always playing at marbles, you know, but they played for keeps, and I was the littlest and always losing – this was the one marble I had left and I wasn't going to let them have it!" She smiled as she said this, but soon heaved a great sigh. "It didn't matter in the end though," she said sadly. "I never did see any of them again".

"Never say never," said Lottie cheerfully, patting Caroline on the back. "Look, here we all are, reunited again – and I say, Josie, Bessie's here too!"

"I am *so* pleased to make your acquaintance," said Bessie, shaking Josie's hand warmly. "I remember you, and I am so glad you chose to stay on; I thought I might have frightened you away. You must forgive me if I did – I'd thought I heard Horatio coming..." She shuddered a little at the recollection. "There was a boy who came once too, a long time ago," she went on, musingly, "but he never came back..."

"Oh, but he does," Josie said, "only now he's all grown-up. He can't see you anymore, but he never forgot you. His name is Casper, and do you know, Lynton was his grandfather – you are his grandaunt. He wears Lynton's half of the locket that you both shared – here is yours".

Josie took the necklace from her cardigan pocket and carefully placed it in Bessie's palm, closing Bessie's fingers over it as she did so.

"Little Horatio helped me to find it," Josie explained. "I brought it up here to see if it might somehow guide you back to this room – I thought you would want to get away from that dreadful place downstairs".

"Oh, I did, I did!" cried Bessie, bursting into a hearty fit of crying. "Ah Josie, I am more obliged to you than I can say. Don't mind me, dears; it is just so much to take in, and I am *so* happy".

She gazed longingly at the tiny photograph in her hand. "But oh, how I should love to see Lynton again," she sighed. "Alas, I fear that is not possible".

"No, not right now, I'm afraid," Josie replied gently. "He died some time ago; Casper said he was already ninety-five. But he never forgot you either, and he told his grandson all about you and how you would come and talk to him in his dreams over the years. I feel certain that you two will meet again soon, just not here".

"Ninety-five," murmured Bessie wistfully. "Ah, that's a goodly age; I am glad of that at least. 'Tis true – Lynton and I did talk to one another in spirit, though our parents laughed at it. But then, people do often laugh at what they cannot understand, do they not? Or they are perhaps so afraid of being thought foolish or absurd that they close themselves up, and never see or hear all the wondrous things right before them. The worst of it is they go on to close their children up too… However, it is plain, Josie, that *your* mamma and papa never did that to you. Perhaps you, too, are what my grandmamma used to call a 'sensitive' – that's what she used to call us".

"Well, I've certainly been seeing *lots* of wondrous things," Josie chuckled, "so perhaps I am! But I'm glad of it – I wouldn't trade any of this for the world. And you know, even if you can't see Lynton right now, you *can* see Casper".

"Ah, that would be lovely," Bessie replied, her blue-green eyes shining brightly. Then she suddenly frowned. "But Josie, did I hear you aright? I do believe you called this sweet little dog Horatio, and yet we all know that Horatio – "

"Is this dog!" Hetty finished Bessie's sentence with a chuckle. "The creature of whom you are thinking – well, we know now 'twas really Robert!"

"Robert?" Bessie repeated, "Robert Bramstone?"

"Aye," Lottie nodded, "Josie here found out everything".

Bessie stared at the girls in bewilderment.

"Hannah and I have ourselves just arrived," said Bridget, laughing, "and Caroline too of course – Josie and the others will have to tell us everything from start to finish".

This Josie did do, as the girls gathered around her bed, listening with rapt attention, and many gasps and exclamations.

"Now," she said at last, "are all of you ready to see Robert again?"

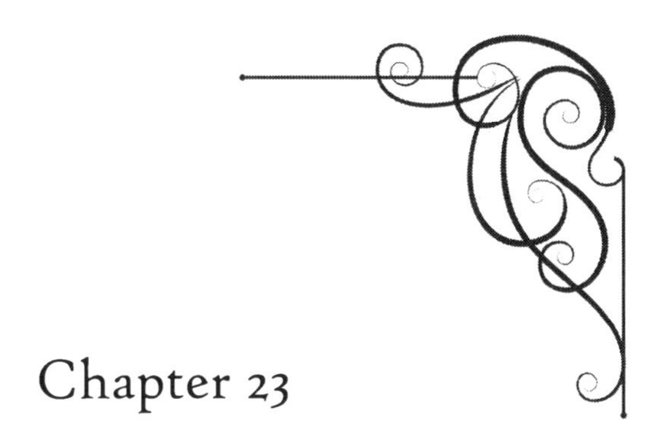

Chapter 23

"We're ready," Bessie said steadily, and the other girls nodded in agreement.

"All right then," said Josie, taking a deep breath. "I haven't the foggiest idea what to do – fingers crossed this works!"

She stood up on her bed, and, clearing her throat a little self-consciously, began calling out Robert's name.

"Robert! Robert, it's me, Josie!" she cried. "We're all here now – do come out please!"

She cocked her ear expectantly, but couldn't hear any sound of movement anywhere. She called again, louder this time, and soon the other girls were shouting too.

Oh, where are you, Robert? Josie thought to herself, wringing her hands anxiously.

Suddenly, from the far end of the room came that curious squelching sound that had once filled her with such dread, but which now she welcomed eagerly with a cry of delight. Robert's tall, ghostly figure pressed through the wall; pausing briefly to sniff at the air, he soon swept past the beds swiftly towards her, while Horatio jumped and yipped at his heels in ecstasies.

"You called, Josie, and I am come," he said gallantly, with a little bow. "Is everyone really here?"

The girls, at first nervous and wary, now leapt up exuberantly at the sound of his voice and there were squeals of elation all round.

"*Robert!!* It *is* you!"

"Oh Robert, how lovely to have you back again!"

"Oh, we *have* missed you! You won't make us disappear again, will you? What a fright you gave us at first, to be sure!"

"Ah, I am sorry for it," said Robert ruefully. "I'm afraid I rather bungled things up for everyone, didn't I?"

"Och, you meant well," said Evie. "We know now you were trying to help. We'd likely all have become frightful phantasms forever if you hadn't".

"Aye," said Hetty. "We'd have had to float about everywhere looking ghastly, and blow down people's necks or rap on tables just to be heard!"

Lottie was standing on tiptoe at Robert's shoulder and sniffing vehemently. "What a delightful smell you have about you!" she remarked. "Why, you make me think of – of – teatime! Almonds and hazelnut and orange cream…"

"Vanilla, roses and lavender!" cried Hannah, breathing in deeply as well. "It makes one feel all warm and snug, like being safe indoors by the fire on a bitter cold day".

"Yes," said Josie, "I noticed the same even in that awful hidden room. It makes me think of my mum and the ginger snap biscuits she would bake! And it makes me remember how she would cuddle me and sing me to sleep at night too…"

"You have a wonderful gift for comforting, Robert," Bessie observed. "You make me feel quite hopeful, I must say!"

"'Tis Josie we must thank for that," said Robert. "She has a plan for setting us free!"

"Aye, Josie," said Bessie, "we are all forever in your debt. Pray, do tell us what your plan is".

"Well, it's not really a proper plan," answered Josie diffidently. She turned to Robert and tapped him gently on the shoulder. "Do you think I might try getting this old sheet off you?"

"I suppose so," said Robert doubtfully, "though I've never been able to myself. Me and the coat stand and the sheet – we're all sort of melded into one another. But you can try if you like though".

"Okay," Josie said, cautiously patting him with her hands. "Oh! You're quite solid in there aren't you," she said in some surprise.

"Well, I should think so," Robert replied. "I do still look like myself, you know, even though much of me has become part of the old stand".

"Um, wonderful," said Josie. "All right, here goes then!"

Grasping the sheet with both hands, she gave it a vigorous yank, and was horrified in the next second to hear Robert give a loud yelp, and more than that, to find that the sheet remained quite firmly stuck.

"Ow," said Robert, rubbing his head.

"Oh Robert!" Josie exclaimed. "I *am* sorry! I'd thought it would just – I don't know – slide off or something; I didn't think it would be attached to you like – like – hair!"

"Well of course it wouldn't just slide off – it would have done that ages ago otherwise, wouldn't it?"

"Oh, I *am* sorry," said Josie ruefully. "I was hoping a good pull would do the trick. You see, I thought that perhaps you were *all* trapped under there – that perhaps your souls were what made it come alive. I was hoping that if we just took off that nasty sheet once and for all, and take apart that horrid coat stand, you might all be set free at last – I guess I was mistaken. Robert, might I – could I – I mean, would you mind very much if – "

"Oh, just say it," Robert sighed. "You want to look under this sheet, don't you?"

"Well yes, if you wouldn't mind".

"Very well," Robert replied, lifting his arms up gamely so that the hem rose a few inches off the floor.

Josie knelt down and gingerly lifted the old sheet. There was a momentary flash of light, and then a cool rush of air, bringing with it a sweet scent of wildflowers that flooded the room; with a cry of astonishment, Josie started backward.

"Why, it's empty; there's no one in there!" she gasped. "It's just the coat stand!"

"But I'm right here!" Robert protested. "*I* can see myself – can't you see me?"

But by this time the other girls had ventured forward to have a peek as well, and everyone had to agree that there really didn't seem to be anything else under the sheet besides the old coat stand.

"Well, that was unexpected," remarked Marianne. "What do we do now?"

"I guess it'll have to be my other idea, then," Josie replied, taking a deep breath. "Robert will have to send me into the darkness like he did all of you".

"What??" cried Robert. "Are you mad? Here are all of us wanting to get *out* of it, and you're asking to go *in*? No, absolutely not – you can't mean it!"

"Oh Josie, it is too much of a risk," said Maggie, "and what good would it do? You would just be as lost as we are – 'tis pitch black in there!"

"And then you would end up being trapped too, with no hope of escape," said Penelope, with a shudder, "and we'd all be finished off as well in the process. No, there has to be another way".

"I don't think so," said Josie slowly. "You see, I've been trying to work out why it is you can't stay out here in the light for very long – why it is you keep returning to the dark – and I think it's because your souls are trapped there; they keep drawing you back. I'd thought they might be with Robert, but they're not; they're somewhere else altogether, and the way there is through him. All this time you've been imprisoned there – you couldn't move, or even touch anything – so you need someone to go there who can".

"But you wouldn't even know what to look for!" Lottie exclaimed. "Why, our souls might look like anything – they might even be invisible!"

Josie paused a little to consider this.

"It's a chance we'll have to take," she said at last. "We won't know till we actually look. And *you* can't find your way in the dark, but *I* can".

"What? But how??"

"Why, with this of course!" replied Josie, taking her pink torch from her pocket. "My mum gave it to me because she said I'd need it on my adventures, and she was right. You can't bring anything into the darkness, but I can!"

"What ever is *that*?" asked Caroline curiously.

"An electric torch," answered Josie, switching it on and handing it to her, while the other girls crowded round to have a look. "It's a lot brighter than a candle, and safer too!"

"And it gives forth light whenever you need – how wondrous!" Hannah exclaimed.

"Well, for so long as it has working batteries!" answered Josie with a chuckle. "I put new ones in before coming here which will last quite a few hours, but I always carry an extra set on me too, just in case".

"It's extraordinary," Agnes marvelled, as she handed it back to Josie.

"Yes," Josie agreed, "and it's never failed me once. I'm sure we'll be able to find what we're looking for. We're so close; we can't just quit now!"

"But this is a place you've never been to, Josie," Evie objected. "Where would you even begin to look? And how would you return?"

"I don't know where I'd begin looking," Josie admitted. "But my daddy says sometimes you just have to step out in faith, you know? I'm hoping it'll become clearer when I'm there. As for coming back though, that's easy – I'll leave someone here who's very special to me".

"Oh! Who is it?"

Josie stuck her hand in her other cardigan pocket and brought out her little jersey monkey. "Meet Monkey," she said, perching him on her pillow. "Mummy gave him to me when I was a baby and I've had him with me ever since. He's my sidekick *and* my good luck charm – I'm certain he'll bring me back. Come on everyone – what do you say?"

The girls looked at each other uncertainly, while Robert shifted nervously on his clawed feet.

"You're our monitor, Bessie," said Hetty at last, "and the eldest here – what do you think?"

"It does indeed seem that we should all be taking an enormous chance," said Bessie musingly. "If Josie were to be trapped, 'twould assuredly be the end of us all as well, I imagine. But I can feel myself growing somehow fainter as time goes by; in truth, I do not think I should be able to last very much longer, and 'tis hardly likely another child will come to the house again soon – certainly not one so bold and plucky.

"On that account, I think this is a chance I'm willing to take – a chance I think we all should. But for Josie – who, as we know, is still very much alive – it is quite another matter. I cannot in clear conscience exhort her to take such a step on my behalf – "

"I'm totally fine with it," Josie interrupted excitedly. "This is the biggest adventure I've *ever* had and I absolutely want to see it through. Come on Robert, we don't have much time – are you ready to send me over now?"

Robert let out a great sigh. "All right then, very well," he said reluctantly. "We will do as you say".

As Josie went forward, the girls came together to give her tearful kisses and fervent wishes for a safe return.

"We shall wait to hear you call for us again," said Maggie, squeezing her hand. "Come back to us soon!"

Josie nodded. "I'm ready," she declared resolutely, holding her torch tightly in her pocket.

With a deep breath, Robert raised his arms and threw them about her in a great bear hug, enveloping her so entirely that she could hardly breathe. There was a dazzling burst of light, and Josie found she could see nothing, so bright was its illumination; then, in the next second, she felt herself being levitated at breakneck speed to what felt like a considerable height, and a wave of intense panic, as of one drowning, swept over her as she struggled to find her footing. All the while, a bracing wind howled about her and the heady aroma of wild flowers and sea spray filled her nostrils.

Then, suddenly, there came an abrupt halt to her breathtaking ascent, and for several minutes, Josie found herself hovering weightlessly mid-air; she could still see nothing beyond the extreme brilliance surrounding her, but she could now hear the wild roar of the ocean and the shrill cries of seabirds, while the pungent fragrance of heather, gorse and other coastal flora made her almost forget her fear – "Mummy," she whispered under her breath, as a vision of the Harwoods' old house by the sea came vividly to mind.

In the next instant, she began to fall headlong, so swiftly that she barely had time to scream or even think, and, keeping a firm hold on her torch, she shut her eyes tightly and braced herself for the impact of what she felt sure would be a startling, painful landing.

But there was no hard landing; indeed, there was no landing at all – the dizzying fall had come to a gentle stop and now Josie felt herself floating along with a curious bobbing sensation. Opening her eyes, she found herself in complete darkness, and quickly pulling out her torch, she flicked it on.

By the light of its narrow beam, she was amazed to see herself in a building of some kind, very large and very old, and clearly in a state of terrible ruin, for there were gaping holes in the roof, and long gashes in the walls from the peeling paint and paper. Yet despite the decay, there was something strangely familiar about it all, and in the next second, Josie gasped in astonishment – *I'm in the Bramstone house!*

As Josie swung her torch about, she realised with a start that she was at least fifteen feet off the dirty, dusty floor – she had been floating above the hallway. The sound of waves lapping, as if against the hull of a boat, now caught her attention, and, puzzled, she felt around her legs with her hand. To her surprise, she felt the cool dampness of rough wood, though there was nothing to be seen – I'm sitting in an invisible boat, on an invisible sea, she thought to herself.

In some perplexity, Josie gingerly arose, but almost immediately regretted it – she felt herself totter and then keel over as if her invisible craft had capsized, and with a squeal, she tumbled downward with arms flailing. Yet curiously, her fall seemed to be slowed by an unseen resistance and, just inches above the floor, she suddenly felt herself buoyed up by an invisible wave; with a great swoosh, it rapidly carried her several feet before depositing her with a thud on the lowest step of the staircase.

"Oof," she groaned, sitting up and rubbing her shoulder. Her torch had turned itself off in the fall, and she was struck by the extreme darkness that surrounded her now; it was of a deep blackness she could never have conceived without having seen it, and there was an uncanny quality about it too, as if a thick crowd of faceless phantasms were pressing closely about her. With a wildly beating heart, Josie hurriedly switched her torch back on.

The little circle of light made her feel very small indeed, and she felt in her pocket for Monkey before remembering that she had left him behind, and for a moment she felt like crying; then she took a deep breath and shook herself. I can do this, she told herself firmly.

Looking about her now, she was appalled to see the dreadful devastation of the Bramstone property. A cold and gusty wind was blowing through, and lent the place an even greater air of desolation.

So this was where Robert had sent everyone, she thought, except it wasn't that "safe, eternal home" he'd imagined, but rather, a deep, dark place within the heart of a lonely, despairing boy. Through years of neglect, it had been slowly falling to ruin – this is why the girls are feeling worse and worse, Josie thought, shivering. Rafters and windows had broken and fallen in, and all was covered with a heavy layer of dust and crushed masonry. Above her, the gallery loomed balefully and it seemed to her dark forms were leaning over the balustrades and looking down at her.

Nerves, she told herself scornfully, as she stood up and dusted herself; then suddenly, in the distance, there came a resounding crash that seemed to shake the very foundations and startled her almost out of her skin.

It seemed to come from the direction of the schoolroom, and Josie swung her light towards the gaping black entranceway. But she was too far away to see anything, and, taking another deep breath, she stepped carefully into the rubble and began making her way towards it. Barely had she reached the doorway when there came another tremendous crash from within the room, and, peering in, she was horrified to see the walls at the far end crumbling in a cloud of dust and falling into the yawning abyss below.

In the next minute, more floorboards began to crack threateningly, and the rows of desks, many of them broken and lying on their sides, shuddered as if at an approaching earthquake. Tattered books and paper were strewn everywhere and, glancing upward, Josie was dumbfounded to see the painted sitters in their portrait frames looking down at her with intense apprehension in their wide eyes. As she stared in astonishment, the buxom lady whom Josie remembered from her last visit to the room raised her gloved hands in warning, and, as if in a dream, slowly mouthed – *RUN!*

Chapter 24

Josie didn't wait to be told twice. Whirling about, she dashed out of the room blindly, stumbling over the debris as the thunderous sound of splintering wood and crumbling plaster followed close behind her. Clambering up the stairs, she paused to look over her shoulder – the hallway was beginning to break up, creating haphazard fissures here and there through which Josie could see the seemingly bottomless chasm beneath.

I'm not supposed to be here, Josie thought to herself in terror, grabbing the wobbling banister and trying to steady herself. *Think, Josie – think, think think!*

Lines from the ceiling were beginning to zigzag down the walls on either side of her and they grew wider and wider as Josie stood on the step looking about her wildly, undecided where she should search first. She had a sickening feeling that her very presence in this other-world was what precipitated this disastrous collapse.

I don't have enough time to search all the rooms, thought Josie in desperation. *Think, Josie, think! Where would something so precious be?*

Looking up towards the gallery, she suddenly remembered Hetty saying that the only path she could see in the darkness always led back to the girls' dormitory. That's it, Josie thought – since this is a kind of parallel world, surely that's where their souls would be!

Excitedly, she ran up the remaining stairs and turned to the first dorm. As with all the other rooms, its door had fallen entirely off its hinges, and the entrance gaped ominously wide and black. With pounding heart, Josie slowly entered, shining her torch over the broken beds and chests of drawers. There were three washstands standing at intervals down the middle of the room, while the open, unboarded windows alternated with two oak wardrobes, and a cracked and foxed dressing mirror leaned against the wall.

It's the girls' dorm as Robert knew it, Josie thought, seeing shreds of fabric and paper peeking out from the cracked and overturned furniture. However, she was soon shaken out of her reflections by the heavy rumbling beneath her feet, and she began swinging her torch about, randomly pulling out drawers and looking under beds. But everything was badly damaged and thickly covered with dust and dirt; it was like looking for a needle in a haystack.

This is hopeless, thought Josie, as she frantically grabbed and kicked at whatever was within reach, while the fearful reverberations continued to shake the house. Looking at the chaos around her, she felt a big sob well up inside her throat.

"I don't even know what to look for!" she cried aloud in despair, wiping a grubby hand across her clammy forehead.

Suddenly, out of the corner of her eye, Josie caught sight of something palely gleaming, moving through the darkness with a strange, creeping undulation, and with a suppressed scream, she swung round in fright.

There, illuminated in the dark doorway, was a tall figure – much taller than Robert or any of the other children – entirely covered from head to toe in what appeared to be long grey hair that seemed to move and ripple with a life of its own. This had a very coarse, filthy appearance, which made Josie recoil in disgust; then, in the next moment, she was petrified to see a bony, ashen arm emerge through the copious, writhing strands. With slow deliberation, the claw-like hand rose, and beckoned Josie to follow; then, turning, the figure made its way out into the gallery.

Breathlessly, Josie watched it go, scarcely daring to move a muscle, but as she felt the entire house shake violently, she hesitated for only a second more.

I have nothing to lose, she told herself, and, gulping, she scrambled over the rubble after the retreating figure. As she reached the gallery, a sudden clap of thunder made her jump back in fright – the entire balustrade had broken apart and fallen to the hallway below.

Josie staggered back from the edge, clutching her torch to her chest and pressing back against the gallery wall in a paroxysm of fear. But she knew she could not stay put where she was – already she could hear the planks beneath her feet splitting apart, and looking up in a panic, she now saw the glowing figure standing several feet away, at the very brink of the passageway, pointing with a bony finger across the chasm to the opposite side of the gallery.

Following the direction of its finger, Josie shone her torch and looked – in the deep gloom she could just make out the cavernous entrance of the infirmary. She stared, momentarily puzzled; then suddenly, gasped.

"Of course!" she cried, seeing in her mind's eye two young children sitting together in Matron's room, comforting each other over their shared collection of treasures.

"The magic box," Robert had said, "keeper of all things extraordinary and mystical; custodian of that other world to which we may at any time escape!" *That's* where something so precious would be!

Keeping close to the wall, Josie began traversing the gallery as fast as she dared. The pale figure made no movement as she passed it, but as she turned the corners and reached the opposite side, she was taken aback to see it moving with bowed head towards what she knew was the ex-headmistress' bedroom – *it was Mrs Bramstone*, Josie thought, electrified.

But there was no time now to dwell on this, for the rafters above Josie's head were falling in increasing numbers, and turning now into the infirmary, she clambered as quickly as she could over the shattered wash stands. The fireplace and doors in the far wall were in pieces, but Josie made straight towards Matron's room, so well did her memory serve her.

Curiously, the room here also smelt strongly of lavender and ginger, as the original room had in the real world, and Josie found this oddly comforting, as if she were visiting an old friend. The beds, too, were still in place, though thickly covered in jagged slivers of paint and plaster, and roughly sweeping aside the debris on the floor with her foot, Josie got down on all fours and crawled under the dilapidated copy of Grace's bed.

There were the floorboards just as she remembered, and indeed, she barely needed to knock on them, for they were splintering apart of their own accord, and the one she was looking for popped up now with only a couple of raps from her knuckles. Excitedly pulling up the planks around it, Josie was thrilled to see the *Hillaby's* tin safely nestled within the hollow, apparently intact and untouched, though very much blackened with rust.

As another rumbling tremor shook the room, Josie seized the tin and wriggled back out, sneezing and coughing as a cloud of dust and dirt hit her squarely in the face. Standing up and brushing herself off, she stared at the box in wonder and exhilaration, but a sudden ear-splitting crash jolted her back to reality, and she saw with alarm that more and more fissures were appearing in the walls and growing wider and wider as they ran down from ceiling to floor.

I can't stay here any longer, Josie thought, tucking the box tightly under her arm, beneath her cardigan. But in the next instant, the plank beneath her left foot suddenly gave way, and with a loud yell, Josie fell to her knees as half her leg went through the opening.

"Help!" Josie cried in desperation, as the neighbouring floorboards began to snap and come apart as well, and with a sudden crack, they too gave way and both Josie's legs fell through. Screaming, she thrust the tin away from her, and made a mad grab at the remaining planks around her, knocking her torch out of her hand.

Clinging to the floorboard by her underarms, while the rest of her body dangled helplessly into the abyss below, Josie watched, panic-stricken, as her torch and the *Hillaby's* tin were tossed about on the heaving planks. As her torch rolled further away and the darkness pressed in upon her, she let out a despairing sob. She was beginning to feel faint and a little light-headed, and a million tiny stars seemed to twinkle before her eyes, as she thought vaguely how lunch seemed to have been a lifetime ago. Somewhere in the distance, she could hear the long call of a seagull, and her hands began to slip…

Then, just as she felt her arms giving way, she suddenly felt something buoy her up by her legs – something malleable and rather slimy; not solid, yet distinctly tangible, with a tangy, salty smell – almost like the sea, Josie thought, becoming instantly alert, and kicking out with her legs as if she were treading water. In the next moment, the invisible substance pushed her up with such force that she was thrown clear of the gaping hole and skidded across the floor on her front, scraping her shins and hands.

"Augh!" she yelped, getting up painfully; her palms and knees were bleeding, and she was sure her chin was too. But as the sound of surging waves reached her ears, she looked about frantically for her torch. She could just make out its small beam trembling against the far wall, and close beside it, the children's tin. Scrabbling across the wreckage, Josie laid hold of them as a dark cascade of water came pouring in upon her from all sides.

It's become real, Josie thought, her eyes widening with terror, and she turned and fled. Out in the gallery, she was horrified to see the water rising up from the hallway, thick with foam and dark, shapeless forms waving their long tentacle-like arms. Stumbling back from the jagged edge, she glanced over her shoulder – water was rushing through the infirmary towards her. With a stifled exclamation, she began running along the gallery, looking about desperately for a way out.

"Help, help!" she cried. "Somebody please help me!"

"This way, honey," came a clear, ringing voice, "this way!"

Josie stopped in her tracks as if she'd been shot, and looked about her wildly.

"I'm here, honey," came the warm, melodious voice again. "Over here; come this way!"

Josie looked across the churning water towards the other end of the gallery. "*Mummy!!!*" she screamed.

Standing beside the doorway of the first dormitory was Mrs Harwood, but not as Josie last remembered her – thin and fragile, with colourless lips, and blue, mottled skin – but strong and blooming, with shining eyes and dark curls and ruddy cheeks, dressed in her favourite vintage blue gingham dress with the mother-of-pearl buttons, and plump arms held out as she used to when Josie was little and they played hide-and-seek in the garden.

Oblivious now to the chaos and destruction surrounding her, Josie scrambled over the broken boards and crumbling debris, narrowly avoiding yawning holes and falling rafters.

"Hurry Josie," her mother urged, "hurry!"

"I'm coming, I'm coming!" Josie cried. "Wait for me!"

She rounded the second corner of the gallery as the dark water rose higher and began to slosh over the edge. Her mother was only several feet away now, arms still held out, beckoning to her; in another minute, Josie had flung herself in her mother's arms, hugging her so tightly she could barely breathe.

"Oh Mummy," sobbed Josie, "you've come back! I've wished for this a million times! Say you'll stay, please please say you'll stay!"

"I can't, honey," said Mrs Harwood softly, smoothing back Josie's tousled hair. "I've only come now to help you. Look there!"

She pointed to the turbulent seawater and Josie was startled to see that a small beam of light seemed to now be illuminating its blue-green depths, throwing the monstrous sea creatures within it into sharp relief. Josie drew back and clutched her mother even tighter.

"That's the way home, honey," said Mrs Harwood tenderly.

"I can't go – I won't!" cried Josie, clinging to her mother's waist. "I won't leave you here!"

"You must, Josie," said Mrs Harwood. "I can't go with you, and you can't stay here – you have something very important to do".

"I don't care about it," wept Josie, feeling as if her chest would explode. She could feel the rounded corners of the *Hillaby's* tin pressing against her side, pulsing strangely like a heartbeat. "Someone else can come get this – I won't leave you here!"

"No one else will, Josie," Mrs Harwood answered softly. "You are the children's last hope, and you promised to see this through. You know we must always do the right thing, and we should always keep our word".

"But I'll never see you again," cried Josie, hiding her face in her mother's shoulder. She smelt wonderfully of ginger and brown sugar.

"Yes, you will," her mother replied. "Not just yet, but one day. We will be together again, I promise".

Gently, she pushed Josie away and pointed to the water again. "There isn't much time left, Josie," she said. "The children are trapped in your world now and they won't last there much longer. That's the way home – Monkey is lighting the way. You just have to close your eyes, and jump".

"What??" exclaimed Josie, incredulously. "In *there*?? With *them*??" She stared aghast at the leviathan-like creatures weaving in and out of the massive fronds of dark kelp.

"They're not as big as they seem, honey," Mrs Harwood said soothingly.

"What? They're huge!! I'm pretty sure I just saw an oarfish and those things are at least twenty-six feet long!"

"Yes, honey, but oarfish only eat plankton, so you'll be quite all right".

"Still!!" Josie retorted. "And besides, I might drown!"

"You won't, honey," said Mrs Harwood. "Hurry now; this world is ending; soon it will no longer exist. You must leave before that happens".

She began leading Josie to the edge of the gallery, when Josie suddenly pulled away. "Wait, Mummy!" she cried.

Turning, Josie began madly splashing through the ankle-high water towards Mrs Bramstone's room.

"Josie! Where are you going?" cried Mrs Harwood.

"Robert's mummy helped me; I can't just leave her here!" Josie called back. "Wait for me!"

It was hard work finding her footing on the uneven, wet rubble, but her mother's presence seemed to fill her with an almost supernatural energy, and Josie was soon outside the headmistress' room. Looking in, she saw a wide chasm where the majestic four-poster had been, with water seething up through it like a fountain, and dozens of books floating about like so many little boats, the beautiful green wallpaper torn and trailing like the seaweed after which it was named. With a gasp, she saw Mrs Bramstone standing before the shattered bookcase.

But she was no longer covered in the nightmarish grey locks, and her hands were slender and fine; though dressed in deep mourning, her hair was lustrous and black again, and curled about the delicate oval face, lovely and youthful now as it was in the early years of her marriage. As her eyes met Josie's, she smiled softly.

"Did you find it?" she asked.

"Yes," answered Josie, showing her the children's tin. "I'll bring it back to them".

"Thank you," Mrs Bramstone whispered.

"You can't stay here," said Josie, "everything's disappearing. Maybe you could come back with me – you could see Robert again".

But Mrs Bramstone only shook her head, and smiled her soft, sad smile. Turning away, she began gliding towards the other end of the room, her heavy skirt spreading out behind her on the water like a sail. The remains of a large window stood in the far wall, its glass panes almost completely gone, and through it Josie could see nothing but a deep, dreadful blackness; it was the window of what had been the secret room, now completely open and uncovered.

In the next moment, Mrs Bramstone put her hand on the window frame, and Josie realised at once what it was she intended to do.

"No!" Josie cried in horror, reaching out, hardly knowing what she was doing.

But Mrs Bramstone looked back at her for only an instant.

"*Remember me as I once was,*" she said in her low, lilting voice; and in the next moment, she lifted her sable skirts in one fluid motion and stepped through the frame.

* * * * *

"Josie! Hurry! You haven't much time to lose!"

It was Mrs Harwood. The water was fast rising and already past their ankles, and swiftly, she took Josie by the hand and pulled her out of Mrs Bramstone's room. All around them, the walls were crumbling with thunderous echoes, and Josie inhaled sharply to see the black nothingness above her where the roof had once been.

"You must go now, Josie," said Mrs Harwood earnestly, hugging her close. "Don't cry; I will always be with you, even though you can't always see me, and one day we *will* be together again – that I can promise you. There's a beautiful garden where I am, and our old house by the sea, and dear old Kenzie-dog is there too. I'll be waiting for you with biscuits and tea, and we'll go exploring in the caves, and nothing will part us again, ever".

Josie held her mother tight and breathed in her warm, familiar scent, and all the memories that came with it, and sobbed a big sob. Then at last, taking a deep breath, she stepped back resolutely.

"I'm ready," she said, tears streaming down her face. "I love you, Mummy. I didn't say it often enough before, but I hope you know I always did and I always will".

"I know, honey," smiled Mrs Harwood, stroking Josie's hair. "Mummy will always love you too".

Then, leaning forward, she kissed Josie on the forehead. "I am so proud of you, my little adventurer".

"I love you, Mummy," whispered Josie. "I'll see you in time for tea".

And without another look back, Josie turned, and jumped.

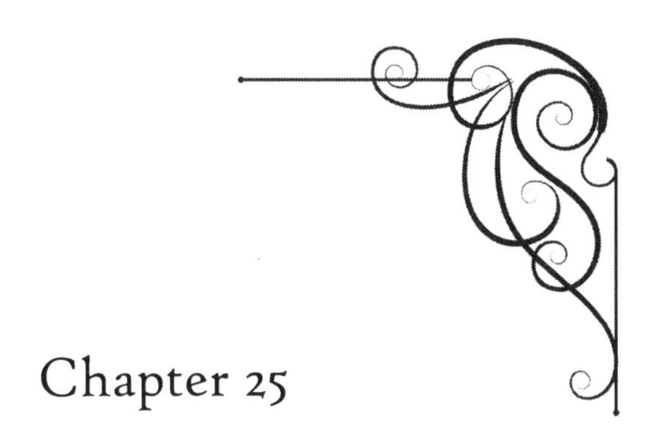

Chapter 25

For at least the first fifteen seconds, Josie kept her eyes tightly shut and her breath held fast; she felt overwhelmingly cold and wet – though strangely, this seemed to be more an impression rather than an actual sensation – while the memory of the colossal oarfish remained vividly fresh in her mind, making her quite unwilling to see it up close.

However, the need to exhale soon pressed upon her too urgently to be ignored, and as she did so, she found, to her immense astonishment, that she could breathe as easily as she could on land, and though her hair and clothes billowed outwards in the current, she herself was quite dry.

It's like being in a bubble, Josie thought incredulously as she sank, as slowly and gently as a feather being borne on the wind.

At last, after what seemed an eternity, her feet touched the seabed, as heavily as if she'd been wearing deep sea diving boots, and sending up a cloud of dust and silt. All about her was the kelp forest of which she had only seen the tips before; now she saw that the dense, stalk-like stipes reached upwards well over two hundred feet, and through the magnificent, wide fronds swam the mammoth sea creatures she had caught glimpses of earlier.

These moved languidly around her, illuminated by the distant beam which shone through the blue-green water, regarding her with some curiosity, but mostly indifference – a strange, seemingly arbitrary collection of extraordinary animals which Josie recognised at once as the very same deep-sea inhabitants that had fascinated her so much as a young child poring over the encyclopedias her parents had given her.

Here was a towering ocean sunfish, eyes large as dinner plates and beakish mouth permanently open; there, two giant manta rays with whip-like tails and fins beating like wings, gliding and somersaulting so gracefully that they quite took Josie's breath away. Above her, a mighty sperm whale, dark and monolithic, revealed its row of fearsome pointed teeth in a wide yawn, casually bopping her on the head with its tail as it passed, while further ahead, a frilled shark moved with serpentine elegance, terrifying to behold.

Staring, unmoving, in open-mouthed wonder, Josie felt as awestruck as a tiny mouse might in the deepest woods. Angler fish, vampire squid, grey whales, orcas, coelacanths, gulper eels, tiger sharks, and other things which she didn't even know existed – all wove effortlessly through the sweeping ribbons of green, red and brown seaweed; and the profound silence lent the dreamlike scene an even more uncanny quality.

Then, all at once, gleaming and dragon-like, an enormous oarfish, at least fifty feet long, emerged through the kelp; coming alongside Josie, it stared at her obliquely, its expression remarkably charged with meaning, before swimming ahead with smooth, undulating movements, the crimson crest on its head streaming like a knight's pennant.

It's going towards the light, Josie thought, her eyes widening; it wants me to follow!

She lifted her feet and was startled to find that her Mary Janes were weighty as lead; she could barely lift them, and after walking several yards with big, exaggerated steps like a clown in a circus, she stopped, panting.

"This is going to take forever!" she exclaimed, her voice coming out in a curious, hollow-sounding echo. The box under her arm was starting to feel increasingly heavy as well, and Josie felt quite ready to sit down and cry.

As she stood there biting her lip, the oarfish came gliding back, regarding her with what could only be described as concern.

"I'm exhausted!" Josie told the fish crossly. "My legs are tired; I ache everywhere, and this box is heavy too!"

Suddenly, Josie felt something pulling at her shoes, and looking down, she was amazed to see a giant pacific octopus wrapping its brick-red arms sinuously around her feet.

"Oh my word – I hope you're not tasting me!" said Josie in alarm, trying to extricate herself. But in the next second, she realised that the octopus had attached its suckers to her Mary Janes.

"Oh, of course, you clever thing!" she exclaimed. "Yes, I'll take them off!"

As the velvety creature obligingly held down her shoes, Josie lifted her feet out; immediately, she began floating upwards like a helium-filled balloon.

"Yikes!" she cried, her limbs flailing. "Help!"

Coolly, the octopus extended two of its mighty arms and dragged Josie back by her legs, nonchalantly thrusting her at the oarfish as it did so.

"I *am* sorry!" she said contritely, as she awkwardly clutched at the oarfish's iridescent body. "I wonder – um, do you think you could possibly – ?"

The oarfish rippled agreeably as it began moving forward.

"Oh, wait, wait, wait," Josie said, turning to the octopus. Its arms were still wrapped around her knees and shins so that she was bent sideways. "I need you to let me go now please".

The octopus stared at her for a moment, its rectangular pupils narrowing as if it were laughing to itself; then, one by one, its powerful suckers detached themselves from Josie's legs with curious kissing sensations, leaving behind multiple rows of large circular bruises.

"Thank you so much," said Josie, as the octopus pulled away.

She would have liked to pat its nubby, voluminous mantle, but – suspecting that it would find such an action offensive – refrained; to her surprise, however, the octopus patted *her* head, while nodding at her in a very old and wise way, and, as she watched it swim away, ghost-like and graceful, she felt oddly reassured. She pressed the children's tin closer to her chest.

"Time to get this back," she said to the oarfish, patting it on its flank as one might a horse. "Let's go!"

With great undulations of its splendid dorsal fin, the oarfish began swimming towards the light, moving with such speed, and so purposefully, that Josie felt certain it knew exactly where it was going.

It's like being on a bullet train with the windows down, Josie thought, hugging the fish in exhilaration.

As they glided smoothly through the vast corridors of swaying kelp, Josie could see the light becoming brighter, and knew she was now fast approaching her destination; the water itself was becoming lighter too, as if with dappled sunlight, and she realised, with some apprehension, that the oarfish was beginning to climb upwards.

"No, no, you mustn't go up there," she murmured anxiously. Oarfish, she knew, ended up at the water's surface only if they were in distress or dying, and she certainly didn't want *that* happening.

"Stay down here," she said, "I'll get off now. Thank you so very, very much for helping me!"

Josie let go of the fish's iridescent body; instantly, she began rising up towards the light. Looking down, past her dangling socked feet, she saw the oarfish swimming vertically as it watched her.

"Thank you again!" she cried, waving. "Mummy was right; you're not as big as you seemed – you're far, far *bigger*!"

In the next instant, Josie suddenly felt herself being pulled upward, so swiftly that she could hardly catch her breath, and she broke through the thick blades of kelp spreading out horizontally at the surface, red-faced and gasping.

Here the light was so bright that she had to squint her eyes, but she could hear the loud crashing of waves and the long calls of seagulls and other birds. A cold wind was blowing sea spray, and all about her were coloured glass bottles bobbing rhythmically. On the distant shore she could just make out the dark, lonely form of a shipwreck, and a fuzzy brown shape running excitedly to and fro.

"*Kenzie??*" screamed Josie in disbelief, recognising her mother's old Cairn terrier.

As the dog began barking exuberantly, Josie was swept up with the bottles on the lip of a huge wave that carried her on her back to the beach, where it broke with a crash, throwing her down roughly on the swash. She hit her head, and for several seconds she lay in the foam, dazed, while the washed-up glass bottles knocked against her. She saw now that the beached ship, heavily-corroded and covered in pink barnacles, bore on its hull the name *World's End.*

"Ow," Josie muttered, trying to get up. But she was hurt, and very tired, and she closed her eyes and fell back limply on the shingle with a groan. Her arm was painfully stiff from having clutched the children's box for so long, and on top of everything, her stomach was growling.

Then, as another wave crashed hard against her side, quite knocking the wind out of her, Josie felt herself being dragged from the water by her collar; in another minute, she was lying in something like grass, and the bright sunlight was eclipsed by something very large and shaggy, and she felt her face being vigorously licked. Opening her eyes, she let out a loud squeal.

"Kenzie!! You're here!!" she exclaimed, and she flung her arms around the dog's neck as he continued licking her face rapturously. The brindle-coloured dog was much bigger than Josie remembered – in fact, much bigger than any dog she knew, for he towered over her now like a grizzly bear – yet his behaviour was as puppy-like as it was when Josie was a baby, and now he bounded away, returning moments later with a bottle in his mouth. This he did repeatedly, till at last Josie slowly sat up, looking about her in confusion – there were bottles everywhere.

Picking one up, Josie gazed at it, puzzled – it was a lovely yellow amber, and tightly corked – to her astonishment, she saw a piece of paper inside, on which was written in old-fashioned script: *Josie, where are you?*

Shivering, Josie picked up another bottle, this time a pale aqua one with a rectangular body and rounded corners. The note inside this one read: *Josie, come back soon; we need you!*

"Where are these from?" cried Josie, frantically picking up the bottles one after another. "Who wrote them??" But Kenzie only stared at her with his shining eyes.

Josie, we're lost! Josie, we're running out of time! Josie, where are you, where are you?

The children! Josie thought, electrified.

"I'm coming!" she exclaimed, scrambling to her feet. She realised now she was in a thick bed of fleshy rock samphire and bird's-foot trefoil; as she got up on one knee, she was alarmed to see the plants disappearing into the soil as if they were being sucked down, and in the next minute, she herself felt the earth giving way beneath her.

"Kenzie!" Josie cried, stretching her hand out to the terrier as her bottom sank down several inches. But Kenzie only licked her fingers once, then bounded away, stopping only a moment to look back at her.

"I'll see you again soon," Josie whispered, her eyes welling up. Along the shoreline, the *World's End* was now sinking fast, and in the next moment, the ground yawned open and Josie tumbled in.

Here the air was strangely thick and seemed to slow her fall, making Josie feel like a blob in a lava lamp, and she found herself surrounded on all sides by blue sky, while bottles, leaves and flowers floated hither and thither, light as gossamer. Everything was bathed in sunlight, and she could hear faint whispers on the wind. Straining to listen, Josie realised they were the words she'd read in the bottles, and as the voices became louder and more urgent – though still very thin and far away – she recognised whose they were as well.

"Maggie! Lottie! Agnes!" cried Josie. "I'm coming!"

As soon as the words were out of her mouth, Josie began plummeting down – clouds rushed past, and even several birds – and she saw with horror that the light was getting brighter and brighter.

I'm falling into the sun! thought Josie, squeezing her eyes shut.

As the blazing white light enveloped her, Josie hugged the children's tin tightly, and breathed in the scent of ginger and tea and lavender talc dusted over her mother's bedsheets.

Suddenly, she had the strangest vision of Monkey – standing on his puffy round feet, stuffed full with plastic poly pellets, and waving his puffy round hands.

"Monkey," Josie breathed, feeling a sudden sense of calm.

Monkey squeaked, and jumped up and down.

There came a mighty rush of wind, and then all went dark.

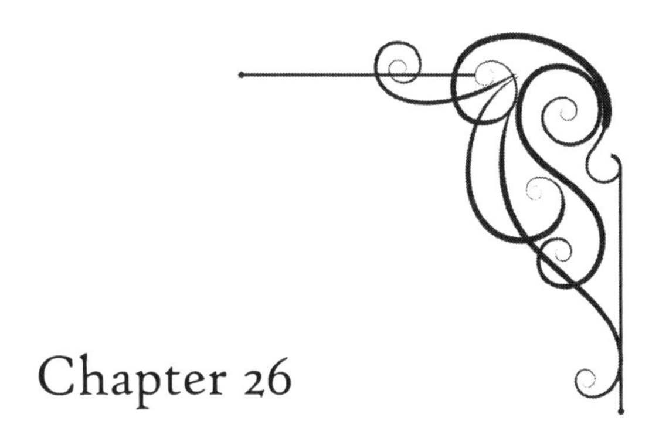

Chapter 26

"Josie! Josie, can you hear me?"

As Josie's eyelids fluttered open, her first thought was that she could no longer smell her mother's biscuits and lavender powder – now it was antiseptic, plasters, old wool and stale cologne – and a tear rolled down her cheek. Looking up in some bewilderment, she saw a crowd of faces bending over her – Casper on her left, Dr Fred on her right; and all around her bed – pale, delicate figures, so indistinct and shadowy, they seemed almost unreal.

Dr Fred lifted Josie's wrist and felt her pulse. He was a mild-mannered, middle-aged man with thick glasses who said hackneyed things like, "How's our patient feeling?" and "You'll be right as rain in no time".

But Josie wasn't listening – staring at the little figures with dawning recognition, she was horrified to see how sickly and wan they looked – they had faded so drastically, she could see right through them. She saw Horatio, too, lying on the floor beside her; he had become so weak that he could not rise, but only looked at her sadly and softly whined.

"They need their souls," Josie said desperately, clutching Casper's hand. "Where is the tin?"

"It's normal to be a little dazed and confused after we've fainted," Dr Fred said reassuringly. "A good meal and you'll be back on your feet in no time".

"No, no," said Josie, struggling to sit up. "Where's that tin? They need that tin right *now*!"

"Shhh," said Casper, pressing her hand. "It's all good. I'll just see Dr Fred out if he's done. You have something to eat – your monkey's been waiting for you".

As Casper led the doctor out, Josie sat up in her bed and looked around her wildly. To her immense relief, she saw the children's tin on her chest of drawers, beside a tray of toast, vegetable soup and lemon water – Monkey was sitting on it. He seemed to be looking at Josie very meaningfully with his big round eyes.

Josie grabbed him with her bandaged hands and gave him a big hug. Then, quickly picking up the tin, she turned to the children. They had gathered closer around her but seemed unable to even speak, so enervated had they become. Looking at Josie with sorrowful eyes, they tried to touch her, but their frail hands passed right though like vapour.

"I'm sorry it took awhile," said Josie, as she fumbled awkwardly with the lid. It was very rusty, and stuck fast. The room was growing dark now, and a chill wind began to blow around them with dismal moans.

"Gosh, that is just *not* helping is it?" Josie murmured, frowning, and trying to use her spoon as a lever. She glanced at Maggie and was alarmed to see her beginning to shimmer as the girls used to just before they returned to the darkness – she knew in her heart that if Maggie were to disappear now, it would be for good.

"Oh, open, will you?" she cried, banging at the tin in frustration.

"Need my help, Josie?" came a voice from the doorway. It was Casper.

"Oh Casper," said Josie, almost in tears. "Yes please – we need to open this tin now!!"

The young man didn't ask any questions. Taking the box from Josie, he set to work prying the lid off, his arms trembling with the effort as Josie watched him with anxious eyes.

Then, all at once, the lid came off in his hand with a loud grating sound, and Josie leaned forward eagerly.

"Huh?" said Casper, looking puzzled. "The thing's empty!"

"No, it's not!" exclaimed Josie, jubilantly taking the tin from him. "Can't you see?"

Filled to the brim with plum-sized orbs that swirled and glimmered like so many silver stars, the box now began thrumming and quivering in Josie's hands as if it were alive. One by one, the luminous spheres slowly rose, expanding and growing brighter by the minute, each making a peculiar humming sound; rising, they paused for a moment before Josie's face, as if in wonder, then soared upwards like birds rejoicing at being set free, while their old, rusted prison crumbled away in Josie's hands like dust.

"Holy sh–," muttered Casper, his eyes wide. "*I see them!*"

Whirling like Christmas sparklers, they flew exultantly about the room in wide, sweeping arcs, leaving a trail of glittering dust in their wakes; then, in a flash, several of them shot out the door with a keen purposefulness, as if in search of something, or someone.

For an instant, the remaining orbs hovered over the children's heads like bees buzzing in a garden of flowers; then, as everyone watched with bated breath, they swooped down as swiftly and precisely as falcons diving, each merging into the child to whom it belonged in a burst of light so dazzling that Josie had to hide her face in Casper's shoulder.

When she looked up again, she found the girls trembling and dumbfounded, staring at themselves and each other in disbelief; for they were no longer faint and flickering like dying candles, but radiant and substantial and bright-eyed and marvellously rosy, and more luminous than they had ever been before.

As they tentatively touched each other's faces and held their hands up wonderingly to the light, little Horatio began whimpering, bewildered by all that was happening, and a last shimmering orb descended speedily upon him, making him sneeze and shake himself as it melded fluidly into his body.

In the next moment, the spirited terrier was on his feet, black eyes shining and thick coat gleaming white; and rearing up on his hind legs, he began to bark joyfully.

"By Jove!" shouted Lottie, whirling around. "*She did it!*"

"Oh Josie!!" Maggie cried, rushing to her and embracing her rapturously.

Within seconds, the other girls were upon Josie too, hugging and kissing her and bombarding her with questions, while Josie herself began to laugh, so great was her relief. But suddenly, she stopped with a gasp.

"Robert!" she exclaimed in consternation. "*You haven't changed!!*"

Indeed, the boy was still claw-footed and covered in his funereal sheet, and, more worryingly, was fading fast before her very eyes. A single glimmering orb remained poised above his head, swooping down eagerly towards him every few seconds, but evidently unable to find a way in.

"Oh no, Robert!" Josie cried. "What's wrong? Why can't it get in?"

"I fear I cannot leave," he whispered weakly. "But thank you, Josie, for all that you've done – it greatly eases my mind to know everyone can go home at last".

"No, Robert, no!" sobbed Hetty. "You can't stay here like this – you'll disappear forever!"

Josie stared at him in despair, uncertain what else she could possibly do to help. Something still binds him to this house, she thought in dismay; what could it be?

"I'm waiting for my sister," Robert said softly, as if in answer to her unspoken question. "I have been looking for Gracie, but I cannot find her. I cannot leave without my sister".

"Oh, Robert," said Josie, her eyes welling up, "Gracie left a long time ago and she never came back".

There was a long pause. "I was looking for her," said Robert at last, in such heartbroken tones that all the girls gathered round to console him.

"I'm so sorry, Robert," said Josie. "Gracie only came back to the house when she was all grown-up, and then it was only to get some repairs done on the house – she didn't stay long. You saw her once, with her little girl, but I guess you didn't recognise them".

"*Forever bound and never to part,*" Robert murmured sadly, almost to himself.

Josie's looked at him, startled, then her eyes widened. "Of course!!" she cried. "Wait here, Robert. Please, just hang on a little longer!"

Throwing off her blanket, she slipped off the bed and scampered out the door at full tilt, making her way round the gallery as fast as her socked feet would carry her. Her bandaged knees hurt, but she was gladdened to see all the room doors well in place, the balustrade and its columns still standing tall along the gallery, and the grand ceiling undamaged and intact.

There was a feeling of lightness in the air – somehow, the house didn't seem as dark as it was before – and she vaguely wondered where Miss Gordy was and if she'd noticed; somewhere in the distance, she thought she could hear a monkey chattering. But there was no time to stop now, and hurrying past Mrs Bramstone's room, and those of the Misses Denton and Aubert, Josie pushed open the door of the infirmary.

Could the children's real magic box still be in its hiding place after all these years? Josie wondered. Maybe not, she thought, biting her lip – Grace herself would surely have remembered it and dug it up at some point, even though it would be decades later before she briefly returned. But what if – ?

I'll just have a quick look, Josie thought to herself, going into Matron's room. Getting down on all fours once more, Josie grimaced as she crawled under the bed; the floor was certainly no longer as clean as it was when Matron was alive, but thick with dust and grime, while spiders and other unrecognisable creepy-crawlies scurried away as her arms reached in.

Trying to recall which planks they were, she began knocking the floorboards with her knuckles; then, as one of them jerked upward with a loud pop, the white, luminous face of a small girl suddenly appeared directly above it, and, with glaring eyes and hair standing on end, let out a piercing scream that rang through the room.

With a terrified yelp, Josie scrambled backward as fast as she could, hitting the top of her head several times against the slats, while the girl continued to glower at her fiercely; but even as Josie reached the edge of the bed, the girl began to grow dim, while her dark eyes welled up. Gradually, she began to disappear, though the sound of her harrowing sobs persisted.

That was Grace Bramstone, Josie thought, her heart pounding as she slowly recovered from her fright; but that was Grace as a child, and Josie knew she had lived well into adulthood. Perhaps it was something of her spirit still attached to this house, or to this spot where the magic box had been hidden, or even to the box itself, that had never quite left.

Gritting her teeth, Josie crouched down and looked under the bed again. The sobbing had ceased, and there was no sign of Gracie. Taking a deep breath, Josie crawled back to the protruding floorboard; bracing herself, she lifted it out – but Grace did not reappear. Then, to her amazement, she saw the red and yellow corner of the rusty *Hillaby's* tin; it was still there after all these years.

In a flash, Josie pulled up the adjoining planks and removed the box. Quickly, she squirmed back out and, without looking back, hurried from the dismal room, her fingers picking frantically at the box's lid as she sped back to the dormitory.

There was a great commotion by her bed, and going closer, she saw that the girls had surrounded Robert and were trying in vain to keep him from fading away – already his clawed feet had entirely disappeared.

"She's not here, Robert!" Josie cried. "You don't have to look for her anymore!"

"Yes, come with us," pleaded Agnes. "I can already hear my brother calling to me – I'm certain Gracie is waiting for you in that other world too!"

"I can't!" Robert gasped, as the long sheet began gradually fading from the bottom up. "I fear it is too late for me now!"

Josie had opened the tin on her bed and was pouring out its treasures – a cracked pocket watch; a silver horseshoe charm; baby teeth, broken shards, torn papers; a quantity of feathers, pebbles and bones; and shells and sea urchins and sea stars. Then, at the very bottom, the dark loop of braided hair. Gently cradling it in her palm, Josie went up to Robert.

"It is not too late," she said, pulling one end of the worn blue ribbon. As the narrow length of silk came undone, the intertwined hair slowly unravelled and fell in dark curls to the floor. There was a loud inspiration, and Robert seemed to sway and totter as if he might faint. In the next instant, the dirty, funereal sheet that had covered him for so very long suddenly crumpled upon itself, and then fell heavily to the floor in a heap.

"Robert!!" the girls screamed, rushing forward. They lifted the thick, grimy cloth – there was nothing underneath. The glittering orb that had been hovering over him had also disappeared.

There was a moment of thunderstruck silence.

"Oh Josie!" Maggie sobbed. "He's gone!"

"No, Maggie," came a soft, kindly voice from behind them, "I'm here!"

There was the fair, slender boy Josie remembered watching in Matron's room, his fine, dark eyes shining and dark hair lightly mussed as if he had just gotten out of bed. Indeed, he was still wearing his nightshirt, and now he came up to Josie, barefoot and shyly smiling.

"I am forever in your debt, Josie," he said, holding out his hand. Josie took it and shook it hard, feeling a lump come to her throat.

"Och, won't ye just give 'er a hug!" laughed Evie. "I'm sure she won't bite!"

"I won't!" giggled Josie as she leaned in to embrace him, turning his face a beautiful shade of pink. "You're the big brother I've always wished for," she whispered.

She turned now to Casper, who had been standing by her chest of drawers with his mouth hanging open.

"I know you've always held your grandaunt's memory dear – wouldn't you like to meet her?"

She drew Bessie forward by the hand. "This is Casper, your brother's grandson. Does he look at all like Lynton, do you think?"

"Aye, he does," said Bessie, her eyes filling with tears. "He's all grown-up, but I can see my brother in his face".

"It is *such* a privilege to meet you," Casper said, choking up as he bent down to give his young grandaunt a hug. "Granddad talked about you all the time; he never forgot you till his dying day".

"And I never forgot him either," Bessie replied. "I was overjoyed to learn that he prospered, and that he has a descendant of whom our family may be proud. When I see him, I shall tell him how well you have grown!"

"Gosh, Josie," said Casper, turning to her. "I don't know how I can ever thank you enough for this".

"Nor I!" said a cheery voice from the doorway. "Where's my favourite girl?"

"Walter!" squealed Josie, running up to him. The young man lifted her off her feet and whirled her around, before planting two exuberant kisses on both cheeks.

"What a doll you are!" he exclaimed. "Absolutely the cat's pyjamas! Gosh, how I shall miss you! I'd play a song for you on the old piano 'cept I don't think we have much time – I could hear my old dad calling to me from the other side; he's been waiting for me a long time I reckon!"

"Oh, I shall miss you too!" said Josie, flushing to the roots of her hair as Walter set her down. "I shall miss all of you! I wish you didn't have to leave forever, but I'm so glad you're going home to your families at last. Where's Miss Gordy?" she asked then, turning to Casper, with a look of puzzlement. "She would love to see everyone off, I should think!"

"I didn't have time to tell you," said Casper. "After you left, she went to rest in her room; when Mrs Edmundson knocked at her door to take her leave and got no reply, she looked in – Miss Gordy was in a faint on the floor. Mrs Edmunson called for the ambulance immediately, and then she called me to come over to take care of you while she accompanied Miss Gordy to the hospital".

"Oh no," said Josie. "Will Miss Gordy be okay?"

"It seems she's better now; she's resting and quite alert. Doctor thinks she may have stood up too fast or something like that, but then you know she also does have heart disease. They said they wanted to keep her for observation, but she made it clear that she doesn't care about any treatments and wants to come home as soon as possible.

"Anyway, it was a good thing I came over when I did; I'd just come in the door when I heard *you* fall on the floor. You looked a mess, so I told Dr Fred he'd better bring a nurse over too; she's the one who helped wash and bandage you up – but I guess you don't remember any of that".

"No, I don't," said Josie slowly, with a frown. "How long was I out for?"

"A couple of minutes, I'd say. I put you into bed and you just rolled over and dozed off. You were mumbling the whole time the nurse and doctor were treating you, but you eventually settled down, and Dr Fred chalked it up to overexertion on an empty stomach – he reckoned you'd come running in from playing outside and fell or something. You must have been exhausted 'cause you slept away most of the afternoon".

"Yes," said Agnes, "we waited for you for hours. We realised after you left that something had happened – we couldn't seem to go back to the dark as we used to. But the longer we stayed out here, the weaker we became…"

"Aye," said Marianne, with a chuckle, "we knew it was not a good thing to be able to see right through ourselves! I think even our minds were becoming affected – everyone was crying, 'Josie, where are you? Josie, we're running out of time!' We were getting quite desperate, I can tell you!"

"Why, that's what the messages in the bottles said!" exclaimed Josie, looking at her in amazement. "How very strange!"

"I should love to hear about what happened to you over there," said Robert. "I should think everyone would!"

"Oh, yes please!" cried Bridget. "What a story to tell everyone back home!"

"All right!" said Josie, laughing. "Gather round, one and all!"

But as she said this, there came a loud rhythmic thumping out in the gallery, accompanied by shrill, ringing bird calls, which made everyone turn in surprise. In the next minute, a large black chimpanzee came bounding into the room on all fours, followed closely by three large brown hares. Overhead, a flock of birds glided in, their stately wings outspread in full splendour.

"Arthur!" squealed Josie, as the chimp made his way directly to her bed; and climbing up to her, the great ape put his arms around her shoulders. For a long moment, Josie hugged him close, remembering how he had helped her.

"I shall never, ever forget you," she whispered, stroking his broad shaggy back, as he pressed his head long against hers.

"And here's Polly, come to thank you too," said Agnes, coming forward with the huge crow perched on her arm.

"Oh Polly," said Josie, "how glad I am to see you out of those awful clothes!"

The magnificent bird leaned forward and gently touched her beak against Josie's cheek.

"She has something for you," said Maggie. "Open your hand!"

As Josie extended her palm, the crow dropped something small and lustrous into it; looking closer, Josie saw that it was a sweet mother-of-pearl button.

"How ever did you find this?" she whispered slowly, staring at its distinctive heart shape and biting her lip. "It's from Mummy's old blue dress. Oh Polly, thank you! I shall put it on a necklace and never take it off!"

She wrapped the button in a tissue and tucked it carefully into her pencil box. Then, taking up her toast and soup, she turned to the little party gathered round her; they made a beautiful, warm glow in the dusky light, and Josie breathed in the heady scent of lavender and ginger and roses.

"Thank you for the adventure of a lifetime," she said, her heart full. Then she grinned. "Okay – story time!"

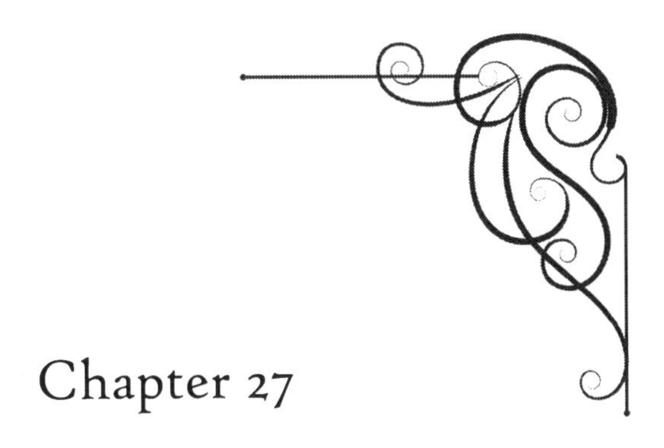

Chapter 27

Twilight was falling as Walter and the children rose to leave at last. Penelope had the brilliant notion of exchanging autographs, and Casper even took several photos, though he said he wasn't sure if any of them would develop, since spirit photography generally had a rather low success rate.

But last kisses and tearful embraces were eventually given, and heartfelt promises to see each other again one day; already the girls were beginning to shimmer with an otherworldly radiance, and, as Bessie pressed her locket into Casper's hand, and Walter finally hoisted up his faithful old typewriter, an orb of light suddenly materialised before them, growing gradually taller and wider till it was almost as large as a door, and glowing with a wonderful brightness emanating from thousands of little twinkling stars.

"It's like a portal!" Josie gasped.

As everyone stared in open-mouthed wonder, a fair, rosy-cheeked lady with a profusion of golden-white ringlets appeared on the other side of the shining doorway – leaning forward, she gazed into the dormitory with an expression of intense expectancy; in the next second, Maggie had run forward and thrown herself into her arms.

"*Mama!!*" she cried, burying her face in the lady's white dress.

"I'm here, dearest," said the woman tenderly, stroking Maggie's hair.

"Oh, Mama, you are just how I remember you best," said Maggie, as her mother took her by the hand. "Am I going home now?"

"Yes, dearest. We have been waiting all this time for you and you are ready at last!"

With a final, long look at her friends, and a softly-whispered "goodbye", Maggie turned to leave with her mother, walking into the brilliant light and vanishing entirely.

"Oh Casper," said Josie, the tears streaming unheeded down her cheeks, "isn't it wonderful!"

"It sure is," said Casper. "Thanks to you, the Bramstone curse has finally been lifted. It's absolutely amazing. I don't know who'll believe us though!"

One by one, the girls' kinfolk appeared, fetching their daughters or sisters home as they had once intended to over a hundred years ago; now, as Hetty's mother appeared, beaming and holding out her hand, they were all startled to hear a frantic shout behind them.

Turning, they saw Mrs Edmundson puffing heavily as she pushed Miss Gordy in a wheelchair, running as fast as her short legs could manage, her face red with exertion and thick grey hair in disarray.

"Wait, wait!" she shouted again, panting. "Miss Gordy said she had to say goodbye, though *why* she couldn't just wait till the morning when the doctors said it was all right to leave, I don't know!"

Josie and Casper exchanged quick glances. It was plain that Mrs Edmundson couldn't see anything that was happening, but what was far more astonishing was that Miss Gordy clearly *could* – she was straining forward in her seat, reaching her arms out earnestly towards Hetty, who stood, puzzled, with one foot in the shining doorway, and her hand in her mother's.

The old lady looked very pale and weak – almost like the girls did when I'd just returned from the darkness, thought Josie with a start, and she jumped up and hurried over to Mrs Edmundson.

"Poor thing's going a bit gaga, I think," she whispered to Josie. "I told her she should just rest, but she insisted on coming home at once

– said she felt it in her bones that she had to be here".

"Don't worry," Josie whispered back. "Casper and I will stay with her".

"Oh, thank you, dear," said Mrs Edmundson with a sigh of relief. "I badly need a bite to eat and a cup of tea. If you two could just keep an eye on her for a bit, I'll go get dinner ready. I've already called your father, by the by; he's on his way home and will come pick you up first thing in the morning".

"Thank you, Mrs Edmundson," said Casper, leading her to the door, as Josie knelt and put her arm around Miss Gordy's shoulders.

"I remember you," the old lady was saying. "Hetty – Hetty Wright. You spoke with me all those years ago, when I was even younger than you. And then I never saw you again…"

"Oh!" cried Hetty, releasing her mother's hand for a moment and taking Miss Gordy's in both her own. "You were the child who slept in my bed! Ah, dear, how long ago that was! The years have passed, and I fear that you are quite unwell now, but I can still see the child that you were, and that you will be again. I am going home at last, and you will too".

She bent and kissed Miss Gordy tenderly on the cheek, then, nodding to Josie with a grateful smile that lit up her whole face, she took her mother's hand again and followed her through the doorway.

Soon, all the girls were gone, and only Walter, Robert and little Horatio still remained; even Arthur and the birds had disappeared through the portal. A stately older gentleman with an impressive handlebar moustache now appeared; he looked very dignified, but his hazel eyes twinkled with an intimation of high good humour. Catching sight of Walter, his face brightened.

"That's my dad," said Walter with a chuckle. "He was in the military, but 'pon my word, he knew how to cut a rug haha! Now Josie, promise me you'll not forget me and will think of me sometimes. Here, it's all I've got on me to give; it's probably too big for you to wear now, but you'll grow into it in a year or two!"

He took Josie's hand and placed a gold signet ring in her palm. Its band was carved with a beautiful wheat motif, and the central plaque was engraved with Walter's monogram in cursive.

"See?" he said, grinning. "It says 'WJF', but you can take the 'J' to be 'Josie'; we're entwined, you and I – friends forever!"

Josie closed her fingers tightly over the ring.

"Thank you, Walter!" she said, taking a deep breath. "I didn't know it would be so hard to say goodbye".

"It always is when we've come to care for someone, kiddo," Walter said with a regretful smile. "I would've liked to have had a lifetime to know you better, but I'm thankful for what I got. See you again some time, kiddo".

He kissed her quickly on the top of her head, then stepped through the portal without looking back. In an instant, he and his father were gone, and Josie was left gazing after them with sorrowful eyes.

"Don't be too sad, Josie," Miss Gordy said kindly. "It's not goodbye forever, and in the meantime, I will give you all my mother's old records".

Josie smiled at her appreciatively. "You can see the lost children now, can't you," she said softly. "Look, here is Robert, who loved your mum so much, he never stopped waiting for her".

Robert came forward shyly, unsure of how he ought to behave towards his elderly niece; but kneeling by her wheelchair now, and looking her full in the face, he suddenly threw his arms around her with a cry.

"You look just like Gracie!" he gasped.

"How can you tell?" asked Miss Gordy in surprise, laughing a little as she hugged Robert close. "I'm well past eighty now you know, and everything is covered in lines and wrinkles".

"I don't know how I can tell," replied Robert, "but I can. I believe Hetty could see it too. Perhaps – "

But before he could finish, Horatio began jumping about and barking excitedly, and as Robert and Miss Gordy looked towards the doorway, a little girl appeared, with very large, dark eyes and curling dark hair – she looked into the room anxiously, and then her eyes met Robert's.

"*Robert!!*" she squealed at the top of her voice.

"Gracie!!!"

In a moment, Robert had leapt into the portal and lifted his little sister off her feet.

"Oh Robert, you've been *such* a time! I thought you were never coming!"

"And I thought you'd gone and forgotten me quite!"

Gracie shook her head.

"The people who love you never stop loving you, don't you know," she said solemnly. "*Never* – not even after they're gone".

"Jove, it's too splendid for words!" said Robert, as he set her down and leaned back to take a good look at her. "You are just as I remember; it's as if we've never been apart. I say, Gracie, do you know who that lady over there is?" He looked towards Miss Gordy, whose hands were clasped together over her heart as she watched them.

"I do," replied Gracie, smiling sweetly at the old lady. "'Tis Ellinor Lucinda Gordy. But I am not come to fetch her now; she has lived a long, goodly life, and will leave in her time, in the usual way, and we will be there to welcome her on the other side". She turned to her brother and took his hand. "Come Robert, we must go now".

"Goodbye then, Josie," said Robert, "and goodbye Ellinor, for the present".

Hand in hand, the siblings walked into the light, with little Horatio gambolling gaily at their feet; in the twinkling of an eye, all three had disappeared, and the portal itself was soon no more than a tiny, marble-sized orb – it danced and glowed fleetingly, like a dying flame, before vanishing as well, leaving no trace behind in the dusky room, save a gentle fragrance reminiscent of summer evenings and teatime.

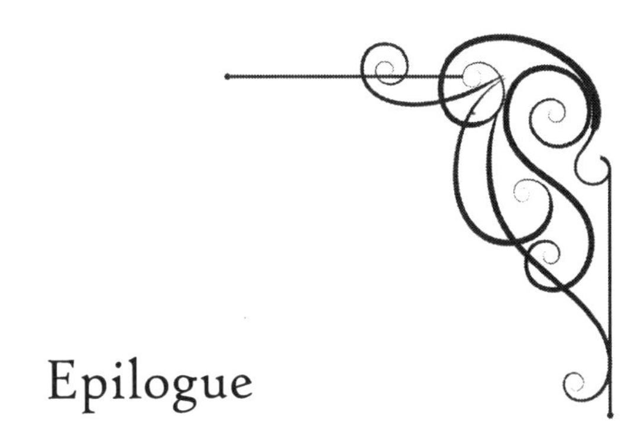

Epilogue

That night, Casper and Mrs Edmundson kept Josie company and they all slept in the dormitory. It was the first uninterrupted sleep Josie had had since coming to the house, and though she felt lonesome without the children, she was too exhausted to think about it for long. She woke up late the next morning, and found her father waiting for her in the drawing-room when she went downstairs. Miss Gordy had passed away during the night.

Having no living relatives, the old lady had bequeathed almost everything to Mr Harwood and his daughter. This was an unexpected, though certainly welcome, windfall, since Uncle Eddie had only left them his collection of '80s soft rock LPs.

In the weeks that followed, Mr Harwood hired Casper and his father to oversee repairs at the Hall, and requested that Mrs Edmundson stay on as their housekeeper full-time.

At first, Josie was worried her father planned to get rid of all the heirlooms and old furniture, but his antiquated heart had already fallen in love with them, and except for the boards on the windows, he said he intended to keep everything exactly as it was. Josie was much relieved of course, but she did advise him to dismantle the secret door – and strip the wallpaper in Mrs Bramstone's room – just in case.

After the funeral, Casper handed Josie a letter addressed to her in a lovely cursive script; he said it had been found on Miss Gordy's bedside table. Later that afternoon, when she was finally at home in her own room, she opened it.

My dearest Josie (it read),

By the time you read this, I will in all likelihood be dead. I suspected earlier at breakfast that I would not last much longer, and when I fainted later in the day, that feeling grew to be a certainty. While I was at the hospital, I began fretting even more about you, and about the children – not knowing what had become of either – and I fell into a very fitful sleep, during which I had a curious dream.

I dreamt that I was a little girl again, visiting the house with my mother. And, as it happened in reality, Hetty Wright came to see me while I was lying in bed, except this time she did not speak to me, but stood at the doorway, beckoning. She looked so sweet and rosy, quite unlike the pale, wan face I remembered from before. The dream was so vivid that I awoke with a start – not in terror or anxiety – but simply with a great conviction that I had to come home right away.

Well, thank goodness Mrs Edmundson humoured me and got me back when she did – I would not have missed anything I saw today for an extra week of this life, or even an extra month; no, not even for the world. You know I'd said I could not die in peace knowing that the children's souls were still trapped – well, now I can. Thanks to you, I am going serene in the knowledge that they are free at last.

You know I always felt in my heart that it was selfish of me to have let you stay on here; I can only hope that you will forgive me any of the hurts that you have suffered – both physically and emotionally – and that one day you will be able to look back on this time as a special one afforded only to the pure and valiant, for such is what you are, Josie Harwood.

In recompense for all that you endured, I am leaving you and your father almost all my fortune and property – the house and all that goes with it. I know your father has been having a rather difficult time of things since your mother fell ill, and I trust that he will now be able to keep both of you more comfortably. I think it is the least we Bramstones can do in gratitude for all that you did.

Well, my dear, I would have loved to hear about all that you saw on your adventures, and to spend more time with you too, but I shall have to be content with what I was privileged enough to witness. Take good care of yourself, dear child, till we meet again,

Ellinor Gordy.

Naturally, Josie shed a good many tears for the worthy old lady after reading this, in addition to the great many she had already shed before; and she took comfort in busying herself with getting the Bramstone house ready for visitors, since her father had decided to open part of it – the lower part – to historical enthusiasts, art aficionados, ghost hunters and the like.

The holidays came to an end and school resumed, but while Josie attended her classes and did her homework much as she ever had, all the children remarked on how changed she seemed; they had always thought her a bit of an oddball – eccentric, unconventional and sometimes just plain weird – but now she had an otherworldly air about her, at once uncanny and compelling, that made her both fascinating and wonderfully fun to be around. Josie suddenly found herself receiving invitations to sleepovers and birthday parties from all quarters, and was even asked to join the school's drama club.

But her closest friend now continued to be Casper Brasket, though he was almost nine years her senior; they had been through too much together for theirs to ever be an ordinary friendship, and it grew from strength to strength as the months and years passed, and the gap between their ages felt smaller and smaller.

He did finally manage to make his tintype of her – and went on to make many more in fact – though, as he had predicted, his photographs of Walter and the children did not develop well, showing Josie seated alone, surrounded by luminous blobs. These, of course, would probably have thrilled many a paranormal investigator, but Casper and Josie preferred to keep the photos in their drawers and say nothing about them to anyone.

By the new year, the Harwoods had taken up residence at Bramstone Hall, since Mr Harwood needed a bigger atelier and the first form dormitory suited him perfectly. Josie chose Miss Gordy's old bedroom as her own, not least because of the antique photographs of Robert, Gracie and the other children displayed on its walls.

Later that January, Mr Harwood invited Casper to use the second form dormitory as his photography studio, at which he also taught classes on tintypes every Thursday. By February, the Harwoods had adopted a dog from the local shelter – a Westie no less – whom they named Horatio.

One evening, as Josie was returning from her bath, she was surprised to hear Horatio barking excitedly in her bedroom; he was generally a quiet fellow, given to long naps and staring thoughtfully into space, so this was unusual. Puzzled, Josie hastened along the gallery, clutching her toothbrush like a weapon. As she stepped cautiously into her room, she was startled out of her wits by a tall figure suddenly emerging from behind the door – it had a profusion of long black hair falling in waves entirely over its face; in another second it had begun swaying, reciting in a high, singsong voice:

A ring, a ring o' roses,
A pocket full o' posies –
Atishoo atishoo we all fall down!

"*Marianne!!!*" screamed Josie at the top of her lungs, laughing till the tears came.

"None other," said she, parting her curtain of hair with both hands, and grinning from ear-to-ear.

"How – ? When – ?" Josie began, then stopped in amazement.

Her bedroom was aglow with children; all ten girls – and Robert too – were seated on her bed, as well as her table, bookcase, drawers and chairs, and both Mrs Bramstone's Horatio and hers were romping together boisterously on the carpet.

And so began the regular visitations of the once-lost children, though what happened after must obviously keep for another book; suffice to say they all enjoyed themselves immensely and their friendship blossomed steadily over the long years ahead. The children later found that Casper could see them as well, but that no one else could, which just served to further cement the bond between them.

That night, Josie went to bed wonderfully happy, hugging Monkey on her chest and discussing with him what they should do over the weekend and whether she ought to accept Sophia Renford's invitation to her party on the 26th. As she finally began drifting off to sleep, there came from somewhere below the dreamy, lilting notes of Satie's *Gnossienne No. 1*, at once wistful and mysterious, and evocative of deep secrets held close.

END

About Josie, Clementine, and the Photography in this Book

Josie and Clementine are custom art dolls made by doll artist Janice Yong. They measure just about 11" tall, and have been carefully carved and painted to develop their unique expressions and personalities. Jan rarely keeps the dolls she makes, but these two somehow spoke to her and so became part of a very small handful that make up her own dolly family.

They are, however, also part of a much larger family of dolls belonging to dolly collectors around the world who come together in this fun, vibrant hobby which wonderfully combines art, craft and play. Toy photography involving miniature handmade props and furniture is an art form in and of itself – the miniature dioramas in this book were all taken on a surface smaller than the average bedside table and everything visible is physically there. Clementine features regularly in her own dioramas on Jan's Instagram page @umami_baby amid Jan's regular dolly adoption posts.

Umami Baby dolls have frequently been described as having an "old soul" quality, which is probably greatly influenced by Jan's penchant for antique things, including authentic found photographic images ("antique" describes items that are at least 100 years old). All the photographs and Victorian lantern slides in this book are from Jan's personal collection and capture the poignant charm and beauty of moments in time long past. Perhaps our modern dioramas, with their thoughtfully posed sitters and scenes, have a bit in common with them.

Dolls for adoption can be found at
umamibabydolls.com

Updates and dolly shenanigans can be found at
instagram.com/umami_baby

All Umami Baby dolls can be found at
flickr.com/photos/114789695@N04/albums

CREDITS

Crow doll by
Chertopoloh Arts

Dolly clothes by
Daffodil's Creations
Moshi Moshi Studio
Petit BonBon
The Pumpkinbelle

Chimpanzee and pangolin figurines by *Mojo*

Hare, swan, cobra, owl, squirrel, pheasant, badger, lamb, fawn, otter, octopus and golden lion tamarin figurines by *Papo*

Crocodile figurine by *Schleich*

Westie figurine by *Veronese Design*